SHE WAS JAPANESE,
BUT SHE WAS AN AMERICAN—
AND HER LOYALTIES WERE TESTED BY LOVE.

When Emi went into her office an enlisted man was packing her things into a corrug[illegible]. "What's happening?" [illegible]

"Comma[illegible] o report to him."

He was i[illegible] ed her in. "You're lo[illegible] iled this morning," h[illegible]

"I feel wo[illegible] she said lazily. She could almost feel Luke Martel's sweet and gentle hands on her glowing skin even then, even after a good night's sleep.

"We're moving you," Braddock said.

Emi was shocked. Surely he wasn't going to send her away from Hawaii, not when she'd just found Luke.

"You'll be pleased to know that you've convinced us of your sincerity, Emi. I think I can say that you've passed the test."

"What test? I haven't taken any tests."

"Just a matter of semantics," Braddock laughed. "Lieutenant Martel is a good man. If he weren't such a good pilot we'd have him operational in intelligence. You'll be moving into a very sensitive area, Emi, but Luke Martel says you've got the right stuff to do it."

"Kind of him," she mumbled hollowly. The wonderful feeling had vanished. All the time she'd been letting herself fall in love with him, he'd just been doing a job. . . .

BITTER VICTORY

BITTER VICTORY

Hugh Zachary

A Dell/Banbury Book

Published by
Banbury Books, Inc.
37 West Avenue
Wayne, Pennsylvania 19087

ISBN: 0-440-00648-1

Printed in the United States of America

First printing—July 1983

Chapter 1

December was the best month of the year for traveling long distances on the island of Luzon. December was the coolest month, but that didn't mean it was cool. It meant that the air rushing through the open window of the old truck was merely hot rather than scorching, bearable, but hardly comfortable.

Father Grand sat behind the wheel, guiding the vehicle over the rough road through the jungle with his strong hands. He'd begun to age and was heavy around the middle. The sleeves of his white shirt were rolled up to the elbows; his black jacket and clerical collar lay on the frayed seat beside him. Periodically he wiped the sweat from his face with an old handkerchief.

"We're making excellent time," he said to Abby Preston. "Have you there in time for dinner."

Abby smiled and turned back to the window, grateful for the breeze, as hot as it was, against her damp face. She watched the jungle passing, catching a glimpse now and then of the bay beyond the dense foliage. Her stomach was in a knot and thoughts churned inside her head like the big truck tires on the rutted road. Going home. But where was home? Was it with her mother and aunt in Charleston, or was it back there at the mission with Father Grand and the other nurses—back there where she was important, where she was needed, where she had found meaning and purpose for the first time in her life.

"I'm going to miss you," she said to the priest.

"Just hurry back to us, my dear."

"I feel as if I'm deserting you."

He laughed. "No such thing. You're young. You need to see your family. You'll be in Australia before nightfall, San Francisco in four or five days."

She picked up the thermos from the floor by her feet and poured sweetened coffee for Father Grand. "I can't thank you enough for all you've done," she said. Father Grand had used his pull as a retired navy chaplain to get her a flight on a navy aircraft. Otherwise she would have had to cross the Pacific by boat, an ordeal that she just couldn't face again. She'd come to the Philippines that way and had endured horrible seasickness.

She and Father Grand laughed as he tried with mixed success to drink his coffee while the truck jounced along. She was going to miss him terribly. She'd never known her own father. She'd been raised by her mother and a maiden aunt, neither one of whom seemed to understand her choices in life. They'd practically been hysterical when she'd come home from college that memorable June of 1939 to announce that she was going to be a missionary nurse in the Far East. They'd gotten over their shock, but during the past two years their letters had pulled at her with gradually increasing force. To read them one would have thought that the two healthy middle-aged women—her mother wasn't even fifty and her aunt was just a little over the half-century mark—were about to plunge into their final illnesses and that if Abby ever hoped to see them alive again, she'd better take the next available flight to South Carolina.

She'd managed to put them off for months, but she finally succumbed and agreed to return for a visit. And that's all it would be. A visit. She was determined to return to the Philippines to fulfill her destiny among these people she loved.

"You have the packet of letters for the home church?" Father Grand asked.

"I won't lose it," she promised.

"I'm sure you won't." He smiled at her. "I know you're looking forward to seeing your mother."

How to explain to the good priest her mixed emotions about the two women in her life. She couldn't. All she could say was, "Yes."

She thought of the last letter she'd gotten from her mother in response to her own letter saying she was coming home. It had been full of fears about all the horrible disasters that could befall a young girl traveling halfway around the globe. Young girl! She was a *woman*! She'd been living on her own under extremely difficult circumstances for two years and doing a fine job in her chosen profession. But, she thought with a sigh, she was destined always to be regarded as a child, barely competent to walk around the corner to the grocery store, by her mother and aunt.

They passed a wallow in which half a dozen contented carabaos lounged.

"That's the life," Father Grand said with a wave of his gnarled hand. "Just lie in the cool mud and soak up the sun."

Seeing the water buffalo, which the villagers used as beasts of burden, touched her deeply. They reminded her of all that she would miss during the three months she'd agreed to remain at home. She thought about the adventures she'd had at the Laguna mission over the last two years—all the pleasures, all the pains, all the satisfactions of helping others; the Filipinos, the children, her fellow nurses and Father Grand. How she would miss it! Yes, she would be back, back in time for the rainy season when they would need her the most, when the rains brought the sicknesses to the jungle.

The rough jungle road gave way to asphalt paving as they neared the Cavite naval base, about seven miles down the bay from Manila. They could see the bay now, shimmering in the unrelenting sun. A small ship was steaming out past Corregidor, the rocky island that split the entrance to the bay into two channels. Even at that distance, they could see the fortifications on the island, the high, thick walls, the bristling guns.

They were soon amidst the bustle of a busy military establishment. A four-engine plane thrummed in low on its way to land at Nichols Field. Olive-drab navy trucks and jeeps rumbled past the wheezing old truck with its strange occupants, a priest and an attractive young woman. Some of the passing men whistled in appreciation.

Abby was worth whistling at. She was a slim woman, five foot four, with a thick head of healthy brown hair loose to the shoulders. She had lively, dancing brown eyes and her smile radiated an all-American friendliness and zest that men far from home in a strange land appreciated.

Approaching the naval hospital, Father Grand had to pull the old truck to one side to permit an ambulance to speed by. He drove onto the hospital grounds and pulled up in the staff parking area.

"I won't come in with you," the priest said. He helped her get her two bags out of the back of the truck. She felt the tears coming now. She brushed them aside as she kissed him on the cheek. They shook hands firmly and she could see that Father Grand was affected too. She hated good-byes.

She was distracted temporarily by the brisk arrival of a bubbly sailor whose wide eyes under a thatch of red hair betrayed his surprise and pleasure at coming upon the lovely woman in a white dress. He insisted on carrying her bags for her.

"You can just call me Red, ma'am," he said, hefting the bags. "And let me say that we're glad to have you aboard. If you need anything. . . ."

Abby turned and waved at Father Grand, who had already gotten behind the wheel of the truck and was backing out of the parking space. He had work to do and no time for excessive sentiment. He returned her wave and she felt the lump growing again in her throat.

Red glanced at her. "As I was saying, ma'am," he went on, "if you need anything, you just call for old Red."

"Thanks," Abby said, appreciative now of the distraction from her sadness in the form of this bouncy sailor with the big smile. "What I need right now is to find Lieutenant Ora Martin."

"She'll be on duty," Red said. "Just follow me."

They entered the hospital and she breathed that odor that hospitals the world over seem to possess. For a professional nurse like Abby, it was a smell of home.

She followed Red past the admissions desk and down a corridor to a ward desk where Ora Martin was filling in forms. Abby knew Ora. Ora had visited the Laguna mission several times to teach Abby and the other medical people there new techniques for combating the persistent tropical diseases that plagued the natives of the Philippines. Ora, about thirty-five, was a career navy nurse who gave the outward appearance of somewhat brusque busyness, but Abby knew that underneath Ora was warm and personable.

She leapt to her feet and gave Abby a friendly hug. "Wonderful to have you here, Abby," she beamed. Then she turned to Red. "Okay, Red," she said, "thanks. Now scram." Red grinned at the two women and reluctantly shuffled away. "Give me a few minutes to finish these papers and we'll go find you something to eat."

As she waited Abby looked about her at the brisk efficiency of the naval hospital. What a pleasure it would be to work in a place like this, she thought. The makeshift facilities at Laguna were sorry indeed compared to what was available here.

The dinner served in the nurses' lounge was so good compared to what Abby had been eating at the mission that she shamelessly stuffed herself. Afterward Ora had to go back on duty, but she first got Abby settled in her room. It actually had its own bathtub. What luxury! At the mission she bathed in an ancient tub which had to be filled with buckets of water carried in from cisterns, often swimming with mosquito larvae.

At lights out she got into the comfortable bed and waited for sleep to chase away all the disturbing thoughts that crowded her mind. One that she had not yet faced fully was the possibility that back in the States she might accidentally run into *him*.

She'd met Frank Charles when she was in her second year of nurses' training. He was ten years older than she and he seemed to her to epitomize the perfect doctor—skilled, dedicated, loving. She'd made her first rounds with Dr. Charles, did her first IV under his direction, and she thought it was safe to fall quietly in love with him in the belief that he didn't know she existed beyond the hospital walls. She was taken completely by surprise one day when he asked her to have dinner with him.

He took her to a fine restaurant and coaxed her to try a glass of wine. It seemed harmless enough then, even romantic. He seemed interested in her only for her professional abilities. Then and on a number of subsequent dates, they talked almost exclusively of medicine and the concerns at the hospital where they worked.

But one Sunday night he invited her to his apartment. She was disarmed by her affection and respect for him and the belief that theirs was but a professional friendship. And then he kissed her and for the first time she dared to hope—to believe—that a man such as he could actually love her. Love! What a bitter joke that had turned out to be.

"Abby," he'd said, "we won't even talk about marriage until you've finished school. I'm just getting established. When you're a registered nurse and I have my own practice. . . ."

How she had allowed herself to dream! How wonderful it had seemed at the time!

Now, there on the bunk in the nurses' quarters on the island of Luzon, she fought back bitter tears. "Father, forgive me for I have sinned," she prayed aloud.

When it was done, Frank Charles had looked at her in stunned surprise. "My God," was all he'd said, "why didn't you tell me you were a virgin?"

Father, forgive me for I have sinned.

She found out on her graduation day that Frank Charles was married. His wife came up from Charleston.

She was a pretty woman who spoke to Abby about their lovely old home in one of the better sections of Abby's own hometown. The fact that the Charleses actually lived in her home city made it even worse.

All the anguish, the torment of that time came rushing back to her and she lived it all over again. Only her faith had kept her from killing herself, had kept her going.

Oh, how he'd smiled, begged, coaxed—and lied! His words came back to her now: "It's all right, darling, we're going to be married." She squirmed with remembered humiliation.

It had been a while since she'd put herself through this pain. Why had it all come back this night? It was the prospect of going home, back to where it had happened and where, as far as she knew, Dr. Charles still lived, waiting to mock her with his secret knowledge of her.

Peace came to her at last and she slept for a time.

She was awakened by the sound of excited female voices. There was confusion and noise in the corridor outside her room. Then she heard Ora Martin's voice raised above the others. "Jesus Christ!" she cried. "What's the matter with you people? It's only six o'clock."

Then Abby heard the words that would ring in her ears for the rest of her life.

"They've bombed Pearl Harbor!" a woman yelled.

Abby clambered out of bed and dressed quickly. She soon found herself in the midst of the confused bustle, the shock and anger that filled the hospital as the word spread. People stood in small groups talking excitedly. A sailor began distributing gas masks to startled workers. Abby held hers in stunned disbelief. It had the disgusting appearance of some grotesque and venomous snake.

"Kid," Ora Martin said to her, "you can forget about going home."

"I know. I have to get back to the mission."

"Yes, I suppose you should." Ora pondered a moment. "I guess Commander Smith might be able to find some transportation for you."

She led the way down a hall to find Smith. A sound froze them in their tracks. It was like distant thunder but more ominous. They went to an open window and looked out. They could see Manila in the distance across the bay. There was another rumble and as they looked, a dark plume of smoke rose into the sky from the other side of the city.

"Oh, God, it's happening already," Abby whispered hoarsely.

"That's probably Clark Field, or maybe Iba Field," Ora supposed.

The thundering continued and Abby felt her flesh crawl. War, the unthinkable, had come to them. It was there, in that smoke, in that terrible sound. People were dying. More people would die.

They hurried on to Commander Smith's office. It was crowded with a group of junior officers. When the two nurses finally were able to get to him with their request, they got an incredulous look in return.

"Great God, Lieutenant!" Smith yelled. "Are you out of your mind? There's a war on!"

Later, they all gathered around radios, eager to catch every scrap of news. The news was devastating. The Japs had caught most of the U.S. aircraft in the Philippines on the ground.

The next day enemy planes came closer. Just after

sunrise they roared in to pound nearby Nichols Field. They were close enough that Abby could smell the smoke, hear the screaming aircraft and the chatter of machine guns as the planes went in low to strafe. The exploding bombs shook the hospital.

Ora Martin rushed up to her. "We're sending all the wounded into Manila, Abby," she informed the younger nurse. "I think you should go with us."

Abby had no choice. It was evident that she wasn't going to be able to get back to the mission, even though that's where she felt she belonged. She considered walking, but decided that such a hike through the jungle would be foolhardy.

Ora found her some uniforms, and although she wore no insignia of rank, at first glance she looked like a navy nurse officer.

As they crossed the bay by boat with the wounded, they could hear Cavite being bombed. They looked back across the water to see both the naval base and the hospital they'd just evacuated burning. The column of smoke was reflected in the rippling waters of the bay.

Abby threw herself into her work and there was plenty to do. Sternberg Hospital in Manila became a mad scene of barely organized chaos. Wounded servicemen poured in from everywhere, from Clark and Iba Fields, from Cavite, from Nichols Field. There were also many civilian casualties.

The air raids went on constantly around them. The hospital building shook repeatedly with the concussions. The windows rattled and bottles of medicine clanked on their shelves. At first it was unnerving, but gradually Abby found to her surprise that she got used to it. She was becoming a toughened combat veteran.

The wounded crowded the hospital rooms and overflowed into the corridors. Red and a lanky orderly named Pete helped Abby and other nurses sort and grade them according to the seriousness of their wounds. There were women and children among the wounded now. The war had reached the innocent.

It was odd, but news that the Japanese had landed at Lingayen Gulf seemed unimportant to Abby when contrasted with the weeping of a little girl with a piece of shrapnel in her stomach.

One hectic day she met Dr. John Fraleigh, one of the surgeons. His tunic was stained with blood and there were deep, dark circles under his eyes.

"Ora Martin tells me you're a good surgical nurse," the doctor said, the weariness evident in his voice.

"Yes, sir," she replied.

"Good. Come with me."

She worked with Dr. Fraleigh in surgery. There was no time to think, no time to be tired. She worked automatically, her hands and body moving in the rhythms she'd been trained to perform. The days merged into nights and nights into days. Dr. Fraleigh appreciated her quiet efficiency but there was no time or occasion to tell her. The wounded, the dying, flowed in and out of surgery in a ceaseless stream.

And then suddenly, almost as in a dream, she found herself in a bus, going somewhere. She looked about her at Dr. Fraleigh and other bone-weary hospital personnel sagging in their seats.

"All we know now," the surgeon announced to the group, "is that we're going out onto the Bataan peninsula. General MacArthur is there."

Pete, the orderly, had a guitar. He sat at the back of the bus and strummed and they all joined in singing songs of home and moonlit bays. It seemed so unreal.

Beyond the bus windows Abby could see the gentle, friendly Filipino people with whom she'd worked for two years streaming down the road, their belongings piled high atop the small carts called calesas, drawn by the little native ponies. They were dazed, frightened, yet one woman flashed a V for victory sign at the bus and gave them a brave, toothless smile. The human spirit did not die so easily.

"Planes!" Red yelled.

The bus jerked to a halt and the passengers scrambled out the front door and the emergency exit and ran for cover in roadside ditches.

An airplane, the Japanese emblem of a red rising sun clearly visible on its wings, came in low, its engine snarling, and stitched a ragged row of machine-gun bullets down the road. Abby pressed her face against the earth of the ditch and every muscle tensed in fear. Farther down the road some civilian refugees who hadn't found cover in time were hit. After the plane had gone, they gave emergency first aid as best they could, then continued on their rocky journey. Nobody felt like singing after that.

They reached Camp Limay after dark. They had to find their bunks with flashlights. A lizard had already found a home in Abby's bunk, but she was too tired to do anything beyond halfheartedly chase it away. She crawled into her sack and was almost instantly asleep.

At Camp Limay there was equipment for a thousand-bed hospital, but it was all in crates in warehouses. Nurses and doctors worked alongside the men to retrieve it. And then came the wounded, in waves, a flood of bloody uniforms and moaning men and malaria and putrid sores which refused to heal. All operating rooms were in continual use, planes roared overhead, tanks rumbled past, men marched, the nights were lit with the flash of cannon and the news was all bad. Quinine was low, often gone, food low, no blood plasma so that everyone who could walk gave blood. When the sterile dressings gave out it was Abby, accustomed to shortages at the mission, who put Red and Pete to work gathering the dried, bloody, sometimes putrid dressings to boil in pots, scrub them, dry them on a fence and sterilize them in a crude rig which used wood as a fuel.

Christmas came, but there was no celebration. Then it was January and the sounds of the fighting came ever nearer. Corpsmen made extra beds by hanging tents on poles and stuffing mattresses with dry grass and rice chaff. Poor food and bad sanitation, dysentery, beriberi, malaria and a growing cemetery. The jungle heat sapped them, dust sifted down over everything. Gas gangrene cases filled the crowded wards with a sickening stench. Men played poker with cards fashioned from pieces of cardboard and painted pennies black and red to serve as checkers. You couldn't keep their names straight because there were so many. And then word came that MacArthur was gone.

A wounded soldier was bitter. "Leave it to old baggy pants. He took a powder. He don't give a damn what happens to us. What kind of a general is it won't stay with his men?"

Another agreed. "General Wainwright, now that's a different story. When I got hit he was no more than twenty yards from me, right up there on the front lines."

The hospital was bombed in March. One bomb scored a direct hit on one of the huge red crosses on the roof. Bombs, Abby discovered, made a sound unlike anything she'd ever heard. After one explosion the jungle screeched pitifully back in the form of a wounded monkey, one of its long, spidery legs blown off.

Dr. Fraleigh was at the operating table during the attack. The room shook from a near miss but he calmly went on with his work. When it was over they heard on short wave that the Japanese had apologized for bombing the hospital by mistake.

Easter Sunday. Red and Pete found a dead mule, hit by shellfire, and the resulting mule stew was delicious. Rank was forgotten. Men and nurses ate where they could, when they could. Ora and Abby were savoring the hot, spicy stew in the company of Dr. Fraleigh and Red and Pete, who'd made it a point to work closely with the two women.

It was Fraleigh who brought up a subject which was often discussed, the expected arrival of a resupply convoy. Pete snorted. "Doc, you can forget it. Way I figure it, the Japs got most of the U.S. navy at Pearl Harbor."

"Shut up and drink your beer," Red grumbled. Pete rolled his eyes. The last beer he'd had was in Manila in late November. "They'll come. You can bet on it. Old baggy pants will come back and bring a couple of divisions with him and wipe them yellow monkeys off the map."

Fraleigh was eating fast. There were wounded waiting. He paused with a bite halfway to his mouth. Aircraft buzzed overhead.

"They wouldn't," Abby said. "Not again."

The all-too-familiar shriek of a bomb sent them scrambling for cover. It ripped apart an ammunition truck near the front gate and flying pieces of steel ripped into the hospital. The wounded in the wards cried for help. The roof of a building was blown off into nearby trees. The planes strafed the smoking ruins. When it was over, the thousand beds they'd once had were reduced to sixty-five and word spread that they would have to leave in half an hour.

Darkness brought mass confusion as hospital personnel, the wounded, retreating soldiers and civilians all headed for the bay. From the dock at the village of Mariveles, Abby and other hospital workers could see the Rock, the island fortress of Corregidor across the open stretch of water. A bombardment was under way. They saw the flash and smoke of bombs on the island. Boats streaming toward it were hit and they could plainly hear the cries of the men in the water. Behind them massive explosions shook the earth as the retreating American and Filipino forces blew up their ammo dumps.

Abby and other nurses climbed dazed into a small boat and motored across the seething waters toward the Rock. At any moment, she feared, they would be blown out of the water. But they made it, scrambled ashore and joined others as they made their way deep into the manmade tunnels of the fortress. There was a peculiar, musty smell far underground and a feeling of great security, for the tons of rock overhead gave them protection from the bombs and shells. There was, best of all, hot food. Working conditions were good.

"Well now, we can just hole up here," Red decided, "and wait for old baggy pants to bring in the Marines."

When the bombers came the entire rocky island seemed to shake and quiver, but it was snug and secure down in the deep tunnels and once again Abby was working in a well-equipped operating room.

The men who straggled in from the Bataan peninsula said that it was all over there. Civilians fleeing the Japanese also found shelter in the tunnels of Corregidor. They slept on the floor in the passageways. A month passed. It was May. No one seemed to remember that Abby was a civilian nurse. It wouldn't have mattered. She worked hungry alongside the rest of them. The big guns of the fort spoke less and less, for ammunition was running low.

She knew something was going to happen when Ora came to her after she'd finished a shift in the operating room.

"We've got to pack up again," Ora told her.

At first Abby didn't speak. Where? was all she could think. There was no other place. Corregidor was the last stronghold. The Japanese had overrun all the rest of the island. The little rocky point of land in the center of the entrance to Manila Bay, the Rock of Corregidor, was the last remaining hold-out.

They knew, the defenders of American honor on Corregidor, that the entire world was watching them. The world heard about their brave stand through the short-wave broadcasts.

"I don't know where we're going," Ora said, answering Abby's unspoken question, "but we're going. All I know is that orders are for all nurses to get ready, to carry only the bare necessities."

"That's no problem," Abby said. She was down to less than the necessities. She'd scrounged a pair of GI socks off a dead soldier so that she had two pairs. She was dressed in oversized GI fatigues, wore GI shorts for underwear.

A bosun's mate stuck his head into their quarters. "Ready, Lieutenant?" he asked. "Let's move it out."

Abby walked with Ora. She had her spare pair of

socks in one hand. The wounded were lying all around on bunks in the corridors. "Are they going to take us off by water?" she asked the bosun's mate.

"That's my guess," the sailor said. "Nurses only. Old Mac left by torpedo boat. They might have a couple of them left."

"What about the men?" Abby asked. "The wounded?"

The bosun's mate shrugged.

"Come on, honey," Ora said. "It's all over. The Japs will have doctors to help take care of the wounded."

The nurses assembled in a large room and there was a head count.

"Ladies," a tired looking army colonel said, "I want to wish you a safe journey, to tell you farewell." He seemed to be on the verge of weeping. He paused and wiped his face with a soiled olive-drab handkerchief. "You'll be in Australia soon."

"Are we going to swim?" someone asked, and there was a nervous titter.

"No, we're handing you over to the U.S. navy," the colonel said. "A submarine, as a matter of fact."

"Oh, Lord," someone moaned.

Abby whispered into Ora's ear. Ora looked at her, eyes wide. "You can't."

"I have a favor to ask of you," Abby continued.

"You're crazy."

"Will you do it?"

"Yes, damnit," Ora said.

Abby gave her Father Grand's packet of letters, gave her instructions on how to get them to the home church.

"In a way I don't blame you," Ora admitted,

holding both of Abby's hands in hers. "If it were up to me—"

"I know, Ora. I know."

"I have to take orders," Ora explained.

For a long moment they clung together, two women in baggy fatigues, one small, the other big-boned and tall. And then the bosun's mate was saying, "All right, ladies, off and on, hit it a lick and move out."

Abby watched them walk down a long corridor and disappear around a corner and for a moment she felt like running after them. Then she turned.

Dr. Fraleigh was not in the operating room. She found him in his quarters. He was propped up on his bunk, a can of beer in his hand. When he saw her his eyes went wide.

"What the hell are you doing here?" he demanded. "You're supposed to be boarding a submarine."

"No," she said.

"I order you to go, Preston," Fraleigh said, throwing his bare feet to the floor and standing.

"I'm not in the navy, doctor," she said. "I'm staying. I *am* a civilian. I'm going to find a way to get back to the mission."

They worked with little sleep for three days and then the news began to spread as the guns fell silent.

Men wept, or cursed, or laughed and made an attempt to finish off the last of the beer before the Japs got their hands on it. The Japanese arrived on May 6. Abby was in the operating room at her usual place beside Dr. Fraleigh. The first she knew of a Jap presence on Corregidor was the sound of a door bursting open.

She looked up. Little yellow men rushed in, brandishing rifles, yelling at them in their incomprehensible language. Fraleigh paused for only a moment. He was in the midst of a delicate bowel resection. A Japanese soldier moved near him, thrust his bayonet toward the doctor and yelled.

"Look," Fraleigh said, "I can't stop now."

A bowlegged Japanese soldier with an insignia on his sleeve yelled at Fraleigh.

"Do any of you gentlemen speak English?" Fraleigh asked, his hands working rapidly.

She knew two or three words in Japanese. One was *kill*. They were threatening to kill the doctor. "Hurry," she whispered to him.

"I have to finish this," Fraleigh said, speaking to the Japanese soldier with the insignia on his sleeve, "or this man will die."

The sergeant—later she would have occasion to identify the insignia of the Japanese army—raised his rifle and smashed the butt down into the face of the man on the operating table, crushing the ether mask. The orderly who'd been administering the ether yelled and leapt up to be met by a thrusting bayonet.

Fraleigh heard the sound of crunching bones, felt the life go out of the man on the table. "You dirty sons of bitches," he whispered. He put down his scalpel and turned. The soldier who'd been punching his bayonet at the doctor moved back. Fraleigh was a tall man, a big man, and the Japanese soldier seemed to be dwarfed. "You killed him," Fraleigh said to the sergeant. The doctor lunged forward and the other soldier's rifle blasted twice. Fraleigh, hit in the chest, stumbled back.

The Japanese milled around, watched Fraleigh sink to the floor. Abby put her fist into her mouth to keep from screaming. The swift dead glaze which came to Fraleigh's eyes told the final story. He was gone.

She stood, hands hanging limply at her sides, and all thought seemed to fly out of her head. Images flowed in ultraslow motion. She saw a parade of faces, the faces all mixed up, her mother, people she hadn't seen since high school, Dr. Fraleigh's dead face, Red's cheerful smile, and all the faces of the dead and the wounded who'd come and gone from the hospitals in that eon of suffering since the first bombs fell on Manila.

She was not, in that stunned, endless moment as she looked down into the doctor's unseeing eyes, concerned in the least about herself. Her thoughts were for Fraleigh, for the other dead, those who filled the dry, dusty graves in that cemetery back at the last camp.

As her mind leapt and shuddered, she wished that she were a man and had in her hands a weapon, a huge and deadly machine gun. She would aim it at the Japanese and fire and it would spit and cough and send the deadly bullets to burst the Japs like melons and to avenge those who were dead or who still lay wounded in the jungles, their wounds infected, maggots working in the decaying flesh.

And as if she had given her mind wings, she seemed transported from the immediate scene. It was as if she *could* see, see the stragglers, the wounded, the sick, the starving. Were the Japs killing all of them, as they'd killed the wounded man, the orderly, the doctor? It was a huge, dusty, malignant panorama—the jungle, the blasted trees, the fleeing men. For that eternal moment she was a part of it, and she would think in later days that she really had gone out of her body, for she was to learn later that what she'd witnessed in her imaginary flight had in fact taken place.

* * *

She had no way of knowing at that time that there were Americans, a few, who fully intended to keep fighting. There were men in the jungle who'd been fighting for weeks on poor food, some suffering the effects of the tropical fevers, who intended to die rather than surrender. It became evident even in the very early hours of the surrender in Bataan that such surrender, to a warrior race that scorned the very idea of giving up while one could still fight, was not the best idea.

Tony Dunking was one such man. He was an Oklahoman, a career man, army all the way. He had three stripes on his sleeve when the bombs fell on the airfields and got two more in the field during the retreat into the peninsula. The stripes didn't matter when the orders came to give up, to lay down arms and seek out the nearest Japanese unit, white flags flying. He doubted that his field promotions had been reported or recorded anyhow, and the stripes of a staff sergeant wouldn't do him any good in a Jap prison camp.

When the orders came he was, by default, senior man in what was left of an infantry company made up of Filipino regulars. They'd fought well, too well in their last engagement. They'd stayed in an exposed position to allow the movement of supply forces and a headquarters, so that their already reduced numbers had been cut to only fifteen men.

They were tough, those little dark-skinned soldiers. Tony had come to have great admiration for them, and he knew that they would, perhaps, get rougher treatment than the Americans in a Jap prison camp. He sought out the Filipino three-striper when the orders came.

"They say we've got to surrender," he said.

The Filipino sergeant spat a stream of tobacco juice, looked Tony in the eye and shook his head. "Yeah, I know what you mean. But we got a couple of choices, bad and worse." The Filipino sergeant looked up and away. He couldn't see the distant hills, only the sere, hot, dying, blasted vegetation of the jungle. "You surrender," the Filipino said. "I go home."

Tony Dunking stood just over six feet tall. He towered over the Filipinos. He had just enough Choctaw blood in him to make his heavy hair straight and dark, his skin swarthy. He had large brown eyes and a long, straight, strong nose. He'd been slim when the war began and now he was skinny, a tall, gaunt, scarecrow of a man whose basic good looks still showed in his high-cheeked face.

"Think you can get through?"

"We get through or . . ." The sergeant shrugged.

Tony wondered if he should go with them. He'd grown up wild as a buck, living on a little house on the edge of Holdenville, Oklahoma. On a fall Saturday he and his little brother could step out into the front yard, guns in hand, and strike out in any direction in search of rabbit, squirrel or a covey of quail. He'd grown up running free and he'd spent the night in a jail once, not as a criminal, but because he'd been stranded out in the wilds of the California mountains with no money and the sheriff had offered him a bunk in the jail. Even as a guest he didn't like closed places. But he was a tall, white man. He might, by his presence, jeopardize the Filipinos' chances of getting through to the mountains.

"You come, too," the Filipino offered after a while.

Tony voiced his worries about not being able to keep up with the jungle-wise Filipinos.

" 'At's all right. We wait."

"Well, buddy, I sure do appreciate that," Tony said. "I don't reckon I'd like Jap food too good."

"Japs eat shit," the Filipino said, and it was decided.

They traveled mainly by night. They had to avoid the roads because the Japanese were there in numbers and the roads were also beginning to be clogged with captive Americans and Filipinos. They waded swamps, plagued by vicious insects and tough-hided leeches and Tony felt the malaria coming back. He'd been out of quinine for weeks and it was God's wonder it had stayed away that long.

"Sarge," he said, "I'm getting the fever. You fellows will just have to go on without me."

They'd been traveling for four days and they'd covered about twenty miles. There was a long way to go. They had to make their way through the whole Jap army and God only knew what else before they got to the mountains.

"Tell me one thing," the Filipino said.

"Shoot," Tony said.

"You're a good man. You know how to fight. You fight Japs?"

"Bet your ass, if I get the chance," Tony vowed. But he was beginning to feel terrible and he shivered in spite of the heat and his sweat soaked his rotting fatigues.

He woke up a few times and thought he was back on a troop ship, for the ship was bouncing, and then he realized that he was being carried by those glorious little buggers, carried through that hell of a jungle on a makeshift litter by two little guys who, put together, would have made one Tony Dunking. He burned with fever and with shame. He tried to get off the litter and they pushed him back on. The boss Filipino had to speak roughly to him, telling him he was holding up the party and to get his ass back on the litter so they could make some time.

Fortunately, the malaria attack was not a full-blown screaming, scalding, trembling, debilitating one. It passed in two days and he was on his feet, stumbling along. They found a couple of dead American soldiers and took their ammo and guns and pressed on.

The character of the terrain began to change and in more open country they had to be extra careful. The Japs must have landed a million men, Tony thought. They were everywhere.

When the last of their field rations ran out—and they'd managed to pick up some extras from the dead on the way—Tony learned to eat snails, and once he enjoyed a steak off the biggest damned snake he'd ever seen. The meat was as good as any beefsteak he'd ever had back in Oklahoma.

He began to feel healthier. They could see the mountains now, rising green—burned green, for the rains had not yet come—low and far off, and he began to think they were going to make it.

They picked up a swabby and an army private in the foothills, both in pretty bad shape, and that slowed them down a little until the Filipinos were able to get enough snail and snake meat into the new arrivals to give them some strength. The growing party pushed on to the relative security of the mountains.

There were no Japs in the mountains. Now and then they got a scare when a group of men would appear, but they turned out, every time, to be other Filipinos. Most of them were just looking for a place to hide from the Japanese, but some were angry, like Tony and the little group of survivors from his company. Some of them were angry enough to fight.

It just seemed to happen naturally that Tony was the man who gave orders and made decisions. He knew the drill. He was used to giving orders and the Filipinos were used to taking orders from white officers.

"What we got to have is some guns and some ammo and some chow," he said, as the group, which had grown to over twenty-five men, chewed on tough buffalo meat over campfires. It was safe to have the fires because they were deep in the hills. "And the Japs got all that stuff now," he finished.

"We go take it," his little buddy said. He'd named the Filipino Sergeant Charlie because he couldn't pronounce Charlie's real name. Charlie didn't seem to mind.

"Yeah, let's do that," Tony said. "How many you fellows want to go back down and kick some Jap ass?"

About a dozen volunteered.

It was a fine trip. The cooler air of the mountains had revived them and the thought of good food drove them. They bushwhacked a convoy of American trucks being driven by Japanese. There was so much food and ammo and guns that they had to burn much of it, not being able to carry it all, and then they went back into the hills.

Tony brought back one item himself. A case of dynamite. He'd had a couple of courses in using it. He could really give the Japs something to think about with that stuff. He wished he had a ton of it because from all indications, it was going to be a long war.

Chapter 2

Emi Pecora heard the news from Ralph Izumi. She was on stage in San Jose at the time the Japanese planes were bombing Hawaii, reciting lines from Ibsen.

Emi had the lead role. There'd been a lot of good-natured ribbing about Ibsen's doll being Eurasian, but she was doing a fine job with the role. The young men who were studying in the drama department at San Jose State liked to come around and watch her rehearse. The fact that she'd been elected as Miss Campus 1941, was a tribute to the willowy beauty she possessed. Her skin combined the porcelain perfection of her Japanese-Chinese mother and the swarthy Portuguese and northern European complexion of her late father. Her hair was the thick, black hair of the Oriental and girls envied her because she could do anything with it. Art students begged her to pose for them and the caption in the yearbook, under her photo as Miss Campus, said without equivocation that Emi Pecora was among the most beautiful girls ever to attend the little college.

When she finished her part she went out front and sat with Ralph Izumi. He was weeping. Ralph was

Nisei, born in the United States of Japanese parents. He had a bit part in the play.

"Ralph?" she asked, leaning toward him. The lights on the stage lit the front seats only dimly.

He wiped his cheeks with the back of one hand. He had the dark, thick hair of the pure Japanese. She'd dated him a couple of times, largely because he was one of the finest jitterbugs in school, but their relationship was more friendship than anything else. He was, she knew, from the valley, not far from her own home in Madera.

"I have freedom here, Emi," he said, his voice choked. "Here I can be anything I want to be. I can be an actor or a businessman. I can earn enough money to own a car and a home. This is my country. I'll fight them."

"What on earth are you talking about?" she asked.

"Yes, I'll fight Japan," he resolved.

"Ralph?"

He told her about Pearl Harbor. She felt a sinking sensation in her stomach. And then a fierce hatred. A sneak attack. Many Americans killed. *Americans*. It hit her hard, because Emi had never considered herself to be anything but American. She'd been born in that little house on the outskirts of Madera, and she'd grown up as a tomboy, playing with boys, mostly, swimming in the irrigation canals, lying on her back in the summer sun to stuff herself with the sweetness of the Thompson seedless grapes her father grew.

Emi Pecora was as American as apple pie and baseball, the all-American girl who wore pleated, wide skirts and bobby socks, who was on the high school cheerleading squad and was always one of the most popular girls in school.

Emi took Ralph's hand. What did it all mean? To her the war had come as a complete surprise. She wasn't much of a newspaper reader and when she listened to the radio it was to Jack Benny and Fibber McGee and Molly.

"But why?" she asked. Ralph just shook his head.

From then on she listened to newscasts. With her roommate and several other girls who didn't have radios, she sat in her room on the bed, Indian fashion, long, slim legs crossed under her, and heard the grim news. The Japanese attacks on Pearl Harbor and the bombing of the Philippines became the main topics of campus conversation. Some of the male students were already leaving, making their way to the nearest recruiting stations.

Emi thought at first that the loss of some male friends would be the only effect the war would have on her. That was before she received the telephone call from her mother. The call, itself, was cause for worry. Macimo Pecora was as old-fashioned woman. She hated the telephone and considered long-distance calls to be the ultimate folly. In Macimo Pecora's mind, there was no crisis too dire to be handled by a three-cent letter.

When Emi was told that she had a call from her mother on the hall telephone, she leapt from her bed and ran for the phone.

Macimo, as usual, spoke in Japanese. Although her mother had been Chinese, she considered Japanese her native tongue. She'd always been Japanese, and always would be, although her loyalty to her adopted country was, Emi knew, undoubted. Emi had heard all the stories, how Sam Pecora, a Portuguese sailor, had found the young Macimo in Macao, where Macimo's Japanese father had settled, married a Chinese woman and reared a large family, mostly girls. Macimo's family had been only too happy to ease the demands on the family budget by selling Macimo to the Portuguese sailor as a wife. And she remembered fondly how Sam Pecora had loved his "little flower," how he teased her about being the perfect, old-fashioned Japanese woman. Perhaps, Emi had come to think later, her father hadn't been teasing when he said, often, "I married a Japanese girl because they are the only women in the world who really know how to value a man." For Macimo had put her husband first in her life, had been a loving servant to him in the old Japanese tradition.

Because of her parentage, because Macimo was more comfortable when speaking Japanese, and because Sam, while becoming a very fiercely patriotic American, still thought best in Portuguese, Emi Pecora was at home in several languages. To her colloquial California English, she could add an educated and sophisticated knowledge of Japanese, fluent Portuguese, passable Chinese, and for her college language requirement, she was taking Spanish, finding it to be so similar to Portuguese that it was a snap course for her, leaving her more time for her dramatic and other extracurricular activities.

"My daughter," Macimo Pecora said, her voice distorted by the telephone, "are you well?"

"I am well, Mother," she replied in Japanese.

"It would please me if you would come home, and quickly," her mother said.

She did not question. She did not ask why. "I'll check the bus schedule right away, Mother," she said. "I'll be there sometime tomorrow."

"Thank you, my daughter," Macimo said. So formal, so polite, so goddamned inscrutable, Emi was thinking.

She had to go back to her room for the coins to operate the pay phone. She found that a bus would be leaving just after seven the next morning and went back to her room disturbed. It had to be bad news. It had to be serious. Her mother wouldn't have wasted a long-distance call without reason, and her mother was the kind of woman who couldn't break any bad news by telephone. But what could it be? She had no relatives, other than her mother. When Sam Pecora brought his Japanese-Chinese bride to the San Joaquin valley they were alone, just the two of them in a strange land.

She had another telephone call minutes later. It was Ralph Izumi. He wanted to see her. He sounded upset, so she dressed and went down into the visiting area. Ralph, wearing a yellow polo shirt and grey slacks, rose from a deep upholstered chair and came toward her.

"Have you heard what they're doing?" he asked. His usually sunny and friendly face was set in a pained expression. He took her arm and led her to a couch. "Men have come to my father's place," he said.

"What men? What do you mean?"

"It's been on the news. In Norfolk, Virginia, they didn't even wait for the F.B.I. They rounded up every Japanese and threw them all into jail."

She looked at him, puzzled. "But why?"

"I just heard a commentator on a newscast talking of how the Tennessee department of conservation has asked for licenses to hunt Japanese for a fee of two dollars each," Ralph reported. "The newscaster thought it was very funny when the request was denied with a note that said, 'It's open season on Japs. No licenses are needed.' "

"Oh, Ralph." And yet it didn't apply to her. She was Emi, the all-American girl. Poor Ralph.

"They're rounding up all Japanese here in California," Ralph went on. "It's said that they"—even he couldn't think of himself as Japanese, in spite of his skin, his eyes, the knowledge that both his parents were Japanese and, since U.S. law did not extend citizenship to Orientals, aliens—"it's said that all Japanese will be put into camps, where they cannot give information to the enemy."

"But not you!" she exclaimed. "You were born here. You're an American citizen."

"What of my parents?" he asked. "What of your mother?"

She took a deep breath. Jesus, was that the reason for the call? No. It couldn't be. Her mother, even if the government wouldn't recognize her as a citizen, was as American as anyone. Her mother, in spite of her humble Japanese female ways, was a little lady with an iron will, a woman who had taken over the ranch when her husband died, kept it going, and was able to save enough money to send her daughter to college.

"I'm going home," she revealed. "My mother called."

"Perhaps the men have been to see her, too," Ralph said.

"What are you going to do?" she asked.

"Go home. I guess I'll join the Marines."

The contradiction hit her and she looked at him, her large, brown eyes wide. He was, as the people who suddenly hated all Japanese would have said, yellow. And yet he was thinking of fighting soldiers of his own race.

She decided that she didn't like this war. She hated this war. She hated it for what it was doing already to gentle Ralph Izumi. And yet, even as she boarded the bus and began the ride down the highway, even as the bus swung east and headed toward the valley, she couldn't believe what she'd read in the morning newspaper.

Attorney General Francis Biddle had made a statement regarding aliens: "As long as aliens in this country conduct themselves in accordance with law, they need fear no interference by the Department of Justice." But then the article went on. All "suspicious" aliens would be given a hearing before they were interned. Interned! The very word horrified her. If found harmless, the aliens would be paroled. Others—harmful ones, presumably—would go to detention camps. There they would be more comfortable, according to the government spokesman, than they would be at home.

She looked up from the paper, musing over that last statement.

"You're a dirty, sneaking Jap!" yelled a small boy from across the aisle. She looked at him quickly, thinking for one horrible moment that he was yelling at her. But he was playing a game with toy guns with another small boy in the seat in front of him. "Bang, bang, bang!" they shot at each other.

"You sneaked up on me just like a yellow Jap," the little boy said, shooting a play machine gun, "Ack-ack-ack."

She went back to the paper. The war was everywhere, front page, back page, middle pages. And the Japanese seemed to have attacked everywhere. Pearl Harbor, of course, was the name on everyone's lips. But the Japanese were also on the move in Malaysia and they'd attacked the American islands of Guam, Wake, Midway, the Philippines. At Wake Island a story was developing which had the interest of the entire country. A small force of U.S. Marines had not only held off attack after attack, but had managed to sink two Japanese ships, a cruiser and a destroyer. The nation was hungry for a victory, eager for heroes. National pride had been dealt a severe blow by the disaster at Pearl Harbor, and the newspaper headlined the cocky answer from the Marines on Wake Island when they were asked what they needed: "Send us more Japs," they'd radioed back.

She dozed and roused during a couple of stops and then the countryside became familiar. She got her small bag down from the overhead rack and walked up to stand beside the driver. She could see the town ahead. Brakes hissed and the door opened.

There was a smell about the valley she'd always loved. Even in winter it was there. She stood beside the road and let the bus move away, then walked across the highway. There, extending on both sides along the eastern side of the road, were Pecora vines, planted by her father and mother working side by side.

The house sat back from the road in a little clearing amid the vineyards—a couple of shady trees, some grass, the porch and the porch swing in which she'd spent many hours, often with a book, often just lying there looking out over the vineyards and listening to the birds sing.

As she walked toward the house she heard her name and looked down toward the outbuildings. It was Thomas Brown. He'd been with the family since before the death of her father, a good man, a good worker. He took care of the vines. He hired the labor needed for pruning the vines and harvesting the grapes.

"Nice to see you home, Emi," he greeted her as he came near.

"Nice to see you, Mr. Brown," she answered.

"I need to have a talk with you before you go inside," Thomas said.

She put down her bag. "Is anything wrong?"

He looked away from her, spat a stream of tobacco juice. "Don't know exactly how to tell you this, Emi."

"Just tell me right out," she said.

"Yep, guess that would be best." He glanced into her eyes for a brief moment, then away again. "I'll be leaving," he said simply.

"I don't understand." She continued to look at him, puzzled.

"Quitting," he offered.

"Is it something we've done? Something my mother has done?" How would her mother ever run the ranch without him?

"Nope."

"I don't know what we'll do without you," she worried.

"You'll manage."

"Won't you reconsider, Mr. Brown?" Emi pressed.

This time he did look at her. "Folks don't take it right, me working for a Jap."

She flushed. He'd been working for a Jap, as he called her mother, for five years, since her father's death—and for many years before that for her father. "Do you always let what other folks say make up your mind for you?"

He spat again. "Don't much fancy it myself, if you must know, Emi."

She wanted to rail at him, but she held back. It would serve no purpose. Because of what people thousands of miles away were doing, because of the policy of the Japanese government, her mother was going to be left without any help around the ranch.

"If I was you, Emi, I'd take my mother and go somewhere," Brown advised. "Folks is riled up. The F.B.I.'s done been picking up Japs and some of the young bloods burned out the Nombura place up the road."

She felt ill, physically ill. Mitsu Nombura was one of the finest men she'd ever known, a kind, considerate man, always willing to help his neighbor. He'd come to the United States when he was a teen-age boy.

"Thank you, Mr. Brown," she said. "We'll manage."

Her mother was in the sitting room. She wore a finely crafted silk kimono, her hair on top of her head Japanese style. She rose and bowed. "My daughter, thank you for coming."

She went to her mother and embraced her. "Don't worry," she said in English. "Everything's all right now."

It wasn't the first time she'd worked in the vineyards, but it had been a long time, and even as a teen-age girl at home her father had never forced her to work. She'd gone into the fields at times and helped with the pruning just to be with him, to hear his salty tales of the seagoing life. Now it was just she and her mother and her hands soon were sore with blisters, her nose red from the sun.

Heroic Wake Island fell. The Japanese were fighting their way through jungles thought to be impenetrable in Malaya, closing on Singapore. The nation had a hero in Colin Kelly, who sank a Japanese battleship.

The telephone rang a lot, for there were other Japanese families in the valley and no one knew what was going to happen. Stories went around. Men simply disappeared. The F.B.I. came and in fifteen minutes a neighbor was missing. Emi stayed close to home. Going back to school was out of the question. No one of Japanese blood knew from minute to minute when the F.B.I. would come knocking on the door.

His Majesty's battleship, *Prince of Wales*, was sunk by Japanese aircraft, the cruiser, *Repulse*, going down with her. The heroic stand of the defenders of the Bataan peninsula and then Corregidor became known, and on the other side of the world the Germans seemed destined to conquer all of Europe. The war. The damned war.

But things were, apparently, settling down. Japanese farmers went into the towns only when necessary, lest they be jeered and sometimes, attacked, but all in all it looked as if they would be left alone.

Executive Order 9066, signed by Franklin Roosevelt on February 19, 1942, ended the period of bucolic peace. The sensitive West Coast of the United States was divided into zones in relationship to Japanese aliens, and all those who lived in Zone 1 would be moved to internment camps within thirty days.

The Pecora family car was an antique Ford. It was seldom driven. Emi, frightened and confused by the news of the executive order, not really believing that it would be applied to a middle-aged Japanese widow, was pleased when the car cranked immediately and got her all the way into Madera without stalling. Her father had done business with a lawyer who had his office in the bank building.

"I'm glad you came by, Emi," the lawyer said. "I've been intending to come out and have a talk with you. This alien scare, you know."

"That's why I'm here," she said. "My mother—"

"Let me finish first," the lawyer said. "You're over twenty-one now, aren't you?"

"By a few months."

"Good. I told you this at the time of your father's death, you and your mother. I was almost sure that neither of you understood, if you even heard. But your father left the ranch to you, Emi, to be yours and under your control upon your twenty-first birthday. That might turn out to be a wise decision on his part."

"I don't see that it makes any difference," she said. "As far as I'm concerned, even if a paper says differently, it's my mother's home as long as she's alive, and it's her property."

"Of course, of course," the lawyer said, "but don't you know that the property of some Japanese aliens is being confiscated?"

She sat down, her knees going weak. "No, I didn't know."

"Either that or they're having to sell for a song when they're taken away as security risks. Now in your case, since you're an American citizen, and since you're only—what, a half?"

"If you're talking about my Japanese blood, one quarter," she answered glumly.

"Okay, good. In your case, I think we'll be able to hang on to the land for you, and if they send your mother to a camp you can stay here."

"Can't you do something?" Emi asked. "She's no spy. She couldn't care less about the war. All she wants to do is stay in her home and work her land."

The lawyer shrugged. "Emi, the Japs and the Germans are very damned close to taking over the world. The Japs have shelled the Oregon coast. You can't go anywhere without hearing rumors of a Jap invasion of California. Now there are a million ways a fifth column can send messages and valuable information to the enemy.

There's no guarantee we're going to win this war, girl. We got cold-cocked at Pearl Harbor. We lost so much of our naval strength that the Pacific is a Jap lake."

"An invasion of California? That's silly."

He looked at her grimly. "Up till December 7 the idea that Pearl Harbor would be bombed was a silly idea. Now you listen. If you don't want to lose your ranch, you'll do as I say. When they come for your mother, you call me. I'll come out. We'll see that you're not taken. You can stay here and hold on. The land is mortgage free. I don't know if you'll be able to hire labor to care for the vines, but at least you'll be able to keep your home and land. You can't fight this, kid. National security, freedom itself, is at stake. You'll just have to roll with the punches and make the best of it."

She waited. In the Stockton-Salinas area there were bombings of Japanese homes and several other incidents of violence. She was living in a state of fear so strange to her that sometimes, at night, she would pinch herself to see if she were awake, and her mother, always strong under that placid, pleasing exterior, had seemed to withdraw within herself.

The men in the neat, three-piece, double-breasted suits came in April. They were very polite. They searched the house for hidden radios and other spy devices and they left a paper which ordered Mrs. Macimo Pecora to report to the train station in Madera on May 10, 1942, for removal to "a safe place."

Somehow she'd known it was coming. She'd made her decision. When the F.B.I. men left, she got on the telephone. She'd already spoken to their nearest neighbor, a man who'd been their friend from the time she was born. He and his sons would lease the ranch. One of the older boys was getting married and he and his new wife would move into the Pecora house.

"Don't you worry, Emi, we'll take care of the place. It'll be here for you when this damned war is over," the neighbor assured her.

"I'm going with my mother," she told the men at the train station. "There's nothing you can do to stop me."

"But you're not on the order," a young man in a three-piece suit said.

"I'm a spy," she announced. "I'm dangerous. I must be put in a concentration camp along with my mother. Heil Tojo!"

In the end they let her board the train. Her mother huddled down in a seat next to the window and watched the familiar, flat, fertile fields of the valley give way to the arid stretches of southern California. The government had taken over the Santa Anita racetrack. Many aliens were housed in stables, but Emi and her mother were fortunate. A new barracks had been built. They were put into a twelve-by-fourteen-foot room with a family of four, a man, his wife and their two children.

There was work for those who wanted it. Emi found herself thinking Japanese, talking Japanese, while she worked with men, women and children at weaving camouflage nets for use by the American troops who would soon be fighting the Japanese and Germans. And the days went by. Her mother, at first, refused to work, but the little room became stifling as summer came and so Macimo joined in the making of the nets. Then it was July, August, and there were endless rumors. They would, according to some reports, spend the war in that racetrack compound. According to other reports they were to be moved to the south, to the Arctic, to the desert, or some other faraway place so that they couldn't stand on the rocky coastline and signal to the Jap submarines or the Jap invasion force offshore.

The move came in October. Once again they were on a train. It had no air conditioning, of course. It was hot. The windows were open and cinders from the engine, soot and dust blew in so that within a few hours Emi felt as if she'd never had a bath.

The camp at Hart Mountain, Wyoming, was enclosed by barbed wire. There were guard towers with armed men and searchlights. There was work. Once again they made camouflage nets. Outside the fence was rocky desert. And as the weather chilled and there was snow, the cold became a kind of hell never known by a girl who'd grown up in the San Joaquin valley. The cold was an insidious force which was bearable, at first, but which gradually crept into her very bones.

She considered escape. It could be called nothing else, because the camp was a prison. The quarters were always frigid. But even if she could coax her mother to leave with her, even if she could get through the fence, where would she go? She'd heard that the nearest town was over twenty miles away. And there would be those loyal, patriotic Americans who would holler "Jap, Jap!" and do God only knew what to them.

Outside, the snow was blown into scattered drifts. Inside, life was nothing more than bare existence. More American ships were lost in the Battle of the Java Sea. The Japanese offensive had moved into New Guinea and their forces had taken many islands—the Solomons, the Admiralty Islands, Bougainville. In the Coral Sea the *Lexington* had been sunk; the *Yorktown* was heavily damaged. Fears of an invasion of Australia were heightened by an attack on Sydney harbor.

The battle of Midway was fought while Emi and her mother were at Santa Anita. It was an American victory, but only high navy brass realized at the time the importance of that battle, in which Japan's first-line carrier strength was destroyed and most of her best trained pilots shot down.

To Emi, there was something unreal about Japanese, imprisoned by their fellow men in the country they'd adopted, cheering the landing of U.S. Marines on Guadalcanal. Many at Santa Anita and later at Hart Mountain seemed to live for the time when they could hear the war news and almost universally were elated when it was favorable to the American side. Emi had developed a hate for both countries, for Japan and the United States, because the war had ruined her life and worse, had made an old woman of her mother. Macimo Pecora went through the motions of living, if life in that concentration camp could be called living, as if in a dream. She did her work on the nets automatically, spoke only when spoken to. She wasn't yet fifty years old.

November brought cold and snow to Hart Mountain. She was at work on the nets when the well-dressed man came for her.

"Are you Emi Pecora?"

"Yes," she said.

"Come with me, please."

For the first time in months her mother showed a sign of life, seizing Emi's arm and looking at her with great fear.

"I'll be back in a few minutes," Emi told her.

The office into which she was ushered was warm and for a moment that was all she could think of, the blessed warmth. Then she saw another man, seated behind a desk. He was dressed in navy blue and had the insignia of a lieutenant commander.

"My name is Tom Braddock," the man in uniform said. "You are Emi Pecora?"

"Yes," she said.

"When the war began you were a student at San Jose State College?"

"Apparently you know all that."

"Miss Pecora, did you know a young Japanese boy named Ralph Izumi?"

"I may have." In prison, one developed the prison mentality. One did not answer questions until one knew the intent.

Braddock made an impatient motion. "Ralph Izumi suggested that we talk with you, Miss Pecora."

"Oh?" She looked at the man in the suit. F.B.I., no doubt. "What about?"

"You speak, read and write Japanese, it says here," Braddock replied, holding a file.

"Yes."

"Chinese, Portuguese, Spanish?"

"Portuguese well. The others?" She shrugged.

Braddock threw a sheet of paper across the table toward her. "Read that and tell me what it means."

She picked up the paper. It was a complicated list of equipment and weapons. "Do you want me to tell you what it is or to translate it?" she asked.

"Translate it, please."

She began. Braddock was following her words by reading from another sheet of paper. "Enough," he said. He gave her another sheet. This one was classical Japanese, a poem, quite difficult to translate. She found herself interested, for she knew the poet. One of her mother's favorites. She read.

"Good, very good," Braddock pronounced. "I guess you think you've had a raw deal, don't you?"

"Why do you ask?" Never, never again would she be able to trust another human being.

"Would you have any hesitation in taking an oath of allegiance to the United States?"

"I'm a citizen. Why should I have to take an oath?"

"All right, Mac, take her away," Braddock ordered gruffly. "Apparently she's not interested in getting out of this camp."

The man called Mac opened the door, stood to one side.

"Just a minute," Emi said. "How about my mother?"

Braddock looked at her for a moment. He nodded to the other man and the door was closed.

"All right, Miss Pecora," Braddock said. "I think you got a raw deal, you and all the others. Naval intelligence has been keeping an eye on Japanese aliens on the West Coast for years. We could have prevented any communication with the enemy by picking up a dozen, a hundred at the most. But it wasn't our idea to take the whole Jap population and ship them to Siberia. They wanted to do it in Hawaii, too, or hadn't you heard?"

"We don't hear much here," she said.

"Then someone pointed out that if they impounded all the Japanese on Hawaii they'd ruin the economy. You should have lived in Hawaii. You'd be in your home right now."

"But I didn't," she said. "All right. I wouldn't

object to taking an oath of allegiance. Until you people told me differently, I was an American."

"Good." Braddock stood up. "Mac, you can go now. Tell someone to bring us some coffee, okay?"

When they were alone he looked at her. "I'll have a lot of questions, Miss Pecora. You'll get damned tired of answering them. I know your history now back to the time you were born, and your family history back to Macao. But I'll need more."

"And if I answer what you want to hear?"

A knock came. He took two mugs of coffee, waved her into a chair. She sipped as he walked around the desk and sat down.

"We'll put you to work," Braddock answered vaguely.

"And let my mother go back home," she pressed.

He frowned. "Not just yet."

"Then it's no deal. I stay with her." She put the coffee on the desk and stood up.

"We can place her in Chicago," Braddock offered.

"Why Chicago?"

"Because it's a large city, lots of people. Because there aren't many Japs there. Because it's where we have a place for her. A little job, a little apartment."

She sat down. It was better, she felt, than Hart Mountain. "Tell me about the work."

"Reading. Translating."

"Where?"

"Wherever we need you."

She almost backed out when she had to put her mother on a train. She did her best to explain. She told her mother that things would be nice in Chicago, that she would have pleasant work, that she would have a nice, warm apartment and people to look after her. And

Macimo didn't weep until it was time to get aboard the train.

"Just take us back to the camp," Emi told Tom Braddock, who'd brought them into the nearest town.

"No," Macimo said. "You're needed, my daughter. If your work helps in some small way to shorten this war, which is so horrible for all, it will be worthwhile. I'll like Chicago. I'll write you long letters."

Tom Braddock rolled his eyes. The two women had been speaking English out of respect for his presence. He could see some navy censor opening a letter addressed to a member of a navy intelligence unit to find it written in Japanese.

Chapter 3

Admiral John Averell was accustomed to having young men around. It was all right with him, as long as they were navy men, preferably academy men, and most certainly they had to be officers. He rather approved of this new one, Lieutenant J.A. Richard Parker, a naval aviator, near the top in his class at the academy. Parker sat at the admiral's table, hair freshly cut, uniform spotless.

They were using the lanai room, a breezy, cantilevered verandah which he always enjoyed. It perched on the side of a steep hill which dropped away to a woody, scrubby slope. The view of Oahu from Averell's Aerie, as it was known, was magnificent. It looked down the gut of East Loch. About two and a half miles away, on that balmy evening, he could see the masthead lights of the *Oklahoma* and the *Arizona*. Overhead a big aircraft, probably a B-17, droned on a circular approach and far off another was preparing to land at Hickam Field.

The aerie had been built to the specifications of his late wife, a woman of excellent taste. Averell property had a deeded history going back to Hawaiian feudal times, before the coming of the Americans, when the brown-skinned natives measured land in *ahupuaa* and land rights extended from the shore to the mountain top, with rights to the adjacent sea waters. There were times, the admiral thought, when he wished he'd been born a Hawaiian nobleman in those days in the distant past when all one had to concern himself with was which maiden to sacrifice to the fire god of the volcano.

He was talking to the officers about his frustration with the navy brass and the politicians in Washington who seemed to be indifferent to the navy's vulnerability in Hawaii.

This young officer seemed to understand. Then again he might have been agreeing only to curry favor with the father of the beautiful girl who sat across the table from him.

"Lieutenant, we *are* at war," he'd been saying. "We *are* shooting. The navy shoots at German submarines and aircraft with each crossing of the Atlantic."

"Yes, sir," Dick Parker agreed, trying to keep his attention on the admiral. But it was difficult to keep his eyes from straying back to Laura.

Laura. Slim, rounded Laura, with that long, blonde hair, those dancing eyes, that teasing mouth.

It was December. Dick Parker had been in Hawaii for three months and he was due an assignment on a carrier any day. He was enjoying the weather. He'd discovered that Hawaii was cooler, more comfortable than it should have been, for other islands at the same latitude were humid, sweltering tropical hells. It had something to do with the mountains, Mauna Loa and Haleakala, and the northeast trades which brought the coolness of the ocean currents. All he really knew was that he loved it and that he envied the admiral. He dreamed that someday he'd have the gold braid and a place like the aerie and a girl like Laura. Hell, why not Laura herself, sitting permanently across the table from him?

"The Japs are going to make a move," Admiral Averell said. "It was damned stupid of the British to cut off their oil. They can't live without it. There's no oil in Japan. They're totally dependent on outside sources and they'll fight to get it. Hell, they're already fighting to get it in Malaysia."

"I've just had a class on the Japanese navy," Dick said. "I was impressed."

"It's a first-class outfit," Averell agreed. "It's efficient. Their sailors live under conditions which our men would bitch like hell about, and there's superb discipline. Goddamn it—excuse me, honey." He winked at his daughter. "They've practically declared war. In effect, what their diplomats are saying is this: One, Japan will continue its alliance with Germany and Italy. Two, Japan will control the Far East. Three, if the United States will go along with one and two, Japan will try to be friendly. In other words, give them everything to the west of Midway Island and they'll allow us to keep Hawaii and California."

"I think they're cute," Laura laughed. "Such little men, and they use such little weapons. Tiny little one-man tanks. Tiny little one-man submarines. Tiny little guns."

The admiral snorted. "And doctors in China are digging tiny little bullets out of tiny little wounds which hurt like hell."

"There's nothing small or tiny about a Zero," Dick said.

"Are you two warmongers ready for dessert?" Laura asked. The admiral considered, looking at his unfinished plate, but he'd been eating too much of late. He nodded. Laura looked up. That was all that was necessary to bring the Japanese waiter scurrying.

They sat over brandy, the food removed, looking down on Pearl Harbor and the jeweled city of Honolulu.

"Admiral, this is the most beautiful place I've ever seen," Dick remarked.

"Not bad, is it?" Averell asked, with a pleased little chuckle. "My wife, Mary, planned it, designed it, saw that it was built while I was on sea duty."

"And I've been running it ever since," Laura put in. She didn't like being left out of the conversation. It seemed to her that every time she found a nice man her father tried to take him over. All they did was talk, talk, talk about ships and the navy and the war which they all felt certain was going to come.

"Mary was *kamaaina*, what the native Hawaiians call a long-settled white. Her people came out from Maine with the first group of missionaries in 1820."

"Father, I don't think Dick is interested in our family history," Laura said.

"Oh, yes," the young officer said quickly. Laura settled back impatiently. She sipped her brandy and waited.

The sky was empty of aircraft now. The velvet night had settled in. Insects chattered and night birds called. The air was a caress on Laura Averell's skin, warm and soft. She felt a little prickle of excitement that raised goose bumps on her shoulders, which were bared by the low, long dress she wore. She liked Dick's profile. Strong face, nice nose. Over six feet tall. Go to bed, Daddy, she said to herself. Go to bed.

But it was after ten before the admiral finally

announced, "Well, I'm going to leave you young people."

Dick leapt to his feet when the admiral rose. "Will you ride with us in the morning, sir?"

Good Lord, Laura thought.

"No, no. I sort of treasure my Sunday mornings, Richard." He laughed. "Not getting old, mind you, it's just that when you're over forty you welcome that one morning of lying in."

Laura refilled Dick's glass. She sat on a broad sofa facing the view. He was in a chair looking at her.

"You can't see the view," she said.

He smiled. "The view I see is finer than anything else."

Yes, he was charming. All gentleman. Perhaps just a bit shy. She patted the couch beside her. "From here you can see both."

She was in his arms within seconds. It excited her to feel him begin trembling immediately.

She felt herself sinking, felt her heart accelerate, her blood pound, her breathing becoming quick and shallow. What a pleasure to be in the arms of a man, to know what she was doing to him. The poor dears. They trembled, they had trouble breathing. They held her as if they were afraid she might break.

She snuggled close. Her bare shoulders pressed against him. She could feel the buttons of his uniform on her chest, just where her breasts began to swell.

"Laura, Laura," he whispered into her ear, breaking the kiss before she was ready. "It's so difficult to keep from saying what I feel."

The last thing she wanted was for him to get serious. Men always did. They began to beg, and begging alienated her. She had a feeling that this one would beg her to marry him. She closed his mouth with hers, let her body fit against his, slid down to put her weight on him. The kiss went on and on, boiling, seething, and then, with a gasp, he leapt to his feet, turned to hide an embarrassing bulge.

"Laura . . ."

Damn! Now he was going to get serious.

"Laura, you're the most beautiful girl I've ever known. You must know that I'm in love with you."

"Yes," she said.

"Is it my imagination, or do you feel the same?"

She rose, put her arms around him from behind, pressed against him to feel him begin trembling again. "Things are so uncertain," she whispered.

He turned to hold her. "I know. I have no right to ask you for a commitment now when I have no idea where I'll be going."

"Don't worry about it," she whispered, lifting herself to be kissed. "Let's just . . . let's just let things happen."

He was lying atop her, a sweet weight, and she could feel his need through the layers of clothing, squirmed to position herself, lifted, pressed and felt his answering pressure. The thrill made her forget all, the beautiful night, the sweet smell of the air. All she knew was that he was *there* and only clothing separated them.

Now, oh, now, she whispered mentally. And she felt as if it were really happening, her dress being slipped from the shoulder. It would glide off her body in a little silken heap and leave her only in bra and panties and then—

A sound came from the house behind them. He jerked, sat up, looked guiltily over his shoulder.

"It's only the house settling," she whispered, reaching for him, but she knew the moment had passed. He looked uneasy.

"Honey, if we're going to see the sunrise we'd best go to bed."

Together, she was thinking, together.

He laughed. "I'd better run before I lose my head."

And he was gone.

No matter how late she stayed up, Laura Averell rose before the sun. Life was just too interesting to spend major portions of it sleeping. She was awake before her alarm clock went off and had her riding habit on when she went downstairs to find Dick Parker already at the table on the verandah. She drank a tall glass of fresh orange juice before sitting at the table to tackle the fresh fruit and eggs Benedict.

It was lighting up in the east when the stableboy brought out the horses. They took the bridle path up the slope and as the sun came up over the mountains they could look down on the aerie, a white, sprawling complex of buildings among which the house stood out as an architectural jewel.

"I'll never leave this place," she said.

They dismounted. The horses stood close together. One blew through its nose, a horsy, homey sound.

"Can't blame you," Dick answered, feeling as if she were trying to tell him something. How could he be so presumptuous as to think that this girl would marry him? What had he to offer? A little house on a military reservation? Months of being alone while he was on sea duty?

"I hope my father lives to be a hundred and fifty," she remarked, "but this will all be mine someday. The man I marry will have to forget his pride and live here with me."

Well, he thought, that wouldn't be bad duty.

A little waterfall trickled down over the volcanic rocks to their right. He knelt and tasted the water. Delicious. And the sunrise was fantastic. Then he was beside her, riding again, and the trails led along the crest of hills in a little semicircle that brought them back to the down trail. It was almost eight o'clock. He was reluctant to go back to the house. He pulled his horse to a halt and got off. She turned her animal and joined him, sat on an outcrop of rocks, legs extended in front of her.

He could see Diamond Head. The morning was crystal clear, the sky cloudless. There was a buzz in the air and he saw a light, private plane climbing up from the direction of the city. He had a sudden urge to be up there in that plane, remembered the feeling of power, the pressure of climbing fast in an F-4F.

"Look," Laura pointed toward the sky.

They were coming from the southeast over Diamond Head, the sounds of their engines not yet audible, just specks. He began to count.

"Probably a shuttle flight from San Diego," he decided, counting fifty, sixty planes. Down below, the ships looked like toys, the monsters on Battleship Row, the strength of the navy.

The little private plane turned and was going toward Diamond Head. The oncoming planes were growing bigger and then two of the specks separated from the main flight and zoomed down toward the light plane. He was thinking that some jokers were going to get chewed out for making a practice run on a civilian aircraft. Then he saw the blinking lights from the wings of the diving planes. He'd seen it on the firing ranges, in practice, the blinking of wing guns from a war plane.

"Jesus Christ," he whispered dryly as the light plane bucked, fell off on a wing and fluttered downward.

He now realized there were at least a hundred and fifty planes coming at them. The lead elements, dive bombers, began screaming down. Laura leapt to her feet, her mouth open in surprise. They saw the mushrooms of flame and smoke rising from the barracks at Hickam Field. Other planes were making torpedo runs on the battleships. A lone gun responded from the harbor.

"What is it?" Laura cried.

I should be there, he was thinking. Oh, God, I should be there!

Smoke and flame billowed up. At least one of the battleships was hit. More planes whined in over Waikiki Beach. Bomb blasts were making a pall of smoke all around the outskirts of the city. The candy-pink Royal Hawaiian Hotel was lost to his view as smoke billowed. He considered leaping on the horse, but he knew that by the time he reached the base it would be too late. Planes were being destroyed on the ground at Hickam and Wheeler and he had no plane. God, what he would have given for an F-4F and a wingload of ammunition. Oh, God, men were dying down there!

Now bombs were falling on the city itself and the antiaircraft units had finally gotten into action. But it was too late. The enemy planes swarmed and dived and released their deadly cargo and he didn't even know for sure who they were.

Thank God the carriers weren't at Pearl. They were somewhere at sea, and as the attack went on and on and the entire plain on which the city lay was shrouded in smoke, he kept scanning the sky for the navy planes.

Laura was standing by his side, holding his hand, squeezing hard. "Keep them away from the aerie," she pleaded. "Don't let them bomb the aerie."

Planes had strayed from military targets and were bombing even the outlying residential districts.

And he was thinking. Good God, the war is starting and all she can think of is her own home! But then he saw the blank panic on her face. She really didn't understand what it meant.

He couldn't tear himself away. He stood frozen as he watched the planes dive and make their torpedo runs. Then there was a fading of sound as the attackers regrouped and went back toward the sea. He guessed that there were at least three carriers out there, then revised his estimate as, just before nine o'clock, the second wave came.

The two attacks had taken just a little over an hour. Now it was quiet. The antiaircraft guns were silent. The sky was empty. And in the harbor, that magnificent natural harbor, through drifting smoke, he began to count. Before the attack there'd been eight of the magnificent old battleships lined up on Battleship Row. He tried to remember their disposition. That was the *Nevada* out there, grounded, at the mouth of the channel. Was that the *Oklahoma* with only her bottom and propeller above water? Where the hell was the *Arizona*? Near the *Pennsylvania* there were two pitiful heaps of wreckage that had been sleek destroyers before breakfast. Five of the battleships were gone.

"It's lucky you weren't down there," Laura said.

He turned to yell at her, to express his contempt for that statement. War had come and men had died and this girl—but he kept quiet. In stunned silence he led her to the horses, boosted her up into the saddle. He arrived at the aerie first, having outdistanced her. The stableboy, looking dazed, took his horse.

"Where's the admiral?" Dick asked.

"Admiral take car, go," the boy said. He was Japanese.

Dick Parker managed to borrow a navy staff car. It was in one bay of the multicar garage. He started to run for it, looked down, remembered that he was wearing riding clothing, ran to the house and his guest room and was hastily buttoning his uniform when Laura came to stand in the door.

"Where are you going?" she asked.

"Down there."

"You don't have to go. You don't have to leave me alone."

"You'll be all right," he answered distractedly. "The attack is over."

"You're a transient officer. You don't even have an assignment."

"Damnit, Laura," he said. She was looking at him angrily. "I'll get in touch when I can."

"Well," she pouted, "*if* you can find the time."

There was nothing he could do down there, she was thinking. The damage was done. The men had the war they'd all seemed to want so badly, but there were plenty of men to fight it without taking away her man, not with her father gone and the house all theirs, with no one around but the servants, and they could be sent away.

She went to her room, removed her riding habit, had a leisurely bath. She had to speak severely to the kitchen staff. They, in the excitement, were late with lunch. Such laziness could not be accepted. The cook was Chinese. Give those people an inch and they'd take a mile.

She turned on the radio. All the news was war. She tried to find some music and got only news, news, news. The Japanese had attacked in other places, too. She went out onto the *lanai* and looked down. There was still smoke in the city and on the military bases. She was sorry that men had been killed. And it made her angry, too. The dirty little Japs had sneaked in and caught Pearl dozing on a Sunday morning. Poor little Japs. God, how they'd pay. The U.S. navy would go after them and have them for breakfast, poor little men with their dinky little toys.

There'd be tremendous build-up in Hawaii, she was thinking. Ships, men, planes. Men. There'd be navy men, army men, Marines, pilots. There'd be a hot time in the old town of Honolulu. Things had been getting dull of late, just the usual parties at the officers' club, and weekend guests, usually older folks, at the aerie, with a new face, a young male face every now and then. But all career navy and gentlemen. All awed by her father's brass. Now there'd be a wave of men.

It was terrible to think of all that damage, all those people who must have died, but maybe war wouldn't be so bad after all. Maybe, at least, she'd meet a man who didn't think that she was some kind of Dresden doll who would break if held tightly.

Chapter 4

It hadn't rained in the Bataan for six months. For four months the jungles had been pounded by guns and bombs. Fires still smoldered in the fallen trees, adding their smoke to the superheated May air. Dust lay thick over everything and was swirled into the air by the slightest movement.

But the worst was the stench. One of the first sights that had greeted Abby Preston after the defeated Americans and Filipinos had been removed by boat from Corregidor was a ditch full of putrefying corpses.

The entire world had changed for her since she'd seen the Japanese sergeant kill Dr. Fraleigh in the operating room on Corregidor.

Charleston was a gentle town. Her family was Old South, and her mother could recite the histories of every Preston and Bland—her mother's maiden name—from the time the first of them had stepped onto American shores, knew the battle history of every male member of the two families who'd fought in the various American wars from the Revolution through the Spanish American, with most emphasis, of course, on that most glorious of lost causes, the War Between the States.

Abby's world had been a world of Sunday dinners for the minister, of carefully curled hair and swirling skirts, of walks along the Battery and quiet teas with her mother's female friends. Each Christmas she spent weeks with her mother making, collecting and distributing gifts to poor families. If the door of the church was open, Abby Preston and her mother walked through it.

All her life she'd been protected. All her life she'd thought of herself as a good girl. Thus it was that her one moment of weakness with the married doctor had had a traumatic effect on her. Those few moments on the couch in Frank Charles' apartment had changed her life, sent her to find peace and atonement in the Laguna mission. But even there she'd been protected, far from any temptation, surrounded by gentle, Christian people, with Father Grand acting as the real father she'd never had.

But the real end of her innocence came in the operating room on Corregidor when she saw the deliberate and cruel murder of Dr. Fraleigh. That moment marked the end of the old Abby Preston.

The shock had left her dazed and motionless. She had stood there, surgical smock speckled with blood, white cap in place. She didn't think of her own death. She saw only the dead man, the patient, the corpsman, the doctor, all moving in slow motion. A Japanese officer came into the room, other soldiers with him. Two other doctors burst in to see what was happening. Everything merged in a swirl of motion and shouted voices, and when she felt hands on her arm she didn't resist.

She didn't even recognize the face until the corpsman, Red, having jerked her quickly through a doorway into the scrub room, put his face close to hers and whispered fiercely, "Come out of it, Abby. Get hold of yourself."

"Umm?" she responded.

Red pulled her. She didn't resist, she was just inert, and her feet didn't want to take orders. Then they were in a supply room and Pete was there. She gazed vacantly at the two men with whom she'd been working for weeks. Red was over six feet tall with the powerful build of an athlete. Pete was a thin man of about twenty with a naturally happy disposition. Even now he was smiling as he spoke reassuringly.

"What are you doing?" she asked when Red pulled off her surgical cap and began to take the hairpins out of her hair so that it fell about her shoulders. "Don't do that." But her protest was mild. Nothing seemed to matter. She realized, as if seeing it from a distance, that her hair was being attacked by Red. He was using a pair of surgical snips and the hair began to fall away in large, severed tresses.

"Abby, they're already beginning to go after the civilian women in the hall," Pete told her.

"Okay," Red said, after a while. "I don't think I'd graduate barber's school, but I'll do." He put a fatigue cap on her head. It was a little large. "Take off your shirt, Abby."

She was dressed, as usual, in GI fatigues. When she made no move Red began to unbutton the fatigue jacket.

"Don't do that," she protested mildly, puzzled. "What are you doing?"

"We haven't got much time," Red apologized. He had the fatigue jacket open. Her last bra had long since rotted away. She felt the air on her bare breasts. "You want to do this yourself?'' He was holding a long piece of gauze dressing.

''Do what?'' she asked.

''We've got to hurry,'' he insisted. ''Look.'' He pointed to her breasts. ''We're going to have to bind them up, make them flat.''

''Why?''

Red made an impatient sound and reached around her, bringing the gauze around, pulling it tight. ''Those little sons of heaven are going to find us any minute and when they do, you're going to be just another GI. A little undersized, but a GI. You dig?''

He pulled the gauze even tighter. She looked down. There was, under the gauze, only swelling. She'd never been overly blessed with development there anyway.

''When they come,'' Red told her, ''you just keep your mouth shut. Stay right with me. Don't look up into any of their faces, because you're too damned pretty even with a GI haircut to be a boy. Keep your head down and keep the cap pulled over your eyes.''

''Yes,'' she said woodenly.

He buttoned her jacket. He was looking at her, shaking his head. ''I hope the bastards are as dumb as I think they are.''

The door to the supply room burst open. Pete threw up his hands. Two Japanese soldiers were in the doorway, rifles trained on them. Red put up his hands and Abby, beginning to realize what was happening, followed suit. The soldier chattered at them and made motions and they went out into the hallway.

In a main corridor they had to step around and over dead and wounded civilians. She saw a woman with her clothing torn away. She was clutching the remnants of her dress to her breasts and was weeping silently. One of her eyes was beginning to swell. It was a severe bruise and would—her nurse's mind seemed still to be working properly—close the eye. The woman needed a cool compress applied immediately. Abby gasped when a passing Jap soldier kicked the woman and yelled at her and, when the woman was unable to get to her feet, yanked her up by her long, black hair. Red put his hand on Abby's arm and pulled her on down the corridor.

The next few days would always be a muddle in her memory. She would retain only a sense of complete chaos. She would remember only a little of what happened there on Corregidor. Often, during those first days of captivity, she escaped into her memories and she found that she could re-create the most minute events of her early life.

She never could remember how they were removed from the Rock, but then things became clearer. She remembered roads clogged with Japanese troops. She remembered wrecked vehicles and the smell of the dead. At some point anger came, and it was a healthy development, for it cleared away the shock.

In that time of trouble, she was to learn later, the main body of American and Filipino troops who had surrendered on Bataan were already involved in that long march from the peninsula to Balanga and then, finally, to Camp O'Donnell, to the north in Luzon. The Japanese were victorious. With the fall of Corregidor, Manila Bay was open to them and all of the Philippines became theirs.

It couldn't be happening, and yet it was.

They didn't know it then, but they were relatively lucky. Most of the defeated troops were ahead of them. The Japanese had not been prepared to handle so many prisoners. The Japanese code of Bushido had taught them that a man who surrenders while he can still resist isn't worthy of consideration. Many of the Japanese soldiers who were detailed as prisoner guards had lost comrades during the fighting and were not sympathetic to their charges.

From the boats, the defenders of Corregidor were marched up the dusty road toward Cabcaben. Like the defenders of Bataan, they were, many of them, weakened by malaria, dysentery and hunger, and as the first day grew hot and the sun broiled them, they encountered what was to be a crueler enemy than the conquering Japanese, thirst.

Abby walked between the two corpsmen. Already her feet seemed impossibly heavy and just the thought of water became an almost unbearable yearning. The sun blazed down on them and she was sure she would be dehydrated in a matter of hours.

The column was not organized. Men slumped, limped, struggled along as best they could without order. Often they had to move to the side of the road to let Japanese vehicles pass.

At first it was only the heat, the fatigue, the thirst. Red and Pete had allowed themselves, with Abby between them, to be pushed to the inside of the moving column of men so that as the Japanese vehicles passed they only saw the glares of hatred, the cold faces, heard the guttural words which they didn't understand. But as one truck filled with soldiers came toward them, she heard and saw confusion ahead and into her dazed consciousness came the realization that the soldiers on the truck were striking out with bamboo poles at the prisoners.

Red saw it, too, and he acted swiftly. He seized Abby, yelled a warning to Pete and tried to force his way to the side of the road through the closely packed men. An officer leaned out from the cab of the truck, a razor-sharp sword gleaming as he swung, the strength of his arm augmented by the movement of the truck. Red threw Abby to the ground and fell atop her and the sword flashed.

Pete wasn't fast enough. The blow severed his neck. His head seemed to leap upward of its own volition, then fell into the dust to roll toward Abby's face as she screamed and Red put his hand over her mouth and hissed, "Shut up. Shut up." The body sprawled. Gushes of red came from the neck. Hands and feet clawed, kicked. Red lifted her forcibly to her feet and they moved on.

Noon. The hottest part of the day. The column of prisoners was in a cleared area. Ahead of them men were being stopped by the guards. To one side a ditch was half filled with green, slimy water. Men ran to it, fell on their faces, began to drink. Abby could almost taste the water. She looked at Red. He shook his head.

Japanese guards were yelling and kicking at the men who were trying to drink. One man was on his stomach, his face thrust into the water. The Japanese raised his weapon and plunged his bayonet into the man's back between his shoulder bones. The man made a sound like a baby crying and was still.

Guards pushed, kicked, hit men with their rifle butts, and it was finally understood that the guards wanted them to sit down. They sat in the broiling sun. A Japanese officer came to stand in front of them and, through an interpreter, told them that they were being punished for not surrendering sooner. For two hours they sat in the sun.

Outside of Cabcaben they were herded into a dry,

hard field, which had been hastily surrounded by barbed wire. The guards came among them and tied their hands with telephone wire.

"Don't say anything," Red whispered when the guards approached. Her hands were tied roughly behind her back, then to Red's hands so that they sat back to back. There was an artesian well to the side of the field. The men closest to it could get water. The Japanese had taken most of the canteens, and throughout the day various passing units of Japanese infantry had taken turns searching the prisoners, looting first the watches, then lighters, wallets complete with pictures of family and loved ones, even dog tags, shoes, everything but the clothes on the backs of the prisoners.

Over by the well two men began to struggle to see who would lap up water first. A Japanese guard shot both of them quickly—two lives gone in a fraction of a second.

Abby thought about sitting in the quiet, old church at home, the minister's voice droning, a pleasant, warm, sleepy atmosphere, the time-honored words in her ears a comfort, the smell of her mother's perfume in her nostrils.

She slept to be awakened by her thirst. Her throat was so parched she had difficulty swallowing.

With an inconsistency which was to be the mark of the next few terrible days, a guard came and loosened their hands. Red whispered to the man nearest him and Abby watched, numb, too tired, too thirsty to be frightened, as some message was passed from man to man. It took over two hours. The canteen cup came, passing from prisoner to prisoner in the closely crowded enclosure, and there was an inch of precious water in it. It had been passed all the way from the well and it had come through the hands of many thirsty men. But word had been passed that a woman, a nurse, was with them.

Other columns joined theirs to the north of the town the next morning. One was made up of Filipino soldiers. Abby was proud of the irrepressible spirit of the Americans. They joked even in defeat, even as men were brutalized and killed by the guards.

The men from Corregidor were generally in better shape than those who'd just come out of the jungle, for those last were the victims of months of scarce rations and hard fighting. Many suffered from malaria. Dysentery was rampant.

Early that morning a man, feeling the symptoms of dysentery, moved to the side of the road to relieve himself. As he was lowering his pants he was shot through the head.

The sick and the walking wounded tended to fall to the rear. Stronger men tried to keep them on their feet, for if a man fell he was shot or bayoneted.

Water. She wanted more than anything on earth to have water, gallons of it, cool, sweet water.

The men had learned their lesson. Victims of dysentery made no attempt to leave the column. The rank smell of the results hung over the straggling group and to that smell was added the terrible and all-pervasive stench of decaying bodies. The whole world seemed to be composed of rot and decay and squirming maggots and stench. And the exhaustion sapped her, sent her back into her memories of a Sunday picnic on the Battery with the bay rippling under a cool, spring breeze.

Just after midday the column was halted by a Japanese officer in a staff car. He stood on the seat of his open car and gave orders.

Abby and Red had flopped to the ground to rest.

They were on a slight rise, looking down toward the front of the group to the Jap staff car. They saw the guards begin to separate the men of the Filipino unit. All officers and noncommissioned officers were lined up, their hands tied with telephone wire, then tied to the hands of the man behind them. The guards then prodded and pushed the men to the brink of a ravine.

"I don't think you'd better watch this," Red told her.

But she couldn't believe it. It wasn't going to happen.

A Japanese officer spoke in English. "My friends, don't take it so hard. Had you surrendered earlier this wouldn't be happening, but many of our soldiers died fighting against you."

Japanese officers began the slaughter with their swords, but it was slow work and tiring in the hot sun. Troops joined in, using their bayonets. It took two hours and it seemed an eternity—the moans of the dying, the screams of agony, the grunts of the laboring Japanese.

She prayed, but she could not turn her face away. She watched. She felt that it was her duty to watch so that she could report the brutality to God. She prayed and then it was over and they were moving again.

Near her, a man who wore glasses caught the attention of a Jap guard by stumbling. He was one of the Malaria victims and he was running a high fever, almost out on his feet, but struggling to keep up because those who fell behind were killed. The guard came to walk by his side, reached out and jerked the man's glasses off, put them on his own face, said, "Ah," and started to move off. The man leapt to grab fling car as fresh air entered. Men tried to push toward it to get away from the terrible stench, but Red was leaning out, looking. She could see jungle outside, a little bank sloping down from the narrow-gauge track, and trees.

"When I say go, you go," Red ordered, moving her to his side, using his strength to push back the men who were crowding to get the fresh air. She didn't hear his voice, felt only a pressure in her back and then she was falling and she felt the jar of something on her feet and a wild tumbling that ended with her looking up at the sky as the train rumbled past. And then Red was there, lifting her to her feet.

He carried her into the concealing jungle undergrowth. For the first time in many terrible days she was able to fall to the dusty earth and rest. He allowed her to have about fifteen minutes and then he pulled her to her feet.

"We're somewhere between San Fernando and Capas," he said. "We've got to make it into the mountains."

She was too tired, too weak to understand. She knew only that she was out of that stifling, stinking boxcar and away from the death and dying.

He found a mango tree. The delicious fruit provided them with both nourishment and liquid. She ate until he forced her to stop, and he was right, for her frail system could not keep it down. Then she ate more sparingly.

They found a stream of clear, cool water. She drank her fill and then took off her boots and went into it clothing and all. She dunked her head, used her hands to wipe water from her eyes. She looked at Red, who was doing the same. He looked so happy that she

him, asking for his glasses. The guard shoved him away from the column, raised his rifle and shot him.

They reached Balanga. Halfway up the west side of the Bataan peninsula, it was a collecting point for prisoners. She could hardly recognize the men who marched there with her as human beings. Most looked like pictures of the victims of long famine. They had been robbed of their boots and marched on blistered, swollen, often infected feet. Their uniforms were in tatters, soiled beyond belief.

And in the quagmire of filth and corruption which was the collecting pens at Balanga, the ground was thick with human excrement, the dead and dying lying in it, the stench of the long dead a miasma. There she saw prisoners being buried alive, trying to raise themselves as others were forced to shovel dirt atop them as they struggled. When one continued to struggle a guard bayoneted him in the face.

She survived. She lived in a sort of coma, only vaguely aware, and always Red was by her side. When there was water he saw that she got some. And he refused to let her drink from the polluted roadside ditches, as many did, thus making their plight worse with the ravages of dysentery and other diseases. She saw men break from the column at the risk of being killed to fall and drink from putrid ditches in which floated the maggot-filled bodies of the dead. Her face was shriveled, thin. She had a handful of dry rice and ate it while wearily putting one foot before the other, holding it in her mouth until moisture formed with great difficulty and softened it a bit. A turnip, small, shriveled, dug from the earth one night, was a blessed banquet for which she offered a prayer of thanks.

Behind them was one long, continuous column,

the same ahead, and all seemed to be walking zombies, witnessing in silence the murder of their fellows who couldn't keep pace, who were ill, or who simply decided that it wasn't worth it and fell to rest for a few peaceful moments before a bullet or a bayonet left them to rest forever.

"We'll leave when we get off the Bataan peninsula," Red whispered to her one night north of Balanga, before they reached San Fernando. "No use getting away here. We'd be bottled up in the peninsula."

She couldn't even think of escape. She was content just to be alive. She walked. She fought for water with the men when they were allowed to drink from a well or from a tap. She picked the small snails from the roadside ditches and ate them raw, found a bush with berries and ate, hoping that they weren't poisonous.

It was in front of San Fernando that Red saved her once again. She went to sleep walking, with her eyes open. She angled to the side of the road and was moving jerkily into a flat area beside the road when a guard saw and yelled and came running toward her. She knew fear then, for he had his bayonet at the ready. She tried to move past him to get back on the road.

But he didn't use his bayonet. Perhaps because she was small, smaller than he, he merely hit her. His fist came toward her as if in slow motion and yet she couldn't move. Then she felt the dull thud, staggered, tried once again to pass him and was hit again. There was a flurry of movement and she realized that Red had punched the soldier and had leapt onto him. She felt a dull pain around her eye and one small part of her mind was thinking that the eye would swell and close and all the while Red had his knees in the small of the Japanese soldier's back and was twisting the soldier's neck until

she heard a sound like a large, dry stick being
Red lifted the man and dragged him into some

He seized her arm and pulled her back i
column. The incident escaped the notice of the
ese, but other prisoners had seen. None had mo
their aid. They could only march, one foot placed
before the other, intent on their own survival,
tated by hunger, thirst, disease, the threat of i
death if they fell or lagged. Abby's eye ached and
she could no longer see out of it, but she was aliv

"They're going to put us on trains," Red told
They were in San Fernando. From the compound w
they'd been placed they could hear the sound of tr
She had half a cup of rice and some precious w
Early the next morning, with blows and kicks,
were herded into boxcars. She felt as if she woul
crushed. Her back was to Red's stomach and there w
a man immediately in front of her and one on eith
side. She heard the thud as the doors were slammed
the heat began to build at once. The smell was atroc

Worse than cattle. Cattle were valuable and wo
have been so treated. Then she found that she
almost relax being held upright by the press o
around her. Near her a man fainted and slowly s
to the floor as his comrades moved just enough
him crumple. Later when she looked down a
seeing only a portion of his face, one lifeless e
told herself, Don't fall. Don't fall.

For hours Red begged, pushed, talked, ins
himself closer to the closed doors, telling Abby
close behind him. The other men were in a da
caring. Finally he was at the door and with his p
hands he broke loose a wooden slat and inserte
pried the door open. A murmur went through

laughed. The sound came back at her, seemingly echoed by the dense growth along the stream, a strange sound, not of her, and then she was weeping.

He let her cry. She waded to the bank, sat on the mossy mud and let the sobs come. She didn't know why she was weeping. Thoughts leapt at her at random. She saw the pink and white, lacy dress she'd worn when she graduated from high school; her mother's German chocolate cake; the headless corpse on the Philippine road; the head rolling toward her face. Then she was finished. Father Grand's face appeared before her.

"Red?"

"You okay now?"

"Yes. Red, would it be possible for me to get back to the Laguna mission?"

"I doubt it, honey," he said. He came to sit beside her. Water dripped from his clothing. For the first time in days there was no stench in the air, only the earthy, rich, smell of the jungle. "The way I figure it, it's going to be a long war. Remember how we used to talk back on the Rock, about how the relief convoy would come and the navy would come and the troops would come pouring ashore and kick the hell out of the Nips? Well, the cavalry didn't come. I guess that means that the Japs control the Pacific. Maybe they hurt us harder at Pearl than we can guess. I don't know. But the way I see it, our best chance is to go up in the hills. My bet is that we'll find other Americans there and some of the Filipinos. You ever been in the mountains?"

She shook her head.

"It'd take the whole Jap army to find us there." He warmed to his subject. "I been there hunting. The hill people are sort of reserved, but friendly enough to

Americans. We go up there and maybe find other folks in the same position, and we just hole up until we see planes overhead with the stars on 'em instead of that damned red ball."

"If I could get back to the mission—"

"If there is a mission," he pointed out.

"They wouldn't."

"Wouldn't they? You saw what happened to Pete."

She saw it all over again, the head rolling toward her. They were human beings, the Japanese, but they'd acted like fiends. The things she had seen were quite beyond her comprehension.

"And maybe we can find some guns and some men and do a little organizing—and then some Jap hunting," Red went on.

Another picture came into her mind. She was holding a rifle. She'd never fired a rifle in her life, but she could see herself holding the weapon and out in front of it was the smiling, bespectacled Japanese officer who'd ordered the execution of the Filipino officers and non-coms. She pulled the trigger and one part of her mind was breathing a prayer even as she saw the Jap officer fall.

Help me, help me, she was praying. Help me not to hate.

Chapter 5

One year after the dawn attack by Japanese planes, the only visible signs of the destruction were the hulks of the *Oklahoma* and the *Arizona* in the harbor, but another direct result on December 7, 1941, was a build-up of forces and facilities which had made Pearl the largest naval base and assembly area of the war.

From all over the United States men and women had been pouring into Hawaii since early 1942. Civilian workers, many of whom had left their families behind in the States to garner the high wages in what was considered to be a hardship location, were still repairing the damage to some of the larger ships hit on December 7. The streets of Honolulu were crowded with men in the uniforms of the army, air corps, navy, Marines. In spite of gasoline rationing, one took one's life in one's hands to try to cross a street. Hawaiian drivers had a reputation of being among the wildest in the world.

Hawaii was the staging base for an effort which, even on the planning boards of the high brass and in the Pentagon, seemed staggering. Never before had a war been fought over such a huge span of ocean. The Japanese empire had expanded thousands of miles during those heartbreaking early days of the war, and now they were entrenched on islands within striking distance of Hawaii. And, in a move which sent chills into the hearts of Americans, the Japanese had taken Attu and Kiska in the Aleutians, within bomber distance of cities on the West Coast.

With a speed and efficiency which would be recognized as the greatest mobilization effort of all time, the United States had committed itself to total war. The results were apparent to Emi Pecora as she peered from the tiny porthole of a PBY approaching Oahu. The harbor was crowded with vessels, and a convoy of ships, leaving white wakes in the blue water, was moving away from the island.

She'd boarded the flying boat at San Diego. She was the only woman aboard. The other passengers in the cramped space available were two navy officers. The crew of the aircraft didn't socialize and the navy officers slept most of the way, leaving Emi to her thoughts. She'd been able to talk to her mother by telephone before leaving. Macimo Pecora had been installed in a little efficiency apartment on Chicago's south side. The job which naval intelligence had secured for her called for her to sit in a chair all day joining one part to another on an assembly line. She'd sounded slightly bewildered, but relatively content. Chicago, she said, was better than the internment camp.

Emi had also had a letter from Ralph Izumi. He hadn't enlisted in the Marines, since they wouldn't take him, but he had been allowed to join the army and had been assigned for training to a special unit made up exclusively—with the exception of officers, of course—of *Nisei*. In contrast to her own bitterness about the treatment of herself, her mother, and other Japanese-

Americans, Ralph Izumi seemed to be well adjusted and eager to fight, even if it meant that he would be fighting and killing members of his own race.

Before leaving the United States, Emi had been interrogated repeatedly, by Tom Braddock and by others.

The problem was that Japan and Japanese philosophy and customs were unknown quantities. A concerted effort was under way to understand more about Bushido and the Japanese quirks of mind which made suicide an honorable death and which made surrender unthinkable while a man still was able to move.

Tom Braddock had helped to debrief a group of American diplomats who'd been interned at the beginning of the war. Among them was Ambassador Joseph C. Grew. The group had come out of Japan on the Swedish liner *Gripsholm* in August of 1942 and the group told surprising and somewhat frightening tales of harsh treatment. Meanwhile, reports were filtering slowly back into intelligence circles of brutal Japanese behavior on various battlefields.

Many Americans, including Tom Braddock, had heard of Japanese atrocities in China, but in those dim, distant days before American involvement, the news was only something which one funny little race of yellow people was doing to another. A man could shudder when he read of Japanese soldiers forcing Chinese civilians to eat huge quantities of dry rice, then forcing large amounts of water down the victim's throat with a hose so that the rice swelled inside and oozed from all orifices of the body. Two soldiers would then put a board across the swollen, distended belly of the suffering Chinese and stand on each end of it until the intestines ruptured. But those things weren't happening to Americans.

And yet thousands of Americans were in Japanese hands in the Philippines and with the American offensive effort getting under way on Guadalcanal, there was growing concern about what American fighting men would face if captured. It was as if a dark curtain had fallen over the American troops in the Philippines and any glimmer of information which further delineated the Japanese character was valuable.

"Explain Bushido to me," Tom Braddock told Emi, back in San Diego.

"It isn't easy to explain," she said.

"I've heard it called the code of Japanese chivalry."

"The Bushido warrior doesn't ride forth to rescue damsels in distress," Emi said. "The emphasis is on loyalty and self-sacrifice. A man's duty is more important than his life and even more important than mercy or compassion. The code doesn't encourage cruelty or deceit, but if they are necessary in the performance of one's duty that is acceptable."

The Japanese hadn't signed the Geneva Convention pertaining to prisoners of war. This worried naval intelligence.

"Would the code be extended to the ordinary soldier?" Braddock asked.

"Yes."

"On Guadalcanal there was an incident where it appeared that they killed their own wounded rather than let them be captured."

"That would be consistent with the code," Emi confirmed. "Suicide rather than surrender. Surrendering while still able to resist is a criminal act and can be punished by death."

Much of what she was saying Braddock already knew, but it was a difficult concept to swallow. He'd read the Japanese army regulations for handling prisoners of war. It was a directive issued in 1904 and it had never been updated as far as American intelligence knew. He could quote Article Two: "Prisoners of war shall be treated with a spirit of good will and shall never be subjected to cruelties or humiliation." And yet there were disturbing rumors going around. He asked Emi what she thought the article meant.

"The Japanese are not barbarians," she said.

"Yes," he agreed, "but what would be their attitude toward a man who surrendered while he was still able to fight, surrendered without killing himself in shame?"

"I think it would be difficult for the ordinary Japanese to understand," she reflected. "They'd be shocked. They would feel contempt."

"To what extent would that contempt be expressed?"

"I don't know. They're not barbarians."

Japanese was a devilish language to one who hadn't grown up with it. To read and write it, one had to retain in one's mind over seven hundred pictographs. To understand subtleties of the language required a knowledge of the traditions and the thinking patterns of the Japanese, and because of those things, Emi found herself in Hawaii.

The PBY made a smooth landing on water, taxied to roll onto a paved ramp and dry ground. She was gathering her few things—Braddock had taken her shopping in San Diego to buy makeup, a few items of clothing, toilet articles—when the pilot of the PBY came back into the passenger area.

"Well, gentlemen," he said to the two navy officers, "we made it." Then he saw Emi. He glanced at her, looked away as the radioman started to open the hatch and did a classic double take. He hadn't seen her board.

"My God!" he exclaimed. "Where did you come from?"

"San Diego." She couldn't think of a simple explanation for her presence and so gave a very literal answer. The pilot grinned.

He was a stockily built man, under six feet, with a full, smiling mouth and a strong nose which gave him an appearance of boyishness by being just a trifle upturned at the end. He had black hair, neatly cropped, heavy eyebrows, brown eyes showing the flyer's crinkle at the corners, giving him the appearance of smiling when his lips were immobile. In his baggy flight clothing he looked strong.

"Let me help you with the bags," he offered. She nodded. The two officers got out first and he seemed to be stalling. "Why didn't you tell me you were back here?" he asked, smiling at her, holding one of her bags but making no move toward the door.

"I beg your pardon?"

"I mean, I'd have been only too happy to keep you company."

"Well, that's kind of you." She tried to move past him.

"Hey, look, what's the deal with you? I mean, why are you flying navy?"

"Because I was ordered to," she said. "I think I'd better go. People are waiting for me."

"God, no, don't go yet."

The way he was looking at her would have been flattering in the past, before the world had changed so suddenly. Now he was only another of *them*.

"I'm going to be here at Pearl for a few days. I can show you the local sights," the young pilot persisted.

"I think not."

"Honey," he said, his voice lowering, "you can't do this to me. Here I've missed the chance to talk with you for hours and then I see you at the last minute and fall madly in love with you and you're trying to walk out of my life."

"Please," she said, trying to push past.

"Where will you be? How can I call you?"

"You can't," she informed him.

"You call me, then." He put his hand on her arm and she looked down at it coldly. "Look, just ask for Luke. Everyone knows me. I run the local taxi. Luke Martel, Lieutenant, U.S.N. You must be with naval intelligence. You don't have to tell me. You are or you wouldn't be on this flight because I only fly the spy boys. So I'll find you if you don't call me. Okay?"

"They're waiting for me." She jerked her arm away.

She was driven in a navy staff car to an office complex. Tom Braddock was there to greet her. And then she was shown her place of work. Her quarters were in the same building.

"You'll be working under tight security," Braddock told her.

"You mean I'll be in another sort of prison."

"Not at all. It's just that the things you'll be reading, hearing and seeing are too important to be at risk. You'll find that we're one little family here. We stick together. There are recreation rooms, a gym too. It's a strict rule. Our civilians can't go out without an officer in accompaniment."

"Prison," she repeated.

"Now listen, Emi," Braddock tried to calm her. "I can understand that you're kind of sore. I would be too. But that's not my fault and it's not yours. It's just something we're going to have to live with. Let me tell you this. I can always send you back to the camp. Some of the others said you'd be nothing but trouble. I disagreed. I thought you were a sensible girl who would recognize the importance of your work and that you'd do it with a minimum of emotion and fuss. Was I wrong?"

"I'll do your work," she stated flatly.

Some called it the Vault. Others called it the Hole, or the Black Hole. Inside, however, the Hole was not black. One entered through steel doors guarded by armed sailors and then there seemed to be nothing out of the ordinary, at first, only offices and a nicely furnished and well-lighted library. There Emi was assigned to her first tasks.

She'd always liked to read and she'd often read aloud to her mother in Japanese. The library of the Hole gave her something which, for long periods of time, made her forget that she'd been rejected as an American citizen, that she was locked inside the Hole and could not go out without permission, could not get into the fresh air, could not go into town on a simple shopping expedition, could not take a walk under the sun without saying, "May I," and then waiting for an escort to watch her and be sure that she didn't run to the nearest telephone and call Tokyo to say, "Hey, honorable members of my mother's father's race, I'm working for naval intelligence and in the library where I work we have just about every newspaper and magazine and book published in Japan since 1930, and some before that."

She read. She'd been instructed to concentrate on several subjects. She was to give particular attention to business publications and news, in an effort to glean facts about Japan's war production capacity.

During the first few days she held herself aloof. There were others of Japanese blood in the facility. A few tried to be friendly, but when she answered their questions in as few words as possible, they left her alone.

At the end of each day's reading she compiled a report, delivered it to Braddock's desk, went to her room to freshen up, had her meal in the dining hall, finding a table by herself when possible, then went to her room for more reading, perhaps some music on the radio.

She'd been working in the Hole, never leaving the complex, for two weeks when she found Braddock at his desk one evening as she delivered the report on her daily translating.

She looked at him coldly, without speaking. He let his mouth twist into a lopsided, wry grin. "Still sore, huh?"

The comment was not worthy of a reply.

"All right, all right. Look, I want to tell you that you're doing a good job."

"Thank you."

"You might guess that I've had your work checked by other experts."

"Of course."

"Now, if I can just get through that defensive hate of yours—"

"I do my job." She glared at him.

"Yes, that's just it. You do the job and that's all. But you're the best we have. I'm told that you get the hidden meaning from that devilish language better than most full-blooded Japs with an education below, say, our Ph.D. level."

She shrugged.

"What you're working on now, Emi, is not very sensitive material. I'm going to be frank with you. I think your talent is being wasted reading material in public print. I'd like to move you into the code room. We have one hell of a time with Japanese military terms and you've shown that you have a command of them."

"My mother is a student of history. And my father, while he wasn't Japanese, was an admirer of certain things in the Japanese character. He used to talk with me about the Russo-Japanese war, and because I wanted to please him, wanted to be able to speak with him, I became a reader of Japanese military history."

"Do you follow what I'm saying?" Braddock asked, moving to put one haunch on the corner of his desk. "I'm saying we could use you, need you, but we don't quite know about you."

She was silent. She was confused, and didn't quite know about her, herself. Braddock was, after all, a likable man. He'd been kind to her since she'd come to work in Hawaii, but still her mother had been forced out of her own home and was alone in a tiny apartment in Chicago and other Japanese Americans were in worse conditions.

"I don't know," she said. "I can say only that I'll do whatever job you ask, if it's within my ability."

Braddock swung one foot and looked thoughtful. "You haven't been out of the complex since you arrived."

"Are you forgetting that we enemy aliens aren't allowed to go out?"

He snorted in disgust. "There you go. Look, it's wartime and this is the military. The orders are that you're not to go out unescorted."

"For me that's the same."

Braddock stood. He looked down at her with what could have been a touch of sadness. "Well, you make your own bed, Emi." Then he was gone.

She began her work. She was cheating a little, reading an article on Japanese poetry, when an enlisted man, one of the men assigned to the intelligence compound, came to stand beside her and cleared his throat politely.

"There's someone to see you, Miss Pecora."

She resented the intrusion for a moment, and then there was a flicker of curiosity.

"He's in the lounge. He tried to barge in here but, well, you know."

She smiled. "Yes, he might steal some valuable secret from last month's Japanese equivalent of *Life* magazine." The sailor laughed.

Well, she was curious. She'd been doing nothing but reading, listening to the radio, sleeping and eating for over three weeks. She rose, brushed the wrinkles out of her tan, gaberdine skirt, walked from the room into a hall and turned right into the lounge.

She didn't recognize the man at first. He was tall, rather handsome, a navy flier. Then when he turned toward her and smiled she remembered. He was the pilot of the PBY that had brought her to Hawaii.

"Aha." Luke Martel flashed her a warm smile. "I told you'd I'd find you."

"So you have," she said.

His was an infectious smile. Her first impulse was

to leave, get back to work, but she did not. She motioned him to a seat on a couch and sat in a chair in front of him.

"So you're a Mata Hari," he grinned at her.

"Sometimes I feel that I'm considered more a Tokyo Rose."

"Yeah, well." He grinned again. "That seaman who brought me in here said that there was coffee and little cakes."

"If you push the right buttons," she said.

She walked to the telephone, feeling his eyes on her, deliberately walking stiffly to reduce the natural sway of her hips. She looked on Luke as merely a momentary diversion from the boredom of endless reading. She had no desire to deepen their aquaintance, was not interested in giving this man-boy the idea that his attentions were welcomed. She ordered coffee. She looked at him. "Do you want cookies?"

He nodded and grinned. He was always grinning. She ordered cookies and sandwiches and sat back down.

"You from California?" he asked.

"Yes."

He seemed to be indecisive. He asked a couple of other questions which she answered with a yes or a no and then a black seaman brought the tray of coffee and food. Luke ate with gusto, commenting on the quality of the food.

"Nothing like this in the officers' mess," he said, "but there's a good little band in the club. I thought you and me might go down and cut a rug tonight."

"Sorry," she said quickly. "I'm busy."

"Yeah, well . . ." He filled his mouth with a sandwich and she felt a little twinge of something, pity, perhaps, for there was a poignant look to his eyes, and then she remembered her conversation with Braddock. It was true. She hadn't been out of the complex since she arrived.

"Actually," she explained, "there are rules here. I'm not allowed out of the complex unless I'm escorted by one of the officers."

He swallowed quickly, his face brightening. "Hey, no sweat. I fly the spy boys around all over the place, so I've got a top-secret clearance. True-blue Luke, that's me. All-American boy. Trustworthy, kind, loyal and all that jazz. They'd let you go with me."

"All right," she agreed.

He beamed. "Say, that's swell."

Swell? She had to laugh. No one had said "swell" since high school.

"I'll come for you at seven," he said. "We'll have whatever they're serving in the club and then I'll show you how I won a jitterbug contest back in good old D.C."

"All right. I should get back to work now."

Twice during the afternoon she picked up the telephone to call someone to deliver a message to Luke Martel that she couldn't go. But each time she put the instrument back on its cradle. Then she went through a crisis. When she'd gone shopping with Tom Braddock in San Francisco she hadn't been in the mood to think of dressy things and she had absolutely nothing to wear. She became very upset and wept because there was nothing but businesslike skirts and blouses. But in the end, she said, "What the hell," and picked a black skirt and a white blouse.

Luke took her to the club in a navy staff car. There

was delicious fish in the club's mess and it was fresh and broiled just right.

Before the war, Pearl Harbor had been a choice assignment, coveted by all navy men, especially officers, because the navy had made the facility into something so special that jealous army officers referred to Pearl as the navy's country club. The main officers' club was a spacious, nicely appointed building. It had escaped damage during the bombing, and although wartime conditions made it a bit too crowded for old timers, it was more like a fancy stateside nightclub than a military establishment. From an adjoining hall came the sounds of a small band. It played songs made popular by Glenn Miller, Tommy Dorsey, Benny Goodman, Artie Shaw and other big bands, and the sound was sweet and pleasant. The food improved Emi's outlook to an extent which surprised her so that, when they'd finished, she gladly accepted Luke's outstretched hand, went with him into the dance area and swung into a medium fast step to "String Of Pearls."

"Hey," Luke said, pleasantly surprised as she followed him flawlessly through increasingly fancier steps.

She hadn't danced since before the war. There was a joyous freedom in it. A Goodman style upbeat gave Luke a chance to strut his stuff. They were still getting the feel of each other's style.

"You're very good," he beamed.

"And you weren't bragging when you said you won a contest," she smiled. The full, black skirt swirled and showed her fine legs. She swung back and away, came dancing back toward Luke, who was doing some very fancy footwork.

"Up and over," he announced and she went airborne, legs out gracefully, skirt flaring. Then she swung off his thigh, onto her feet, up and over to the other thigh. A circle began to clear around them and the band leader, seeing two real hepcats on the floor, extended the upbeat number until the floor was cleared and the two dancers put on an exhibition for the others. When it ended, they were given enthusiastic applause. Then the band, to give the older officers a chance, eased into a soft, reedy verson of "Moonlight Mood."

"Mercy," Emi panted.

Back in the relative quiet of their table she fanned her face with her hand and laughed. Luke was grinning, all toothy and boyish. "You're terrific!"

"Thank you. That's a compliment coming from you. You're almost as good as a boy I knew in college."

He made a mock, fierce face. "What do you mean, almost as good. Who was this joker?"

"His name was—is—Ralph Izumi."

"Ah," he said, looking away.

"Japanese-American," she went on. "He tried to join the Marines and they wouldn't let him, so he's in a Nisei unit in the army."

"Good for him." He leaned forward to pour her some wine. "Look, Emi, I know it won't mean much, but I think the Japanese-Americans got a raw deal."

"Thank you."

"No, I mean it. I think I can imagine how you feel. I've had a little taste of what you must have gone through, but not as rough. When I was in school in D.C. there were those who called me Abie and Jew boy."

She looked at him quickly. "I wouldn't have guessed."

He grinned. "Somewhere back in the past I think

some of my fine Jewish forefathers took a fancy to an Irish lass, and it's been a family curse ever since. I guess I got about as much pure Jewish blood in me, if there is such a thing, as you have Japanese. But once a Jew always a Jew. I did my thing in synagogue, went through all the rituals. I guess I felt about as Jewish as you feel Japanese."

"We're just a couple of downtrodden minority members," she said, not liking the serious turn of the conversation. The band was bouncing again.

"I got turned down by a fraternity in college," he said. "I didn't let it ruin my life."

"Are you sending me a message?"

He shrugged. "Thought maybe I could help."

She put an end to it by standing. "We came here to dance, didn't we?"

"All *right*!"

He drove slowly on the way back to her quarters. She was pleasantly tired. He parked in front and killed the motor. She reached for the door handle and he stretched over to pull her hand away. "Don't go yet."

"It's late."

"I want to see you again."

She was silent for a moment. "It was a nice evening."

"Tomorrow night?"

"Okay."

"Swell." He looked at her and grinned. "But if you have any idea of kissing me, forget it. I'm not that kind of a boy. Never, never on the first date."

She laughed. "Thank you, Luke," she said. He opened the door, walked her to the entrance of the building, took her hand for just a moment and pressed it gently.

"Seven-thirty sharp."

On the second night in the club there was real steak and the same band playing the same tunes and the dancing was even better. Once the band leader challenged them with an impossibly fast beat, but they flashed and pranced through it, exhausted at the end. They took a break and sat at the table and laughed. He reached across to hold her hand for a moment and told her that she was very, very beautiful with her face flushed from exertion.

It was past midnight again when he drove slowly to her quarters, then parked. She made no attempt to open the door.

"Tomorrow night?" he asked.

"Lord, Luke, I got only five hours sleep last night and it's almost one now."

"Hey, we can sleep when we're dead."

"Well, tomorrow night, I think I'd best just stay in and practice for the future," she said.

"Heartless wench. Look, I'll have you in by eleven."

"Ten," she said.

"Ten-thirty."

"Ten."

"Killjoy."

"Say good night, Luke."

"Good night, Luke."

"Arrrg."

"I kiss on the second date. Do you?"

"Only tall, somewhat silly lieutenant jg's who dance well."

He put his hands on her face and looked at her. A

dim light from a streetlamp illuminated the interior of the car. His lips were surprisingly soft and gentle and the kiss ended rather quickly.

The next day, she was leaning back in her chair, dozing, when Tom Braddock came into her area. She wasn't fully asleep and when he cleared his throat, she sat up with a jerk. She smiled sheepishly. "You caught me."

"I had assumed you were concentrating on a difficult phrase or something."

"Now why didn't I think of that?" she asked.

He put a small box on her desk. "I'd like for you to work on these."

She opened the box to find a small packet of letters, thumbed through them. They were all written, she guessed from first examination, by the same hand.

"We think they're from a Jap officer to his family."

"I'll get to work."

"Make special notes of any mention of strategic information about troops, units and so on. But mainly I'd be interested in what a Jap officer on Guadalcanal was thinking. Give me your analysis of his character, his thought processes."

"You're still looking for something different in the Japanese," she sighed. "And you're wrong. They're just people."

"People who put a human life on a par with that of, say, a rat."

"We've talked about their belief, their code." She placed the letters in front of her.

The man who'd written the letters wasn't an officer. He was a private, but a well-educated man. He was writing to his wife and children. There was no military information. Once he mentioned that there was severe fighting, but mostly it was just a man writing to his beloved family. And he was such a lonely, lost man who dreamed of going home but had a feeling that he never again would see the land of the rising sun. The melancholy mood of the letters seeped into her, and when Luke came for her she was still thinking of that lonely soldier. She could assume that he was now dead, that his premonitions had come to pass, for how else would the letters have come into the hands of American intelligence?

Luke didn't head for the club. He drove off base, through the outskirts of the city, and took a road into the hills. He chatted merrily along the way, telling her of a quick flight he'd had to make to one of the other islands and how beautiful the island had been. He said they'd have to go there someday and then he was pulling off the road onto an overlook.

"Instead of the officers' club mess I thought we'd rough it," he proposed. "I made a raid." He reached into the back seat and came up with a picnic basket. "I outdid myself, and I'm a great chef. Would you prefer a Spam sandwich and a peanut butter and jelly sandwich for dessert, or just leave off the dessert and have this?"

He produced a bottle of champagne, iced down in a silver bucket. The drive had caused some water to slosh out onto the back seat.

"Why not all?" she asked.

"Glutton."

She took a sandwich. It wasn't Spam. It was sliced chicken breast, with fresh lettuce and tomato, and it was delicious. As she ate, he reached into the basket and showed her a handful of Hershey bars.

"You are, indeed, a great man," she admired.

''Not all of them,'' he said, as she reached for the candy. ''This is a partnership, lady. I demand my half.''

''And I thought you were an officer and a gentleman.''

''Give 'em an inch,'' he muttered. ''Okay, you take three and I'll take one, glutton.''

''I suppose I can be fair,'' she smiled, giving him back one of the candy bars.

It was easy, being with him. How things had changed in just a few short days. Even her work had seemed to be more interesting, and she'd actually been civil to Tom Braddock that day.

He finished first. They'd decided to save the champagne. He opened a candy bar and ate it in a few bites.

''You're supposed to savor it,'' she scolded, taking a small bite and letting the rich, sweet chocolate melt in her mouth.

''I'm an all or nothing guy,'' he said. ''No patience.'' He leaned toward her. ''Want a sweet kiss?''

She laughed. He had chocolate on his lips. She had the rich taste of the candy in her mouth. She puckered, he touched, and she had the taste of the candy from his lips.

''We sound like two school kids,'' she laughed.

''Well, this time last year I *was* a school kid,'' he said. ''I was well on the way toward being a genuine George Washington U. grad.''

''Come to think of it, me too,'' she said. ''Now I'm translating Japanese, reading private letters from some poor soldier who was probably killed on Guadalcanal.'' She gulped in an exaggerated way. ''Whoops, classified material.''

''No sweat. Remember, I'm cleared top secret.''

''Well, it's silly to classify those letters anyhow.

They were just letters from a lonely guy who happened to be a Jap—'' She paused. That was the first time she'd ever used the shortened, contemptuous version of the word. ''—who was a long way from home, missing his family, afraid he was going to die.''

''I wonder how many of our guys he did in before they got him.''

''He quoted poetry, love poetry.''

''Touching,'' Luke said. ''No, really, I can dig that. I guess all men are somewhat alike. It's just that we didn't start this war, and when we take a Jap prisoner we don't mistreat him. We're getting some weird reports out of the canal, and some rather disturbing reports are leaking out of the Philippines.''

''They're different in their thinking,'' Emi said, ''but they're not barbarians. They have a very old and a very well-developed culture. They're among the finest poets and painters in the world.''

''And they're pretty good at killing people. Whose side are you on, lady?''

He had asked the question jokingly, but she chose to answer it seriously. ''Since you asked, I'll say this. I'm an American. In spite of what they did to us, I'm still an American. I hate the war. I hate it that anyone, Japanese or American, has to die. But I'll do what I can to help win the war for America.''

''Good show.'' He took her hand. ''Word around the complex is that you're very good at your job—and that Braddock has bigger things in mind for you.''

''I thought everything was so hush-hush.''

''Office gossip. Remember, I fly all the brass around. After a while they begin to look on me as a piece of the furniture and talk in front of me.''

''I don't have that problem. I'm an enemy alien.''

"They don't want you to be, Emi. They want you to be a part of the team. If they were sure—" He stopped.

"Sure of what?"

"Well, of your inner thoughts, of your true feelings, of your sympathies."

"Do they ask the same questions of Ralph Izumi, who's Japanese, and who volunteered to fight against the Japanese?"

"I don't know the cat. But let's take an imaginary situation. Suppose you were working in some very sensitive area and you found hidden, say, in a teacup's leaves, a secret message that would help the Marines kill a half million Japs without losing a man. What would you do?"

"I'd do my job."

"Not even considering that you were going to help kill a lot of Japs?"

"I'd hate it, but I'd tell myself that it might help to shorten the war and save lives in the long run."

"This is just me and you," he said. "If you're resentful, I'd understand. Remember, I've had some of what you got. You can level with me. Wouldn't you like to see the bastards who put your mother in a camp get theirs?"

"If I could have the power to put the man who gave the orders behind barbed wire, I'd do it. But not the men who did nothing but follow those orders."

"Very sensible. How about another sweet kiss?"

But by then they'd been sipping champagne from the two glasses he'd brought and there was no taste of chocolate, only the taste of his masculine mouth. His arms were warm and strong around her and she let herself sink into it. She'd been kissed before. Smooching, as the college crowd called it, was not unknown in California. And she'd known the thrills before too, that sweet, forbidden feel of wanting, that growing excitement, that slight trembling, that awareness of a man's body heat and his strength. There'd been times when her mind examined the idea of the *next* step. But she was completely unprepared for what happened to her in the arms of Luke Martel. At first it was just a gentle kiss, growing gradually deeper and stronger, and then as he pulled her closer and his arms tightened and her breasts were pressed against him, she experienced a kind of explosion in the area of her midsection which sent rays of an unknown, exciting energy to all areas of her body. It made her toes tingle and her knees weak all at the same time. She felt a sweet and overwhelming sense of urgency.

She pulled away with a gasp. "What?" she asked.

"What what?"

He did it again. This time he slipped his tongue into her mouth and then she surrendered. With an inner shock, far away in some dim recess, she knew that whatever he chose to do she would be unable to resist. His hand closed gently over her breast and she sighed and squirmed, pressing into his hand.

Yes, yes, yes, her mind and body were saying.

She had no strength to stop his hand reaching between her thighs. Never had she been so weak. His fingers pulled aside the delicate lace of her panties and she was gasping, his, all his.

"Lord, Lord, Emi," he moaned and he was gently pulling her skirt back down and moving over behind the wheel of the car to light a cigarette with shaking hands.

No, no, her body and mind were screaming. Don't stop.

"I promised you I'd have you in by ten."

"Yes."

"It's nine-thirty." He cranked the car.

The kiss of parting was long, deep, and there was a residual of the need she'd felt, the helpless feeling of total surrender, and then he was gone and she was telling herself, Girl, that was a narrow escape. The problem was that she wasn't sure she was glad she'd escaped.

When she went into her office an enlisted man was packing her things into a corrugated box. "What's happening?" she asked.

"Commander Braddock's orders. You're to report to him."

He was in his office. He rose and escorted her in. "You're looking bright-eyed and bushy-tailed this morning," he noted.

"I feel wonderful," she said lazily. She could almost feel Luke's sweet and gentle hands on her glowing skin even then, even after a good night's sleep.

"We're moving you," Braddock said.

She was shocked. Surely he wasn't going to send her away from Hawaii, not when she'd just found Luke.

"I hope you'll be pleased to know that you've convinced us of your sincerity, Emi. I'll have to admit that I had my doubts about you, but the reports on you are excellent. I think I can say that you've passed the test."

"What test? I haven't taken any tests."

"Just a matter of semantics," Braddock laughed. "Lieutenant Martel is a good man. If he weren't such a good pilot we'd have him operational in intelligence."

He looked up at her. "He must be very good," he said, "if you didn't even realize that he was questioning you, probing you."

Oh, no! Oh, Luke!

"You'll be under a magnifying glass for a long time, Emi, because you're going to be moving into a very sensitive area, but Luke Martel says you've got the right stuff to do it."

"Kind of him," she mumbled hollowly. The wonderful feeling had vanished. All the time she'd been letting herself fall in love with him, he'd just been doing a job.

"Well, into the breach," Braddock said.

She followed him into a part of the building which previously had been off limits to her. From somewhere they'd gotten a picture of her, and it had been reduced onto an identification badge which Braddock gave her and she pinned onto her blouse.

A total of three guards, one of them an officer, examined her badge and her face before she and Braddock were admitted into a vault much smaller, much more complex, than the one in which she'd been working. Only a few civilians were in the secure room, along with some huge and strange looking machines. All the others were navy men.

"Emi, this is the inner sanctuary," Braddock said. "You'll be working under the direct supervision of Lieutenant Commander Smith." She was introduced. Smith was an older man with a scholarly pair of glasses and a quizzical look on his face.

"You will look only at material which is given you by Commander Smith," Braddock instructed. "You'll translate it and give it back to him. You will not breathe a word of anything which takes place in this room to anyone other than Commander Smith or me. You'll be under close guard at all times, not because we don't trust you, but because what you'll learn here would be devastating to the war effort if it leaked to the enemy. I won't say you'll be in danger, but I'm sure the Japs suspect such an operation as this, and if they got onto it, knew who worked in this vault, they'd risk a dozen divisions to take you and question you."

"Right here in Hawaii?"

"We have to assume, Emi, that the Japanese have spies here. We have them in their territory."

"These guards—"

"Oh, they won't intrude. There'll be a man outside your door at night. You'll have different quarters, right here in the building. And the rule that you can't go out alone holds, of course."

"Of course." She was looking around.

"Smith, you brief her," Braddock said. He left.

Smith waited for a full minute, his eyes examining her. She began to feel uncomfortable. "You're staring, Commander," she said.

"Sorry," Smith said. "I was just trying to get a reading, Miss Pecora. It's highly unusual to have a woman, a civilian, in here." He sighed. "Oh, well, I must assume that they know what they're doing." He turned and indicated one of the strange machines. "What you see here is a code machine. We use them throughout the services and they're quite complicated, but you need not concern yourself with its workings. Just take my word for it that it does work. This one, however, is a very special machine. With it we broke the battle code of the Japanese imperial navy."

"Are you saying that you know what the Japanese are going to do, even before they do it?"

"In effect. There are limitations, of course, because not all Japanese orders are broadcast. But if it's put on radio, we get it and this machine breaks the code."

"It's the complexities of the Japanese language which makes it necessary to have someone like you here," Smith went on. "For even when we break the code and get the orders in plain Japanese, we sometimes have trouble with words or pictographs which have multiple meanings. Take this one, for example." He handed her a piece of paper with writing in Japanese.

"It's a field order to the commander of a Japanese destroyer force," she said.

"Yes, we know that."

She read it through. "Pending a closer study, I'd say that they're going to reinforce Guadalcanal by landing men from destroyers," she interpreted the message.

"They tried," Smith said, with a tight smile. "We were prepared."

"I see."

"All right, then," Smith said. "There, in the corner, is your desk. We have a snack bar inside the vault. If you want something else it can be brought in, but we don't like to open the door too often."

"I can manage with what you have."

"Good, good." He seemed ill at ease. "There is, ah, a minor problem. There's only one head."

"Head?"

"Toilet."

"Oh, well."

"There's no lock, as yet. We'll have one installed."

"Thank you."

"On your desk you'll find several texts. Please work on them and give me a report when you've finished."

Since the texts were dated days, weeks in the past, she assumed that they were merely going to check her work. But she did her best. It was amazing. Every time a Japanese radio station broadcast an order to ships at sea it was picked up by American receivers, preserved on wire recorders, run through the code machine and transcribed into Japanese.

It was unbelievable and it was fascinating. She was reminded of Luke's question. *What would you do if you had a chance to give information which would lead to the death of a half million Japs without the death of a single American?*

Luke. She pushed thoughts of him from her mind. At the end of the day a Marine guard escorted her to her new quarters. The window overlooked Pearl Harbor, but it was protected by thick steel bars. The room was pleasant, the furniture comfortable, clean, new. There was a little library of books, a record player and about a hundred records. A quick look told her that they were mostly of big band music. There was a telephone and when she picked it up she was connected with a security switchboard.

"Just testing," she said, and hung up. Had she really been thinking of trying to call Luke?

Luke, you son of a bitch!

He'd made her weak, made her so passionate that she'd been ready to give herself to him—and all the time he was just doing a job, finding out if the little Jap girl was really loyal.

A part of her was still loyal to Luke. That part told her that he may have been doing a job, but that he'd been sincere. At least he'd made no real effort to deceive. After all, he hadn't mentioned love. He'd merely danced with her, kissed her. Oh, Lord, that kiss. And he would call. He would come.

She sat down with a light novel and fell asleep in the chair. It was after ten when she awoke and Luke hadn't called.

Well, he would call tomorrow.

The next day she watched the words come from the code machine, fascinated. According to Smith, the Japanese had no idea that the Americans had broken their code. That machine was a very important and a very deadly weapon. Of course, most of what came through the machine was routine. Major battle plans, Smith said, were almost never broadcast, but handed to officers by hand. And yet there was always the chance. So each broadcast order had to be carefully examined and speed was important. It wouldn't do any good to find out, for example, that the Japs were going to make a raid on the California coast after bombs had started falling on Market Street in San Francisco.

Another night and no call from Luke, and another day. The job was becoming more and more fascinating. It was as if she were a major piece in a giant, deadly chess game. Emi Pecora, campus queen, had never in her life been in so important a position, and it couldn't help but affect her.

At the end of the week she had a conference with Braddock. Not even he had access to all the information which came out of the code room vault. He seemed to have a new respect for her.

"Smith says you're good, Emi. Any problems you'd like to discuss?"

"No."

She wanted to ask where Luke was, but it was evident now that it had just been a job for him, and the truth was that he didn't care enough about her to come back, even to call, now that his job was over.

"Listen, if you want to go over to the club for dinner or something, just yell, and we'll assign an officer."

"Thank you. I'm concentrating on the job right now. But I may take you up on that later."

She had never really been in love before. Oh, there'd been the usual high school and college crushes. But never, never had a man devastated her the way Luke had that night while parked on the overlook after a meal of chicken sandwiches and candy bars and champagne.

After a time, she accepted Braddock's offer of a night out and he took her to dinner himself. They talked shop. They danced once to a slow two-step.

There was a little lounge in the complex which was secure. It had a jukebox with some records. The Marine guards took their breaks there and she learned their names, allowed the braver ones to flirt a bit, but she treated them in that I'm-just-a-friend way which girls have of informing a guy that he has no hope of dating her. Her protective self-image had taken over. It hadn't been love, after all, with Luke, just, as the kids used to say, hot pants. To put it less crudely, there'd been a certain chemistry between them. It was just another learning experience. Now she knew what happened to her when she kissed a man with the right chemistry.

Now she knew what to look for in the man with whom she'd eventually fall in love. But it would have to be more than chemistry alone. There would have to be—well, there'd have to be in the man she loved something which wasn't in Luke. But what was it?

Goddamnit, the Jew bastard with his boyish grin and his tousled hair and that sweet manner. *Want a sweet kiss?*

Damn, damn, damn.

Chapter 6

According to Admiral John Averell, Marines had their place. The navy used them to protect ships and, in this war, to put them onto landing craft and thereby extend the arm of the navy to the islands. But his dining room, he felt, was not the place for a Marine, not even a polite, head-skinned Marine captain named Ivan.

The Marine was just the latest of the men his daughter kept dragging home for dinner.

Only that morning, at breakfast, the admiral had brought up the name of one of the navy boys he would have liked to see at his table.

"You'll be reading this in the papers soon," he said. "We knocked the hell out of the Japs off Midway."

"Good for you," Laura said. She had other things on her mind.

"Young Dick Parker was there."

"He would be."

The admiral snorted. He'd expected, at least, to have her ask if Dick was all right. "Distinguished himself. Got two Jap torpedo bombers before they sunk the *Yorktown*." He paused. "That you won't read in the papers for a while, so forget it."

"Is Dick all right?" She had letters from him regularly. They were usually breezy and chatty, but sometimes he got a little sticky.

"Yes, he's fine. He landed on another carrier."

Damnit, he was thinking, it was time for her to settle down. Marrying a pilot in wartime wasn't ideal, but it would beat the hell out of her hopping to every officers' club on the island with a series of escorts.

There were times when Averell wondered where he'd gone wrong. This girl was nothing like her mother. He was reasonably sure that she did more than just club hop, but she was, after all, twenty-one years old, a woman. He just hoped she wouldn't be careless. The last thing he needed was a shotgun marriage to some jarhead like that Marine captain she'd picked up in a club.

He was a practical man. He hoped that she was a chaste girl, but if not, well, he didn't think it was a good idea to have a talk with her about the birds and the bees at this stage of the game. He just hoped that she'd find some nice young academy man like Dick Parker and cut out the crap.

Throughout dinner, Captain Ivan Mitchell, U.S.M.C., kept hoping that the old man had something important to do on the other side of the island, or back at the base, or even upstairs in his bedroom, because just the night before he'd danced so close with this blonde knockout and had gotten definite indications. The writhing pressure of her hips had made a man out of him and she hadn't pulled back, had, instead, smiled up at him and pressed harder. He knew his women and he wanted to get this one alone as soon as possible.

If he could have read Laura's mind he'd have become a man right there under the dining room table, because she, too, was willing her father to finish his dessert and retire.

The admiral stayed for his customary cigar and brandy and then made his usual statement about leaving the young folks alone and departed. She rose, took Ivan's hand, and led him to the glassed-in room overlooking Pearl Harbor. The windows were open. It was cool and comfortable. She sat on a sofa and Ivan sat next to her.

"Beautiful view," he said.

He wasn't looking at the harbor. His eyes were on the finely tanned skin which showed below her neck. She smiled, knowing that now it was going to happen, that he would kiss her and soon he would be panting and trembling and then he'd start to beg.

He made no uncertain moves. He merely put-out his cigarette and reached for her, gathering her up into his arms. He was a large, strong man, and she felt her breasts push hard against his chest, gave him her mouth. It took only a few minutes for her to be lying on her back on the large sofa, he on top, hardness revealing what was on his mind.

This one was very businesslike. He knew just how to kiss, how to brush his lips over her neck down to exposed cleavage, just how to position himself so that his hardness pushed at exactly the right spot and then she was feeling that wonderful thrill, that working, that climb.

"No, my father might come down," she whispered as his hand went down her dress, under her bra. But she didn't mean no and he knew it.

He lay beside her and moved his hand, stroking the skin beneath her dress. Oh, God.

She put her own hands down and clasped his as he

inserted his fingers under the waistband of her panties and began to slide them down.

"No, no, he might come down."

"Beautiful," he whispered, and she began to writhe under his skilled manipulation. A fine, golden feeling of sensuality rose in her, and it was going to be glorious because he was still dressed and she was bare, dress up around her waist. It was near, so near, when he stopped, his lips on hers, and he shifted his weight and—

"Oh, God, no!" she cried with swift alarm, for in the moments of glorious feeling she'd missed his movements, and she felt what she'd never felt before, that hardness, probing around the vulnerable area which, in spite of what anyone thought, had been penetrated only by male fingers, not that huge and heated thing which now demanded access as he pressed atop her, his trousers open. Panic seized her.

"Stop it!" she gasped, jerking her hips to try to escape. "He'll come down any minute."

"We'll hear him," Ivan whispered.

"No, damnit," she insisted, her voice rising. She felt it slide in and jerked away after partial entry.

"It's all right," he whispered. "We can hear him coming."

Tears came. Never before had an officer and a gentleman been so insistent. Her father had made remarks about the crudeness of Marines, and now she knew it was true, because he was using his male strength, his hands under her hips now, holding her still and in a moment it was going to be too late.

"Stop or I'll scream," she panted, still fighting.

"You wouldn't."

"I will." She opened her mouth. "I will," she said, quite loud, her voice rising.

"Baby, you know you want it as bad as I do."

"No."

"You think I can't tell? You want it. Now be still and I'll make it very good for you."

Oh, God. She fought desperately to move aside. That small bit of entry before she jerked could have been enough. She could become pregnant.

"Stop it, you son of a bitch!" she hissed, and her fingernails made red marks down the side of his face.

He jerked back and in a reflexive action struck her on the side of the face. Her ears rang.

He had hit her. And he wasn't stopping.

"You're going to get it, you goddamned tease," he grunted. He lunged and she felt it, felt the thing she'd never felt before. It hurt. She screamed. It was a loud and piercing scream and it seemed to go on forever before he had his hand on her mouth. But she'd managed to buck him off, to have that thing out of her.

Oh, God, maybe it wasn't too late!

"All right," Ivan growled. "You *are* a goddamned tease. Keep your mouth shut, I'm leaving." He pulled away, his hand still on her mouth.

When he stood and took his hand away she saw it and it was moist and glistening.

"Listen, you dizzy little bitch," he spat out, looking down at her with his face contorted. "You're just lucky. You pull that stunt with someone else and you'll get raped."

"I hate you!" she hissed. "God, I hate you! Get out!"

She soaked in a bath, washed herself, inside and out, and wept. Oh, God. It had been all the way *in*. Oh, God. Please don't let me be pregnant.

She would hate Ivan Mitchell the rest of her life, she decided. She lay on her bed, face down. He'd taken the fun out of life. Never again would she feel safe in enjoying the thing she loved most, of being in a man's arms, of feeling his hands run over her, his weight on her. Never again would she dare to let herself go, to let that glorious passion build up in her to have it released, body to body, hardness insulated from her, made safe by layers of clothing, but the pressure, the friction, and occasionaly, a man's nice, gentle hand bringing that passion to a finish.

And now for weeks she'd live in terror of her stomach swelling.

It took a few days for her father to notice. "You're not going out much lately," he said one night when they were alone at dinner. She didn't answer.

"When is Dick coming back?" he asked. He saw the letters.

"Soon," she said.

"Nice boy, that one."

She'd been thinking a lot about Dick. She'd never allowed herself to spend too much time with any one man. If she went out with the same man too many times he got too excited by the way she liked to make love and wanted more and got to be a bore with his begging.

She thought about Dick because, for some reason, he was the only one whose letters she bothered to answer. Did she know herself less well than she thought? Was there something special about Dick Parker?

To take her mind off her pressing worry, she threw herself into planning her father's annual Fourth of July party. Because of the war, the guest list differed from those of the past, and there were names given to her by the admiral that were unknown to her. That, getting out the invitations, planning the menu, seeing to it that the booze stock was ample, killed a few days and then, on the third of the month, she was taking a break, lying in the sun on a patio, when she heard her name being spoken.

"Laura?"

She removed her sunshade and squinted. He was standing in the doorway leading into the house, tall, his face in shadows, and it took her a moment to recognize him. She rose and saw that it was Dick.

"My God, girl, do you know what you're doing to me?" He was grinning. Her skin was glossed with suntan oil. She'd chosen an old bathing suit, so that one of her new ones wouldn't be stained by the oil, and it was tight, faded. "You look good enough to eat."

She was surprised. She was genuinely glad to see him. She smiled and went to him and he took both her hands.

"You'll mess up your uniform," she protested as he tried to pull her into his arms.

"I don't care."

But he settled for leaning forward to touch his lips to hers.

"I'll call the boy to mix you a drink while I run up and get this grease off and change."

"Don't stay too long," he said, kissing her again.

She came down dressed in a halter and a pair of white shorts, blonde hair loose, skin golden. The look on his face was a reward for her, and this time she went into his arms and was thinking, hey, we're alone. Just the servants. Because she knew Dick was safe. But he soon pulled away.

"It's been a long time," he said. "Tell me all about what's been happening here."

"Yours would be a more exciting story. Father says you're quite the hero."

He shrugged. "I don't consider it a fair trade, two Jap planes, with me losing my ship."

"Not your fault."

"Maybe not."

He'd changed. There was an air of seriousness about him. She began to tell him about the plans for the party. He would, of course, be there. "And you can spend the night," she invited.

"I'll try."

"Try?"

"The navy might have plans for me. In fact, Laura, I've got to run. I came directly here without reporting in."

"Poo, that's all right. They don't even know you're here. You can stay." She was looking at the big, comfortable couch. She was feeling, in her mind, his arms around her. Good old, safe Dick.

"I'll call," he promised. "I should be able to come out tomorrow, if you don't mind my coming early."

"If it suits the convenience of the navy—and you," she said.

He laughed. "I'm flattered. I think you don't want me to leave."

"Suit yourself," she said.

She awoke the next morning with an uneasy stomach. She was never ill. She hated it when she had a case of the sniffles. The feeling stayed with her as she dressed and then as she started from the room she had to make a dash for the bathroom.

It was impossible. It was too soon. Morning sickness, she knew from listening to married women, did not come within two weeks of conception. But she was scared nevertheless.

She felt a little giddy and slightly uneasy all that day, but it seemed to pass as the evening came and the party, well organized, began. Then Dick arrived and he was the only one she'd invited. She sat next to him and listened as he talked about the Battle of Midway and Jap losses and the good old *Yorktown*. But the Japs had lost four carriers and that was a blow to their front line carrier strength. She couldn't have cared less. Of course the U.S. would win the war. What concerned her was morning sickness.

Since it was a special party many guests stayed late so that it was after one when the three of them, the admiral, Laura and Dick, were left alone in the wreckage of the large sitting room. Then the admiral wanted to talk more and she, disgusted, said she was going up to bed. She changed into a sheer nighty and lay down and the fear came to her again.

She heard the men come up, still talking, heard her father's gruff, "Goodnight, Dick." Heard his door slam. Then footsteps.

And the answer to her fear came to her instantly. She leapt from the bed. He was already past the door when she reached it and opened it, heading for one of the guest rooms. She hissed at him and he turned. She knew that the flimsy gown showed a lot of Laura Averell, and that was all right. She motioned to him, and he, his face showing a questioning smile, came to her.

"Come in. I want to talk with you."

She took his arm and pulled him in. The room was in darkness when she closed the door, only the glow of a Hawaiian moon giving light. She felt her way to the bed and turned on a bedside lamp. She saw that he was uncomfortable, knew that she was standing in front of the light, her lithe body showing through the sheer material.

"I've missed you," she murmured.

He took her in his arms. She'd never had a man hold her when she was so nearly naked.

"Don't you want to put on a robe?" Dick asked after a long, torrid kiss.

"Want me to?"

"No, but you'd better."

She slipped into a robe, sat down. "I'm sorry if I made you feel uncomfortable."

He grinned weakly as he sat beside her on the bed. "I'm not made of ice, Laura."

She gave him her most blazing smile, then pecked him on the cheek. "I should hope not."

"I'm trying to hope that this means what I hope it means," he said.

"Dummy. I'm not in the habit of inviting men into my bedroom." True. He was the first who'd ever been there.

"All right," he said. "I'm going to hope."

"Want to shut up and just kiss me a few hundred times?"

"Sounds good, but not before I—" He seemed to lose his voice. She put her arms around him. He could feel the softness of a breast against his shoulder. "I love you, Laura. You know that."

"Yes," she whispered.

"It's a hell of a time to get married."

"Why?"

Dick moaned in mock pain. Then he looked at her, his eyes wide. "Hey, do you mean?"

"Make you a deal," she said.

"I'm listening."

"I'll give you my answer *after* you kiss me."

She pulled him down onto the bed. He seemed uncomfortable at first, glancing toward the door. She closed his mouth with hers.

He was only a man. No man had ever kissed a more willing woman. He would have said, had someone been in a position to ask, that he was the one who instigated their position, he atop, she underneath, clothing between them.

Damn, she was thinking.

Nothing was happening. Nothing. There were the heated kisses, the weight of his body, his male hardness, all as it had been before with him, and she was standing off to one side watching and there was no feeling.

"Okay," he whispered. "Laura, I love you. I love you with all my heart, and I'll be the happiest man in the world if you'll marry me."

She held her breath, wanting that thrill, wanting to feel something.

"Laura?"

"Yes," she said. Because of that miserable feeling, because she'd leaned over the toilet and vomited. Because she'd heard horror stories about illegal abortionists and she was the daughter of an admiral and she would never risk doing *that* to her own body and to her father.

He was crying. He was kissing her and weeping big, silent, male tears and then he was laughing into her mouth and telling her how happy she'd made him.

"As quickly as possible, darling," she begged. "I want to marry you tomorrow."

"It might take a couple or more days."

"As soon as possible, then." Because Laura Averell would never, never put herself into a position where there could be doubt. If she waited until she was sure she was pregnant the child would be born in six or seven months and the speculation would begin. At the time she couldn't be more than three weeks pregnant, and an eight-month baby was rather common with a first child.

But still there was nothing, although now he seemed to change and his male hardness pressed into her and he was devouring her and she let herself sink down, down, and willed it to come and made up her mind that if he wanted to go all the way she would, because it was all right now.

"Unless you want to be deflowered before we get married, I'd better go," Dick whispered, his voice hoarse.

"Do you want me?"

"God, yes."

"If you want me . . ."

He pulled his head up and looked at her. "You love me that much?"

"Yes."

He lay beside her, his arm over her stomach. "I respect you too much," he said. "We can wait."

She giggled. "Maybe *you* can." But she was faking it. For the first time in her life she was faking it.

"It'll be better if we wait," insisted Dick.

"All right."

She looked at him. He grinned at her in a silly way, as if his eyes couldn't get enough of her. "One thing," he said.

"What?"

"I'd like to see you."

Her eyes went wide.

"Just look. I want to see you naked."

"All right."

He removed her robe and gown tenderly, she rising up on an elbow, rolling to help him, and then she lay there, whiter areas indicating the shape of her bathing suit, and his mouth was open in wonder.

"Oh, Lord, you're so beautiful." And he couldn't keep his hands off her. He let his fingers trail down her neck to her breasts, to her stomach. "Oh, Lord."

He kissed her quickly and said, "I've got to get out of here." He ran.

She couldn't help laughing. And there was a fondness in it. He was the first man who'd ever seen her naked and his reaction was pleasing to her.

She waited outside the admiral's den while Dick went in the next morning and then she heard her dad bellow, "Laura, get in here!" She wondered what had gone wrong, but when she opened the door the two men were grinning foolishly, both smoking huge cigars.

"By God," her father shouted, "I'm glad you've finally developed some sense!"

"Is that approval?" she asked teasingly, winking at Dick.

"Don't think you could have picked a finer man," the admiral boomed. "By God, it's about time. I'll help iron out some red tape. You just be sure you have a couple of weeks, Dick." He poked Dick in the stomach with his finger and grinned. "I don't want you going back to sea before you've had time to make me a grandson."

Dick looked at Laura and rolled his eyes.

"We'll have the wedding here, of course," the admiral went on. "Girl, you get out of here and start your planning. Dick and I'll take care of the red tape. You get the reception and everything organized, or whatever it is you do." He rose and clapped Dick on the back. "By God, son, you don't know how happy this makes me."

"Don't I have anything to do with it?" Laura asked.

"You know what I mean," her father said. "I have always been fond of this boy."

"And you want grandchildren?" Laura asked.

"Well, I never talked about it, because you didn't seem to be ready."

"If you're in a hurry, if you'll excuse us, we'll go upstairs and start one now," Laura offered with a little smile.

"Get out of here and start picking out your dress or something," the admiral roared.

It was a wedding with all the military flair—swords, men in dress uniforms, ladies in long dresses. It was wartime, travel was difficult and time was short. The admiral had delayed the posting of orders for Dick, but for only two weeks. The admiral moved out. He went down to the base into quarters, leaving the house to them, and then they were alone, with only the servants in the house. Laura found herself overcome with a shyness she'd never felt before so that when they retired, with champagne on ice on the serving table in her bedroom, she felt slightly awkward and strange.

But this time she didn't have to manipulate. This time she was his, and it was honorable, legal, wonderful.

She found her heart beating fast as he kissed, fondled and explored her. She waited for that surge of passion, but it didn't come. Instead there was doubt and fear. She remembered well that one thrust by the Marine captain, and how it had sent a stab of pain through her. At the last moment she wanted to cry out, No, no.

But he was so gentle, so patient, and then it was done and he was in her, using her, and she was detached, wondering what he was thinking. Did he know? Could he tell?

He lay beside her, whispering to her how wonderful she was. And then, very malelike, "Was it good for you?"

"Yes, of course, darling."

"I mean, was it, did you—well, did you climax?"

She was silent for a moment. "Well, I guess I was a little frightened."

He held her tenderly. "Of course. Oh, God, I'm sorry. I shouldn't have been in such a hurry."

He seemed to be so disturbed, so genuinely sorry, that she was touched. She raised herself on one elbow and smiled and then kissed him and said, "I'm not frightened anymore."

Now it was her turn. She'd been in the arms of many men. She'd kissed most of them, had felt passion with many, had felt the hands, the weight. But she'd never had an opportunity to examine a man closely before. He laughed as she toyed with him, kissed his stomach and coaxed him into playing with her with his hands until that glowing, wondrous feeling came. And when he entered her for the second time it was there and more satisfying than she'd ever imagined.

For two weeks she thought of nothing but Dick, wonderful Dick, her husband. His needs seemed to match hers and hers were great, so that lovemaking sprang up at odd times—while they were swimming in the moonlight, on a float beside the pool, on a blanket on the beach and in her big bed. For two weeks she forgot the war.

When he got up one morning and began to pack it hit her. They were going to take him away from her.

"I'm not going to let you go!" she cried, running to cling to him.

"I don't want to go."

She went downstairs and found her father. "Daddy, I want you to arrange a shore job for Dick."

"Somehow I've been expecting this," her father said.

"Then you'll do it?"

"No. No, I won't, Laura. He's a flier. We need fliers. He's a navy man, and my bet is he doesn't know you're asking me to take him off sea duty."

"No, but that doesn't make any difference. You can't let him go. I won't let him go."

"Laura, if I did this for you I'd never have a moment's peace with my conscience. No woman wants her man to go off to war."

She couldn't believe that he was refusing her. He'd never refused her anything.

"I've got to go," he said. "We'll talk about this tonight."

She wept when Dick left. She wet his collar with her tears and he left with his own eyes misting. Then she spent a miserable afternoon and was in a determined and angry mood when her father came home. She confronted him immediately.

"Have you given any more thought to giving Dick a shore job?" she asked.

"I've thought about it."

"And you're not going to do it?"

"No."

She knew that it would be useless to weep, or scream, or get angry. She planned her next move carefully. Her father had a bottle of sleeping pills on his bedside table, which he used occasionally. She knew that he'd miss the bottle immediately. The very presence of the bottle on the table assured him quick sleep most of the time. She went to his room just before he retired. She dumped all but two of the pills into the toilet and flushed it, took the other two and lay down on her bed, still clothed. She left the empty bottle, lid off, lying beside her.

She wished that she could stay awake to watch, but the pills soon sent her into sleep and she awoke feeling as if she couldn't open her eyes, being bundled about, still unable to come out of the stupor. Then there was something down her throat and it was uncomfortable and then she was being walked around by two men. Finally she could focus and she saw her father and a grey-haired navy doctor, an old friend of the family.

"Tired," she moaned, but they walked her and she drank gallons of black coffee so that she vomited again and when at last she was allowed to sleep she knew she'd won, for she'd seen the look on her father's face.

"I'm sorry," she told him, when she was awake. "I just couldn't face it. I just couldn't stand the thought of his leaving, of his being killed."

"You scared me, honey. You scared me bad."

"I'm so sorry."

"You'll never, never do anything so dumb again."

She turned her head and willed tears to come.

They did. She slept. When she awoke again Dick was there.

"Hey, dummy," he greeted her.

"Oh, Dick."

"I'm here." He sat down and held her. "I won't leave you."

It was two days later when her father said, "Listen, honey, there's a doctor I want you to see."

"I'm not sick."

"I'd like for you to talk with him, anyhow."

He came to the house. He was a civilian, a dark little man who stared at her and began asking silly questions.

"I'll be damned," she said. "You're not a doctor."

"Oh, but I am."

"You're a shrink. They think I'm crazy."

"No. Disturbed, perhaps. You'll have to admit, Mrs. Parker, that it isn't normal to take a full bottle of sleeping pills."

"Damn!" she muttered. She'd just have to put up with it. She had Dick. He'd been given an assignment at the base. He was home every night, a bit late sometimes, but he was there in her bed and they discovered that champagne and sex make a great combination if the champagne is not overdone. One night she was feeling grand, and had just one more glass, and then another and she was giddy and happy as he made love to her. A lot of things were going through her mind when it was over.

"Dick?"

"Ummm." He was half asleep.

"Why haven't you ever asked me about other men?"

Dick looked at her, surprised. "What other men?"

"You know. You've never asked."

He turned to put an arm around her. "Didn't have to."

"What do you mean?" Laura persisted.

"Sure you want to know?"

"Yes. I'm sure."

"Well, to be vulgar, there's a navy expression: Tight as a virgin's twat."

"Hmm," she said. "Think you're so smart. I've kissed a lot of men."

"I've kissed a lot of girls," Dick laughed.

"Bastard!"

"Then, too, you didn't know much, Laura. A man can tell when a girl's been around. Not that I ever had any doubts. Do you want me to ask you about other men?"

"Yes."

"What about other men?"

Laura snickered. "I let a couple play with my breasts."

"Naughty, naughty."

"And once I let a man feel my, well, you named it, my twat."

"I'll kill the bastard."

She held him close. "But you're right, darling. You were the first."

"Bet your bottom. The last, too."

"Well, *if* you keep up the good work." She put her hand down. "You're not sleepy, are you?"

"Arrrg," he groaned. "You're a slave driver."

"Don't complain." She felt giddy and wonderful. "I could have let you go away, and then you'd have only your airplane to kiss."

He went stiff. She held her breath, knowing that she'd said too much.

"Laura, I think you'd better explain that," he said.

"Nothing. I was just talking."

He leaned up on one elbow, looking into her face. "You're the world's worst liar. I never did swallow the idea that you'd try to kill yourself. You didn't, did you?"

"Let's not talk," she said, trying to work on him. He held her hands.

"You had it planned, didn't you? You didn't take that whole bottle. I talked with the doctor and he said that you had a magnificent constitution, that you recovered from that overdose so rapidly it astounded him. How many? Two? Three?"

"Dick, please—"

"Tell me, damn it," he said. He was squeezing her hands.

"You're hurting me!" she cried.

He turned onto his back. "I went through hell for a while, blaming myself for even wanting to leave you. I'm right. You faked it. You just took a couple of pills and then your dad arranged my orders."

"I'm going to sleep," she said, but when she closed her eyes the room swam and she was getting angry. He was being mean.

"Laura, you're going to have to learn to think of someone besides yourself."

"Look who's talking."

"Did you think, for a moment, how you'd frighten your father, not to mention me?"

"Oh, shut up," she said.

"Just tell me the truth and we'll forget it. We'll never mention it again."

She'd had enough. She was bored with his criticism. "All right, damnit."

"How many?"

"Two."

He didn't speak again. But she knew he was awake. When she finally could close her eyes without getting sick he was still awake, but it was done and he could do nothing about it.

Dick was in the admiral's office shortly after the workday began next morning. "Admiral Averell, I want it straight. I know that my orders didn't come from your command, but did you have anything to do with my being put on shore duty?"

Averell took time to light his first morning cigar before answering. He had established a good relationship with his son-in-law and he was a man who valued honesty.

"Admiral?" Dick prompted.

"Let's say, Dick, that I made a value judgment."

"Because of Laura," Dick concluded. "She worked us both pretty well."

Averell frowned. It was difficult for him to admit that his daughter was weak enough, or crazy enough, to try to kill herself.

"She admitted to me last night that she took only two sleeping pills, that she faked it," Dick continued. "Then she begged you to put me ashore, right?"

"Damn," Averell said.

"It isn't right," Dick went on, unrelenting.

"I know, boy. I know. Why don't we just let it ride for a while."

"You had my orders cut."

"Yes," Averell admitted.

"I think I'll have one of those cigars," Dick said, sitting down. Averell handed one over and they sat, in silence, while Dick lit it. Then he said, through a cloud of smoke, "We both love her, and we both know that she's got some growing up to do."

Averell nodded.

"I don't blame you." Dick shook his head. "She can be damned persuasive."

"She has a way of getting what she wants," the admiral agreed.

"Okay. Now there's nothing I'd like better than to stay here in Pearl for the duration and be with my wife. And your bed and board ain't bad, Admiral."

Averell chuckled at that.

"But I'm a career man," Dick went on. "I grew up in a navy family. My father was retired a commander after W.W. I. He spent most of the war in Washington. If I spend this war here in Pearl I'll retire a commander, and you know it."

"Well," Averell puffed on his cigar. "I know what you're saying, son."

"I was trained to be a combat pilot. I'm good at it, and God help me, I love it. I want to go back, Admiral, and as much as I admire and respect you and love your daughter, I'm going on record to say that if you don't do something I'll have to do it myself."

Averell nodded. "You'd be within your rights. I guess I was thinking of Laura and myself and not of your career. It will be slightly embarrassing, but I'll do it."

"Thank you, sir."

"Jesus Christ," Averell muttered, putting his cigar into an ashtray and reaching for the telephone.

Experienced fighter pilots were in short supply. It was easier than Averell had thought. Then he had to face his daughter. He went home early, to see her and tell her before Dick could get home. She was beside the pool. He had the man fix him a drink and took it out with him.

He'd come home angry, but seeing her cooled that passion. She wasn't that far removed from the little girl he'd reared alone after the death of her mother. She was weak, spoiled—but what the hell. He could afford to spoil her and she deserved it. She looked at him with a smile.

"Honey," he began, "I came out here to chew you out."

"I didn't do it," she said, smiling. "It was the cat."

That made it even worse. When she was just a child that had been a joke between them. Anytime she'd done anything wrong she blamed it on the cat and it was so cute she usually got away with it.

"I guess we can get rid of that shrink," he said. "Or put him working in a different direction to find out why you'd pull such a dumb trick."

"Whoops," she said. "I guess you've had a talk with my loving husband."

"What you did was stupid and very wrong."

"It seemed to be a good idea at the time."

"Well, aside from showing that you're not quite as grown-up as I thought you were, no harm's done."

She went pale. "What do you mean?"

"He's getting new orders."

She looked up toward the blue sky. It was fluffed

with white clouds. She felt a moment of loneliness, but that was quickly replaced by anger.

"Laura, he's a good officer. He is an academy man, a career man. He needs a good combat record."

"Goddamn the navy," she said.

"Sure. It hasn't been good to you at all." He waved his hand. "You've lived in poverty all your life."

She was silent. Goddamn Dick. He was thinking only of himself and the navy. And she was pregnant. By now she was pretty sure.

"Laura, are you all right?"

"Don't worry," she snapped. "And you can have your prescription refilled."

The casual reference to her stunt, which had taken five years off his life, made his face go red.

"And now you're going to start yelling at me," she said. "Well, go ahead. I don't give a damn."

He rose, killed his drink. When he spoke it was with his officer's voice. "He'll be leaving in two days. I suggest that you remember who you are."

She smiled, but she didn't feel like smiling. "Oh, I won't make a scene. If he thinks more of the navy than of me, so be it."

She was cool, polite at the dinner table. Dick said he was tired. She told him to go up alone, punishing him. She sat on a balcony and watched the moon. When she went into the bedroom he was in bed reading.

"We've got to have a talk," he said.

"I know all about it." She undressed quickly and got into bed.

"It has to be this way." He tried to catch her eye, but she wouldn't face him.

"Sure." Damnit, she needed him, and she couldn't stop herself from responding when he held her close to make love to her.

He got up first. He came out of the bathroom with his face showing alarm. "Something's wrong," he said. He threw back the sheet. It was stained with blood.

She began to laugh. She wasn't pregnant after all. She'd jumped into marriage because she *knew* she was pregnant, but all along she hadn't been pregnant. And now she'd found that she loved married life and that was going to end because her husband was a patriot and a navy man.

"Silly," she said, "my period just snuck up on me, that's all."

He held her close and told her of his love and there was an encore. It was so good and she was so confused, wondering why she'd married a man who thought so little of her that he'd voluntarily give up a safe shore job and being with her to go off and risk being killed. Knowing how much she'd miss *this* made it all the worse.

"God, I love making love to you," she sighed.

"I've noticed," he grinned.

"I don't know how I'm going to live without it," she whispered sweetly.

"Oh, you'll be strong." He matched her teasing tone.

"I'm not so sure. I've never been strong. I have an addictive personality. I eat too much candy, smoke too much, drink too much. When I find something I like, I tend to overdo it and I just can't deny myself."

"We'll write each other steamy letters." He nuzzled her behind the ear.

She changed the tone of her voice. ''Maybe I won't want to deny myself this pleasure, Dick. Maybe I'll tell myself, hey, girl, your husband could be with you. He chose to go. I want you, when you're up there being a grand hero in your little plane, to think about that. Think and wonder. When night comes, I want you to wonder where I am, what I'm doing.''

''Jesus, Laura!'' There was real pain in his voice.

''Because if you really loved me, you'd have stayed here. You'd have said, hey, great, I can stay right here in Hawaii and give my wife what she loves.''

''Laura, don't say that.'

''Just think about it, buddy boy.'' She turned her back. She pretended to be asleep when he got out of bed and walked to the balcony and stayed there for a long time, his cigarettes glowing in the dark.

Chapter 7

For the first time in weeks Abby Preston's stomach was comfortably full. They'd been walking for three days when Red spotted a small farm in a jungle clearing and left her in the brush while he stole a chicken. The fowl was delicious when roasted over an open fire a few miles away from the farm. A little pile of bones was all that remained.

"You're a great chef, Red," she said.

"I used to hunt when I was a kid," he said. "Sometimes I'd be out in the woods all day and I'd kill a rabbit or a bird and build a fire and have a feast all by myself."

"I don't even know your name."

He grinned. "That's for the best."

"Ah, come on."

"Okay. I'll trust you. It's Clyde."

"Nothing wrong with that."

"Depends on how you look at it. I'm a Long, not of the Louisiana Longs."

"Well, Clyde—"

"You're a nice lady, but I'll toss you in the nearest creek if you call me that."

"Red," she amended. "I haven't thanked you."

"No need." He saw her scratching her ankles. "Bugs?"

"Itchy little varmints."

"Here, let me see." He pulled up her trouser leg. Above the fraying GI socks there was a red rash. She'd broken the skin in spots. He picked up a gnawed chicken bone and rubbed the grease from it onto the rash.

"Better?" he asked.

"A little." She was leaning against a big tree. "Red, do you have any idea where we're going?"

"Toward the mountains."

"Will we get there?"

He shrugged. "Worth a try, isn't it?"

"And once we're there?"

"These Filipinos are tough. I know a lot of 'em surrendered, but my bet is that there'll be a passel of 'em up in the hills, hiding out. Maybe a few Americans. I think that would be better than being guests of the Japs for the duration."

She shuddered. The horrors she'd witnessed seemed to have blown a fuse somewhere in her. It was difficult to believe that her memories were accurate. Surely she couldn't have seen men shot down without mercy, such filthy compounds or the train so crowded that when a man fell he couldn't rise again.

"When I got assigned corpsman duty I was relieved," Red said. "I didn't join the navy to kill people. I came in to get away from a sharecrop farm and to see the world. Back in Louisiana I thought Pearl Harbor was a girl."

She laughed.

"But now I want to get my hands on a gun." His

voice grew low and intense. "The biggest, most deadly gun I can find. And I want to kill Japs."

She'd never spent so much time alone with a man. They walked by day, keeping to the jungle, avoiding roads. The roads were full of Japanese, in trucks, tanks, marching, jabbering. Day by day, hour by hour, sometimes hungry, always suffering from heat and the attacks of insects, they pressed on. They had no way of telling how many miles they'd covered. They used the sun to guide them and spent the nights huddled on makeshift beds of leaves and branches. From moldering dead men Red looted canteens and weapons. He walked strongly, although he was laden down with belts of ammunition for a Springfield ought-one. Then, in a blasted zone where the dead men were already beginning to merge with the mulch of the jungle floor, where the old, dead scent was fading, where small predators and scavengers had feasted, he found a "grease gun." It was a not very accurate, one-man machine pistol that sprayed out rounds with a force that drove the barrel upward, so that to hit a target it was necessary to start low and let the natural recoil of the weapon carry the stream of slugs upward.

He tried to get Abby to carry the rifle.

"I can't," she said. "I just can't."

He tried once again. This time it was an officer's forty-five, that old and impressive handgun which was more ceremonial than worthwhile.

"Abby, take it," he urged.

She looked at the weapon in distaste.

"Well, I guess I understand," he said. "But I just want you to think a little. Think what would happen if we ran into the Japs and they got me."

She remembered the woman back in the tunnel at

Corregidor. Still she couldn't bring herself to touch the pistol. Red strapped it around his waist. Now he carried several clips of ammo for the grease gun and extra boxes of bullets for the forty-five.

It was odd to begin to feel better. It seemed that she'd been walking forever, but the tiredness she felt was purely a physical tiredness, more bearable than the strained exhaustion of those last days on the Rock when she'd spent as many as sixteen hours a day in the operating room. And Red was the finest man she'd ever known. Not once in those days and nights, those days which became two weeks and then three, did he depart from his gentle, protective, big-brother manner.

One day they climbed a long hill and through a break in the forest saw the mountains. They walked for an entire day without seeing or hearing a Japanese vehicle and slept beside a stream. She awoke with the feeling that someone was watching her, opened her eyes and sat up, startled. A Filipino boy, not over fourteen, squatted on his heels and was looking at her, his face impassive. She nudged Red. He came awake with a flurry of movement, had the grease gun in his hand.

"Don't shoot, Joe," the boy said quickly.

Red looked around. The boy seemed to be alone. "You live around here?" Red asked.

"Yes. You're Americans."

"You bet," Red said. "Any Japs around here?"

The boy shrugged. "They come. They go. Kill all animals." He pointed up toward the higher hill. "You go there?"

"That's the idea," Red confirmed.

"I show you the best way."

Red looked at Abby.

"My brother fight Japs," the boy said. "He's dead."

"Okay, friend," Red agreed. "I guess we can trust you. Any other Americans up there?"

"Maybe yes."

"We could use something to eat," Red told him.

"Don't feel like a lone ranger," the boy said.

Red grinned. The boy definitely had been around Americans to pick up slang like that.

They set out. The boy walked easily and they had to walk faster than was their custom to keep up with him. At a burned-out hillside farm he showed them where to dig to find runty turnips. It was a feast.

"Where's your family?" Abby asked the boy, when they stopped for the night.

He shrugged.

"No family?"

"Mother dead. Papa, he try to stop the Japs kill our animals. Brother in army, maybe dead."

His name was Carlos. He was fourteen. When they awoke shortly after sunrise, he was gone. "Well, that's that," Red sighed. He gathered up his ammo belts and weapons and suddenly Carlos was back. He was carrying a freshly killed monkey.

"You hungry, Joe?" he asked Red.

The dead monkey looked almost childlike, limp, pitiful.

"I couldn't," Abby said, but Carlos took no notice. He began to dress the monkey with swift strokes of a sharp knife. Red shrugged and began to build a fire.

"No, I couldn't," Abby refused, drawing back when Carlos cut off a piece from the roasted haunch of the monkey and extended it toward her on the tip of his knife. But there was a delicious smell of cooked meat in the air and she extended her hand, jerked back a singed finger, then took the piece of meat between two big leaves pulled from a nearby tree by Carlos. She found that she could after all, and soon she was tearing at the meat with bared teeth, ravenous. In her mind's eye, she saw how the group would look to the little ladies back in Charleston, three savages in ragged clothing squatting around a smoking fire eating with their hands, tearing at the meat like animals.

The brains, cooked inside the skull over coals, were saved for last. Carlos made it clear that they were the best part. She scooped them out of the skull, topped skillfully by a slash of Carlos' machete, and found them to be strange, but delicious.

Now the hills were higher, the going slower. "No Japs," Carlos said. "Use gun to kill monkey now."

The deed was done in late evening. It took a short burst of the grease gun to bring down one of the monkeys. They were eating when three silent, grim-faced Filipinos appeared. They stepped silently from the trees, weapons at the ready. Red froze, a piece of meat in his mouth.

"Hey, Joes," one of the Filipinos said.

"These good Joes," Carlos spoke up. "One Joe, one woman."

The newcomers looked from Red to Abby. One came and removed her hat. "Welcome, lady. You a nurse?"

"Yes," she said.

"Good. Okay. You finish eating."

They walked into the night, following the Filipinos. Then they saw, in a mountain glen, a group of huts and some tents. They were led to the largest hut. The door was open. Someone inside was singing "Camptown

Races." Abby entered first. A group of Filipino men were playing cards at a table. A lanky, dark American lay on a bunk. He stopped singing and got to his feet.

"More babes in the woods," he said. He extended his hand and Red took it. "Tony Dunking," he introduced himself. "Sergeant."

"Red Long, Seaman Second."

"A swabby. Jesus, you're pretty well armed for a swabby. You know how to use that thing?"

"I can manage," Red said.

"Well, well, well," Tony Dunking said, as he shook Abby's hand and felt its smallness, its softness. He lifted her hat. Her hair was beginning to grow back and it was a mess. "What have we here?"

"This is Abby. She's a nurse," Red answered.

"Very good," Tony said. "But don't try to pull rank here."

"I have no rank," Abby spoke up.

"Civilian?"

"I was at the Laguna mission, down past Manila."

"Jesus, you've come a long way."

"She was with us on the Rock," Red explained. He looked around the room. He was the biggest man there. "I just want to make it clear, gentlemen, that she's my friend—and a lady. Do you read me?"

"Loud and clear," Tony affirmed. "No sweat. Well, Abby, I guess you're a little pooped, but when you can, I'd appreciate it if you'd take a look at a couple of the guys."

"I can do that now," she volunteered.

"It can wait. First some chow."

It was clear from the beginning that Tony Dunking was the leader of the small group in the hills. He was the only American. The others were Filipino, from various Filipino units in the American army.

The meal was rice and a stew. Monkey meat again. When they'd eaten, Tony took them to another hut and there were some clothes. Abby found a fresh pair of fatigue pants and a jacket. There was nothing big enough to fit Red.

The makeshift infirmary was in a separate hut. Two men lay on bunks made from shelter halves. A few items of medical supplies were available—bandages, some iodine, a small kit of surgical instruments. One of the men had an infection in his foot. He'd driven a large thorn into it. The other had a broken wrist. Abby saw that the wrist had been set well. It was splinted with pieces of cut bamboo. The foot needed attention.

"I'm going to have to clean that wound," she told the man.

The Filipino soldier nodded. "It's bad."

"Do you have any ether or morphine?" she asked Tony.

"None."

"It's going to be very painful," she told the soldier. "But if we don't clean it, it'll get worse."

When she lanced the wound it spurted pus. The man grunted with the pain, but held very still. "I think there's still something in it," Abby said. "Red, you and the sergeant hold him, please."

The man screamed. His muscles tensed and still he didn't move. It wasn't necessary for Red and Tony to hold him. She had to dig deep into the infection, had to cut away flesh, and there, almost to the bone, was the tip of the thorn. The iodine had to do, and there was another scream of pain when she poured it into the cavity. Sweat was pouring down the man's face, but when she finished bandaging the wound he looked up and forced a smile.

"Thank you," he said.

Abby was assigned a pup tent by herself. Carlos, the boy who'd been their guide, set about building himself a lean-to near her tent and was still at it when she fell into the tent onto a bed of grass covered with a GI blanket and lost all knowledge of the world.

The sound of the men's voices woke her in the morning. She'd slept in her clothing, as usual, and her hair was a tangled mass. She crawled out of the tent. A fire was going and the smell of real coffee was in the air. Eggs had been boiled in a pot.

Ted and Tony sat on a log beside the fire and sipped coffee from tin cans. Carlos handed her a GI mug, steam rising from the fragrant brew.

"Juan had a good night's sleep," Tony said. "You did a good job."

"We'll have to watch closely for a return of the infection," she said.

Carlos peeled a boiled egg and handed it to her. She took it eagerly, hardly noticing that his hands were a bit grimy. Niceties were not a part of her life anymore.

"We need something a little better than iodine," she said.

"We need a lot of things," Tony answered.

"The Japs hauled off all the medical supplies," put in Red.

"And everything else," Tony agreed.

"We saw a lot of convoys on the way up here," Red said. "Mixed Jap and American vehicles. Truck-loads of food and supplies. If I'd had a few men I could have knocked off one."

"We get a few patrols into the foothills," Tony said. "They don't carry much. Those little .22-caliber Jap peashooters, some rice."

"We crossed a main road about four days back," Red said. "A man who knows the way could probably cut it to two days."

"You sound like a man ready to go for a walk," Tony said thoughtfully.

"It's gonna be a long war, Sarge. I'm a little tired of monkey meat."

Tony stood up on the log. "All right, all you little tigers," he yelled, "come over here and listen up."

The Filipinos gathered around.

"The swabby and I are thinking about going down the hill to kill a few Japs. Any of you tigers want to go along?"

"I'll go," Carlos yelled, and there was a laugh. The other men merely nodded.

The man with the broken wrist said, "Give me a pistol I can use with one hand."

"Naw, you stay," Tony said. "And you, little man," speaking to Carlos, "you stay and give Abby a hand and take care of her."

There was little preparation, because there was little to prepare. They were gone within an hour and the camp seemed suddenly lonely. Carlos and Abby sat by the smoldering fire. It was cooler in the mountains than in the heated jungles, but soon the warming day drove them away from the heat and she went to check on the man with the infected foot. She changed the dressing and saw with satisfaction that a clean scab was beginning to form.

It was while the able men were gone that she was

given the name which would stay with her for a long time.

"Thank you, lady," the wounded man said.

"Lady, you want food now?" Carlos would ask.

"Lady, how long it take this bone to mend?"

"Lady, coffee."

There was a stream near the camp, a good water supply, and a deep pool of good water. She posted Carlos just up the slope and ordered him to warn her if anyone came. She stripped and used sand to give herself a good scrubbing, then dressed in the fresh clothing.

At night the birds of the hillside forests made strange sounds. Bats, attracted by the campfire, swooped down, up and away. The man with the wounded foot hobbled out, using a makeshift crutch, and the four of them sat around the fire and drank coffee, compared notes. The two soldiers had seen what the Japs did to those who surrendered, had thrown away their rifles, their uniforms, and made for the hills. The man with the broken wrist had been a corporal. He seemed to burn with an urge to kill Japs.

"I went first to my village. All my people lived there. Most were dead. The houses bombed, burned. All my family. My wife, my children."

"Old Mac, he come back," Carlos said. "I be big, then, and I help him fight, kill Japs."

"Lady?"

"Yes."

"You got family? Man?"

"No," she said. "No man. I have family in the United States."

Juan, the man with the wounded foot, said, "Don't worry, you'll go back someday."

"We take care of you, lady, till then," Carlos said.

She wiped her eyes with the back of her hand.

"Why you cry, lady?" Carlos asked.

"I'm not crying."

"Eyes watering?"

"Yes, wise guy."

Three days went by, then four. They dined on monkey meat and rice. There was good water and she slept a lot. Then on the fourth day, toward evening, she began to listen, to look. Carlos, too, often looked off down the slope. After the fifth day she began to worry. There had been only about thirty of them and they had a makeshift assortment of weapons. They would be no match for even a squad of well-armed, well-trained Japs. She prayed. She prayed for all of them, the men whose names she didn't yet know, but she prayed especially for big, gentle Red.

On the sixth night Carlos sat on the ground by her feet as she sat on a log beside the fire. "Don't worry, lady, they come. They bring many goodies."

She almost gave up as the seventh day turned to darkness, and then Carlos jumped to his feet, listening. She heard it then, the bray of an animal, a mule.

"Hot damn," Carlos said. He ran from the camp and down the slope.

They came in a long line. There were four mules. One mule was packed with an American-made mortar and rounds for it. The others carried bulky packs. She began to count, her eyes failing in the dim light. She counted into the twenties and then Tony Dunking came into the camp area leading a mule and she ran to meet them.

"How'd you like to have a full can of peaches, all by yourself?" Tony asked, grinning.

"I'd kill for them," she said. She was looking for Red. He was midway in the column, leading another mule. She ran to meet him, threw herself into his arms. He squeezed her.

"Hi," he said. "The conquering heroes return."

"So much," she breathed. "Food?"

"Little bit of everything," he said. "We hit the jackpot. The Japs were moving captured supplies."

They gathered around the fire. Peaches, tinned Spam and, wonder of wonders, chocolate bars. They hadn't lost a man. They'd hit the convoy from ambush and the Filipino soldiers vied with each other in telling how Red's grease gun had cut down the small contingent of soldiers in the lead truck and how they'd taken out the drivers one by one.

"Anyone here read Japanese?" Tony asked. He had a newspaper. One of the Filipino soldiers knew a little Japanese. The paper was an army publication. The soldier read from it haltingly. If the paper could be believed, the Japs were victorious everywhere, the U.S. navy destroyed and the war almost over.

Tony jerked the paper out of the soldier's hand and threw it into the fire. "The war's not over yet," he growled.

"Hey, Sarge," Carlos asked, "I go with you, kill Japs next time?"

"We'll see, rooster," Tony said. "Meantime, pour me a cup of coffee."

"Okay," Carlos said, leaping to the task.

Gradually the camp settled down. Here and there groups of men sat and talked and smoked. There'd been cartons of American cigarettes in the convoy. Abby found Red sitting on the ground, hands on his knees, looking off into the night.

"I was worried," she said.

He was silent for a long time. She sat beside him. When he spoke his voice was low.

"I'd never killed a man."

"You don't have to talk about it if you don't want to," she said, putting her hand on his shoulder.

"They didn't know we were there. They were laughing and talking as the truck moved up this hill, slow. Six of them in the back of a six-by."

"Red, I'm sorry."

He shrugged. "I'm not. I got sick for a minute when the rounds began to plow into 'em, but I got over it. I just remembered Dr. Fraleigh and those Jap officers cutting off men's heads during the march and I kept on holding this sucker down. It was trying to come up and then I swept it back to the second truck and took out the driver and a passenger, and the truck plowed off the road into a tree."

"Red, why don't you go get some sleep."

"We were talking on the way back, me and the sarge. There are probably other groups like us up here in the mountains. And they'll need food and supplies and they'll kill a few Japs. Then the Japs will know we're here and it won't be easy to get them, and if any of us ever get captured—"

"We've got food. You won't have to go down again."

"The sarge and I made each other a promise. If one of us gets hit and can't move—"

She shuddered. He didn't have to finish.

"The men heard us. They all made the same pledge. No one will fall into Jap hands alive."

She shivered.

"But that's not what worries me, Abby," he went on. "What gets to me is that I enjoyed it. After that first moment of being sick in my gut, I loved it and I wanted to go on killing. I wished there'd been a thousand, ten thousand Japs in front of the gun."

"Don't think about it."

"We went through a little hill village on the way home. They'd been there. Bodies all over. Bayoneted. Women and kids and even pigs and dogs. I'd been feeling a little bad about myself up till then, after I got over the killing, back on the road. Then when I saw that, I wanted to kill again. They've brought me down to their level, Abby. They're animals. Savages."

He sighed, lifted his shoulders. "How was it with you?"

She forced herself to laugh. "I've got a protector. We did fine."

"Yeah, he's quite a kid, that Carlos. I told him to take care of you or I'd kick his a—" He coughed. "Kick his backside when I got back."

As if the mention of his name had made him materialize, Carlos was there. "Lady," he said, "you go to bed now? I made you new bed. Good, fresh grass."

"Thank you, Carlos," she said. "I'll be there in a few minutes."

Carlos left, looking back.

"I'll be darned," Red said. "I think the little joker is jealous."

Chapter 8

The Zeros passed over the camp at about one thousand feet. Abby was in the infirmary. Conditions were much better there, for Tony and Red had led the men down out of the hills twice more, each time bringing back material and supplies, the last trip gaining much-needed medical supplies including quinine.

The gain had not been without a price, however. Two of the sturdy Filipino soldiers had been hit in an encounter with a Japanese patrol and they were in the infirmary. One had been shot in the shoulder, the other through the fleshy part of his thigh.

"God takes care of us," Carlos had said, when the wounded came back and a mule pack contained everything Abby needed to treat the wounds and guard against infection.

There were times when Abby felt guilty for being so content. It wasn't a luxurious life, but it was decent. The shacks were always being improved. Red had fashioned her a real bed out of bamboo. The mattress was stuffed with grass and rice chaff and was quite comfortable. The men had "liberated" chickens and the camp had its own growing egg and meat supply.

There was a casual routine about life in the hills. Tony ran things with a minimum of quasi-military discipline. As long as there was food and it was cooked and the place was kept clean he demanded nothing else of the men. Except when he decided that it was time to go down the hill and remind the Japs that not all of the Americans and Filipinos had surrendered.

The men were away the day the Zeros came over, their engines announcing their presence even before they burst into sight over the top of a hill to the east. Carlos heard them coming and ran to the infirmary.

"We scram, lady," he yelled. But by that time the planes were past.

Abby ran to the window and looked out. She could see them, high, making a turn over the hills to the west, coming back.

"Help me," she told Carlos. "You men, quickly, quickly."

The sound of the aircraft engines grew louder as the two wounded men scrambled out of bed, the one with the leg wound grimacing in pain. He leaned on Abby's shoulder. Carlos led the other man out into the clearing.

"Run!" she yelled. "Carlos, you go on ahead."

It was slow going with the wounded man. He was in severe pain, leaning on her, trying to make his stiff leg work as the planes snarled down. A tent disintegrated as the wing guns winked and the planes swept low into the little valley. The shack in which the spare ammo was stored blew up with a blast which helped propel Abby and the wounded man into the shelter of the forest.

The two Zeros made four runs on the camp. All of the shacks were demolished, the final touch being added when the two planes dived and released small wing bombs to score a direct hit on the infirmary hut.

All of her life Abby had had a problem. When she got angry she wept. There'd been times when she had wanted, so badly, to say something scathing in anger, but she'd always been unable to speak. Anger to her simply equaled tears and she was in that state with the planes gone and the infirmary in splinters. Now she was, once again, without medical supplies, and it wasn't fair. It just wasn't fair.

"Okay, lady," Carlos soothed. "No need to bawl now."

"Oh, shut up," she threw back, finding her voice at last. "Get out there and see if you can salvage anything. Then we'll have to move out of here."

"No. We don't go till Red and Tony come," Carlos refused.

"They know where we are now. They'll send a patrol."

"Naw. Take them days to get here. Men be back 'fore then."

At least there was food. The chicken pen wasn't in the camp and it was intact, although there were some excited fowl there. "Bombs scare out eggs," Carlos laughed, picking up some fresh eggs.

They salvaged some bullet-riddled canvas and rigged a shelter, hidden under the trees, for the wounded men. Then it was just a matter of waiting. The sound of a mule's braying was the most beautiful music she'd ever heard. She ran to meet the men. Tony, as usual, was in the lead.

"We'll have to move," she said. "Planes came—"

"Yeah, we saw them," Tony said. "Figured they hit you. Everyone all right?"

"Yes."

Red was coming up and she turned to give him a fleeting smile. He halted his mule at the edge of the clearing. "They did a good job."

"Nothing left," she reported. "And they ruined all the medical supplies."

"No sweat," Red smiled.

"Okay," Tony said, turning to yell orders.

The men milled around in the camp for a while, salvaging what they could use, and then they were moving. Abby walked beside Tony as he led his mule.

"I've been expecting this," he said, "or something like it. We're not hurting the Japs, but we're a nuisance. And they can't afford to let the population know we can get away with it. They'll be putting a large force into this area very shortly."

"Where will we go?" she asked.

"Some of the Filipino civilians said there's another group operating from deeper in the hills. I thought we'd go north and look for them."

She walked in silence. It was not easy going. Almost immediately the terrain steepened. Carlos, her ever-present shadow, was just behind her. They went up and over a ridge and in the adjacent valley they found a mountain stream, wide and shallow. Tony halted his mule and let the others pass. Red winked at her as he waded into the stream. It was only when the others were across that Tony made a move.

"Lead the mule, kid," he told Carlos. Carlos, pleased by the attention, leapt to take the mule's reins. Abby started toward the bank of the stream. She gasped when Tony picked her up in his arms.

She laughed. "Really," she said, somewhat flustered, "this isn't necessary."

"No need you getting wet," he insisted, wading into the stream.

"I won't melt," she protested, but he was moving through the swift water carefully. She put her arms around his neck to hold on.

"Back where I come from we take care of our women." He grinned down at her. "And, lady, you're worth taking care of," he whispered, so that only she could hear.

She felt a warmth in her face and neck. "Thank you, Tony," she said, and then she looked away.

"Hey, Sarge!" a Filipino yelled. "Next time you carry all of us, okay?" There was a general laugh.

"Trouble with you monkeys," Tony said, "is you got no couth."

"I got plenty," Carlos protested. "What was it you said?"

It was almost like a picnic outing. They traveled at a leisurely pace. The men, pleased with the success of their last raid, were in high spirits. They vied with each other to be the first at the top of the next hill to see what was on the other side. At the rear came the men carrying the chickens. A crate had been made for them, so that some of the chickens were atop the back of a mule, but others had to be carried, and a half dozen men walked with two chickens in each hand, held by the legs, the birds dangling and squawking at every step.

She fell back and walked beside Red. She was thinking of the miles they'd covered together in getting to the hills.

"You ever see such a mess?" Red asked, with a grin. "A dad-gummed Chinese fire drill."

"How many Chinese fire drills have you seen?" she asked.

She could see Tony up ahead. Tall, dark-skinned. Now and then he'd look around, or back, and she'd see his strong profile, his full, masculine lips which always seemed to be on the edge of a smile.

"He's quite a guy," Red said.

She knew what he was talking about, but was surprised that he'd noticed her watching Tony.

"They talk a lot about leadership in the service," Red remarked. "I've always thought it was something you either have or you don't, and you can't teach it to a joker if he doesn't have it. I've seen officers who've been in for years who couldn't handle this outfit. Old Tony just *expects* people to do what he says and they do it."

She didn't know what to say. His notice of her attention to Tony had created a question in her mind. Why was she always finding her eyes drawn to Tony?

"Like this last time," Red went on. "We decided we'd take out a train. Some of the guys were scared, but Tony said it was a piece of cake and they believed him. It was."

"I worry about you when you're gone," she said.

He grinned at her. "Just me?"

"You especially," she said.

"I'm very, very careful. My part of the job wasn't bad. I just set the charges and blew the track and then got under cover and used the old chopper." He patted his grease gun. "It was Tony and the men who cleaned up the job."

"I want you to be careful always," Abby said.

"Yeah, I'm sorta fond of this old carcass."

She asked the question before she realized how it would sound. "Does Tony take risks?"

"Not really," he said.

They camped beside another stream. Soon chicken was stewing in a pot and the smell filled the evening air. She walked down to the stream and washed without removing her clothing. Carlos finally had been allowed to carry a gun. He sat on the bank, looking very alert, guarding her. When she finished she passed near him and ruffled his hair. "Thanks for guarding me, buddy," she said.

He grinned sheepishly and got up to walk beside her. "Hey, lady," he said, "next time we cross river I carry you, okay?"

"Well," she said. She was larger than he and she was a small woman. "We'll see."

"That Sarge, he thinks he owns everybody," Carlos groused.

"You shouldn't talk like that. Tony's a very good man and a good leader."

"Yeah, well," the boy muttered, looking away. "He don't own you."

Tony and Red were sitting together, eating. She filled her mess kit and walked over to sit with them, leaning against a tree.

"This is a beautiful place," she said. "Too bad we can't stay here. The water is good and we could build shelters under the trees."

"You're not tired of walking after one day?" Tony worried.

"Oh, no."

"She walk all the way from Corregidor," Carlos said loudly. He'd followed her and was sitting on the other side of her tree. "She walk good as you."

"Hey," Tony said, laughing, "don't get huffy, tiger. I think this lady is just as great as you do."

"Yeah," Carlos said.

He was looking at her when he said it and there was a quality to his smile that made her look down and away.

Red finished eating first. He went down to the stream to wash out his mess kit. "Carlos got your bed fixed?" Tony asked.

"Sure," Carlos answered.

"Listen, kid, you're a good guy and I'm plenty fond of you, but how about you bug out?" Tony rose, put out a hand to help Abby to her feet. Carlos, a sullen look on his face, stayed seated as they walked toward the stream. Red winked at her as he passed them on his way back to the campfire.

A sweet and velvety darkness had fallen. The sound of running water mingled with the chatter of night birds. She knelt and rinsed her eating utensils. He was at her side.

"Were you a cheerleader in high school?" he asked.

"No. I was the studious type."

"I dunno. You're built for it. Small and cute."

"I used to dream that I was," she admitted. "But I didn't have—well, whatever it takes. Push. Popularity."

"I'd have voted for you," he said.

She was getting a bit uncomfortable. She was one woman alone with over thirty men, and yet, until that moment, she'd never been concerned. After all, she'd traveled for weeks with Red. Not once had he said or done anything to make her uneasy. She remembered well how he'd told Tony and the others that he was, in effect, her protector. Carlos had also appointed himself to protect her. It seemed that everyone did his best to look after her and Tony among them. So why was her face flushing?

"Listen, when I scouted this place I found a nice little waterfall about a quarter mile downstream. What do you say we walk down and look at it by moonlight?"

She felt a sinking in her stomach. She wanted to, but there was a feeling of disappointment too, for he'd violated the code. He'd stepped outside that unspoken agreement not to let the sexual equation intrude. They were all in an unusual situation. No one had any idea how long the war would last, how long they'd be in the hills, or for that matter, whether the Japs would find them and kill them all tomorrow. And she resented this new element, Tony's departure from a norm to which she'd become accustomed.

"Tony, I'm tired. I think I'll find that nice bed Carlos made for me and sack out."

"Ah, come on. It's early. We'll be back in less than an hour."

He took her hand and she very calmly put down her other hand and pushed his hand away. "Let's don't, please, Tony?" Let's keep it the way it's been, she meant. Don't make me start thinking of myself as a woman among men. Let me hold onto this comfort, this feeling that I can say what I want and do what I want without some man beginning to get ideas.

"All right, kid," he gave in. "All right." He started walking toward the campsite. She let him go and then, alone, walked up the slight slope toward the trees. In the glow of a fire she saw Red. He waved and grinned. Carlos was waiting for her where he'd prepared her bed.

"You okay, lady?" he asked.

"I'm fine. It's a beautiful bed. Thank you, Carlos."

"I right near if you need me."

"Yes, thank you again."

The fire died down. Around her the mountain jungle was filled with the sound of nocturnal creatures. From the area where the men were sleeping there was a chorus of snores and it was almost comical. One man, she decided, had a problem. He sounded as if he might suffocate at any moment. Others buzzed regularly. She turned onto her stomach, snugged the GI blanket around her and closed her eyes.

The smell of coffee woke her. It was barely dawn and the fires sent their smoke straight up into the still air. She went to the stream and splashed water into her face and then there was Carlos with her coffee cup. She walked to the area where the men were eating and saw Red and Tony sitting together, as usual. She started to go toward them, remembered the incident of the night before and turned away. She sat with Carlos and he seemed pleased.

During the day's march she stayed away from Tony. She walked with Red and Carlos, and the going was getting very tough. Once, on a very steep hillside, Tony reached back and took her hand. He'd halted and was helping others up the slope. The mules were struggling and several men pulled on ropes to help them. When it was her turn to go up, there was Tony, smiling, reaching out. She took his hand and was upset to find that his touch sent a tingle through her. And she knew that he could tell. His smile faded suddenly, his eyes widened and he looked at her quizzically.

When they camped for the night she once again kept herself apart, but she knew that he would come to her. When he did he was carrying a jagged can of peaches, which he'd opened with a knife, all the can openers having been lost in the air raid.

"Thought you might need something a little extra." He sat himself down beside her. "It's been a tough day."

"Ah, lovely," she said. She spiked the peach halves out of the can with a fork. She held the can out. "Have some?"

He shook his head. "All for you."

"Peaches must be good," the ever-present Carlos said. Tony gave him a frown.

"I'll save you some," she promised.

"Yeah, then you can take them over with the men to eat them," Tony suggested none too subtly.

So there it was and she couldn't do much about it. It was time to face it. She ate a couple more peach halves, turned up the can and drank some juice—sweet, thick, so delicious—then handed the can to Carlos.

"Go," Tony ordered. Carlos looked at her questioningly.

"Go ahead," she said gently.

"God," Tony groaned when Carlos was gone, "he's worse than any kid brother I've ever known."

She steeled herself.

"Abby, I don't want to push myself on you. If you want me to leave you alone, just say so."

She opened her mouth to speak, to tell him that it would be best for him to leave her, but he went on talking.

"It's just that I get tired of being around the men all the time. Heck, I grew up with six sisters. My old man was hardly ever home. I like girl talk. I like being around girls."

Perhaps, she was thinking, that was all there was to it. Perhaps she'd been imagining things. She smiled.

"Shall I talk about making lace-ruffled curtains or something?"

"Whatever." He stretched out, put his hands behind his head and looked up at the sky. "Tell me how you looked as a little girl."

"Skinny. I was always small for my age."

"Cute, though."

"No."

After a while he said, "If you don't talk I'll have to, and you'll be sorry."

"What about you as a little boy?" Abby suggested.

"Mean as hell. I collected snakes and scared all the girls with them."

"You were the kid in my fourth grade, nasty little boy. Always carrying snakes into the classroom."

"That was me. Then one of my older sisters had enough of it and one night she put this big old blacksnake into my bed and covered him up. When I ran and jumped into bed there that joker was. He was scared, I guess, and he bit me on the toe. I came out of that bed like a striped ape. After that I didn't try to scare my sisters with snakes anymore."

"Serves you right."

"I'll bet you had a lot of boyfriends in school," he probed.

"No."

He rolled to his side, raised his head on one elbow and looked at her. "Too bad I wasn't around."

"I think I'll have another cup of coffee before I turn in," she said. She started to rise and he reached out and caught her arm.

She sat back down. There was that thrill of contact, that little tingle, that electric awareness of his touch.

"There's no waterfall on this creek, but there's a nice little glade down there. Let's walk."

The problem was that she wanted to go with him, wanted to be alone with him. That scared her. Reason told her that to complicate the situation that way was not only foolish, but dangerous. And yet she wanted to go, to walk by his side and feel her hand in his.

"Not a good idea, Tony."

"I think it's a wonderful idea," he pressed.

"The men would know. Red would know."

"So what?"

"Tony, we're going to be here a long time."

"I want to kiss you."

She felt her heart flip. She gathered her strength and said, "Tony, I feel very close to you. I feel close to you, and Red, and Carlos and the others."

"I don't care what you feel about the others," he said earnestly, his hand still on her arm. "I know how you feel about me."

"I don't know what you think you know," she said. "I look on you as a friend, as our leader. That's all, Tony."

He sat up and grinned at her. "Liar."

He moved before she could stop him. He put his arms around her. She tried to push him away, but his mouth reached hers and held for a moment before she turned her face.

"We have all the time in the world, Abby," he whispered.

"Please don't do this," she said, pushing. He let her push him back and released her.

"I'm not just thinking of now," he said. "I want you to know that. I want you to know that I wouldn't do anything to hurt you or embarrass you or cause you pain. I want you to know that I've never felt about a girl the way I feel about you. And whether you think so or not, at this moment, you're going home with me when this is over. You're going to live on a cattle ranch in southeastern Oklahoma. I'll teach you how to ride. There's this little creek runs through the place, all clear and cool, and we'll dam it up and make ourselves a swimming pool."

"Tony, please. It's just that I'm the only woman here, that's all."

"Nuts," he said. "Just down the hill there are lots of Filipino girls who think Americans are hot stuff." He grinned again. "Nope. I've got my mind made up and you really have no choice. Besides, I felt you tremble when I kissed you, girl."

He went away. She shivered in the darkness. She crawled to her bed and lay down and pulled the blanket over her and shivered more. She knew he was right.

She tried to reason it out. Actually it wasn't sudden, his revelation of his feelings about her. They'd been together for some weeks now and even Red had noticed, that day on the trail, how she couldn't keep her eyes off Tony. So that was it and it was her fault. She'd been the one who instigated it, by being attracted, or fascinated, or curious, or whatever it had been. She'd always been looking at him and what did that mean?

She'd been in love a couple of times in high school, those enchanting young loves which make one ache for the mere sight of the other. And then there was Frank Charles. What kind of woman was she?

She lay awake for a long time, long enough to hear the chorus of snores from the men's section of the camp. She concluded that she wasn't, after all, a very nice girl. It had been easy enough for Frank Charles to get her into his bed. For a long time she hadn't even been exposed to a man other than Father Grand and the Filipino men at the mission. And then the war came and now the first time a man looked at her and flattered her she felt the butterflies in her stomach and was ready to go walking off into the night with him.

Was she in love with him? Well, what difference did it make if she was? The question was the purity of her thoughts. She wanted his arms around her and wanted his kisses and she knew that if she allowed that more would follow. It had with Frank Charles. That was the way she was—weak. She was part Eve the temptress, the sinful.

All right, girl, she told herself. From now on you will simply stay away from him. If he comes near you will be nasty to him. And if he still persists. . . .

Red. There was always good old Red. But that wasn't a good idea, either, because Red was like the big brother she'd never had and if she told Red that Tony was bothering her there'd be trouble.

For a moment she had a terrible vision of the two Americans fighting over her. She told herself that she could never allow that to happen.

Chapter 9

Landing on a carrier never became routine. No one ever admitted it, but no matter how many times a pilot came wafting down like a dead leaf, flaps extended, aiming for that tossing, heaving, postage-stamp-sized area of wooden deck, he knew that visceral tightening. Even with the F-4F lightened, almost out of fuel, ammunition gone, the bird's weight and the speed of the approach always made it a chancy experience.

Dick Parker had been on what should have been a routine patrol, but then, up around the canal, nothing was ever routine. The Japs were trying to hang on to that blasted, disease-ridden, ruined island, and to do it they were trying some pretty daring stunts, like putting men ashore from fast destroyers. Even though previous attempts had been costly, they'd managed to land some men and Parker's patrol that morning had found that they were at it again, this time in larger numbers. He was remembering how they'd looked down there, a huge Jap fleet with carriers and battleships and cruisers and more destroyers than he'd ever seen in one place.

He concentrated on watching the paddles in the hand of the officer of the carrier deck and keeping the feel of the dying bird with the seat of his pants. The carrier was moving and the ocean was moving and the plane was moving and the hard, wooden deck was coming closer and closer. He didn't want to go short and ram under the flight deck, or overshoot and go wafting off without air speed to splash down in front of the oncoming bow of the big ship.

Each landing had to be taken in turn, one at a time. Live through one and there'd be another coming. That's all there was to it.

Kick her a little left, cut back, let her die in the air. The ideal approach was to stall with the wheels an inch off the deck. Looking good. Good as Laura looks in a bathing suit. Beautiful. Jesus, Laura. Maybe there'd be letters. No time to think of Laura. The plane hit the deck with that bone-jarring jolt. The cable took hold and it jerked to a stop. He'd lived through another one.

At debriefing he confirmed the flight leader's estimate on ship sizes and numbers and got a few claps on the back afterward because he'd splashed another Jap, a Zero.

He'd written dozens of letters. He'd done his best to try to make her understand how he felt about his duty. He'd told her of his love. He'd told her that the navy and a family could work together. He'd begged her to understand. He'd had two short notes from her since returning to duty in the Solomons.

He had a letter, but it was from his mother back in the States. He threw it violently against the partition over his bed. He stretched out on his back, still in his flying togs, and was lying there with his eyes open when his flight leader put his head in the door.

"Get some sleep, Dick. We're putting up a maximum strike. You've got about an hour."

An hour. Hell, he wasn't tired. His eyes didn't want to close because when they did he could see Laura and hear again her cold, angry words. He knew that girl. She'd as much as told him that if he didn't choose shore duty and stay with her to satisfy her sexual needs, she'd find another way to get the job done.

No booze on a navy ship. No escape there.

He hadn't slept when the horn sounded and it was time to saddle up again. The rest of the guys were in the ready room when he arrived and the flight leader looked at him. "You're looking bad, boy. Didn't sleep?"

"I'm fine," Dick said.

He heard the briefing and then he was back in his plane on deck, its engine idling, waiting his turn. The planes ahead of him left one by one. The torpedo bombers and the dive bombers were already in the air, forming up overhead. The fighters waddled out and raced their engines and roared down the deck and struggled up, up, so slowly. The man ahead of him dropped down out of sight, below the level of the deck, and he held his breath until, after what seemed like an eternity, he saw the bird struggle up into the air. Then it was his turn to feel that dropping sensation in the gut as the plane left the deck. Then he was looking up and around and forming up on the flight leader.

They were riding shotgun in a torpedo group. They climbed high and began to fly through puffy little clouds. Through the clear areas he could look down at the sea and far off see the low, rank darkness of Guadalcanal.

Trouble was in this war a guy always had to commute. Be more convenient if the Japs would come a little closer to home, to the carrier. That way it wouldn't be necessary to use up half the fuel getting to them and then be plagued by the hidden, nagging little worry about not having enough juice to get home. What the hell. The drone of the engine and the rush of wind made him drowsy. He enjoyed flying. The problem was that the moments of beauty had to be earned by going and coming from a bouncing carrier and by tangling with the Japs now and then. He wished Laura could know the feeling.

Goddamn her.

So good together. She wouldn't betray him, would she? She was spoiled and beautiful but she wouldn't do a thing like that.

"Parker!"

The voice snapped him awake just as the wing tip of the flight leader's F-4F was about to come through his canopy. He jerked his plane away and jockeyed it back into position.

"Do your goddamned sleeping in the bunk," the flight leader warned.

Keep alert, boy. Forget Laura. You almost killed yourself and another man. Hell, there was no need to worry. She was just being herself, spoiled, she wouldn't. Hell, not even Laura would do that.

"Whoooooeeee!" He looked down through the clouds and it looked like the whole damned Jap navy was down there. The torpedo bombers, poor bastards, were beginning to tilt and fall away.

"Two o'clock low," the flight leader said, and there were Yamamoto's flying heroes coming up to play games, climbing hard. "You awake, Parker?"

"Bet your tail."

Enough gas for fifteen minutes and then stretch it home.

"Would you gentlemen please join me in giving

thanks for altitude and please stay in formation, if it isn't too much trouble?''

''Sir, I have to go to the bathroom.''

''Put a string around it. Okay. Heigh-ho, Silver!''

Down they went, engines singing. The Japs got bigger and bigger and there was a whole herd of them.

''Okay, kiddies, you're on your own.''

His plane seemed to want to halt in midair as the guns opened and the tracers flashed, missed, then adjusted.

''I'll have to flip you for that one!'' the flight leader yelled as a Zero disintegrated and a prop, still spinning, flew just a few feet over Dick's head.

''Look at that bastard turn.''

''Look out, Tom. Look out, Tom.''

G forces built as he turned hard and climbed and a red, rising sun appeared in the sights. He missed and the nimble Zero flipped away.

''Parker, it seems that there's a Jap intent on shooting my tail pipe off,'' the flight leader called.

Tracers framed the leader's F-4F. Hold her steady, pretend the son of a bitch is one of the barracks commandos back in Pearl. One of the bastards seeing that soft, white skin where the bathing suit cuts off. Take that, you bastard, and seeing him just sort of slump over. The Zero fell off on a wing and went screaming down but there was no time to watch him splash.

''Charlie, mark that one for me!'' he yelled.

He got a glimpse of the waddling, fat, slow, clay pigeon torpedo planes. First one, then another were caught in the dark and red flash of the Japanese antiaircraft guns. Poor jokers, and thank God for being in a fighter and not one of those flying coffins. If he got splashed would she even care or would she then feel free to do as she damned pleased? Jesus, knock that off! While he was daydreaming and watching poor bastards get killed down there and seeing the curtain of fire coming up from the battleships and cruisers there was this Nip son of a bitch trying to kill him. He jerked into a roll and fall, knowing that the Zero could outmaneuver him, but not scared yet. Pound, pound, pound, a line of bullets spotted his port wing and then there was a satisfying burst of flame just behind him.

"You owe me one, Parker."

" 'Preciate it, buddy."

"Blue flight, blue flight, form on me."

Zeros breaking away, scooting for their home—if it still floated. There was a lot of smoke coming from down there. At least one battleship was hit and hit hard.

"Gentlemen, needless to say, I have my own opinion, but I would like your educated guesses as to the sufficiency of the goddamn fuel."

"Oh, Jesus, I *do* have to go to the bathroom."

Someone sang, "Coming in on a wing and a prayer."

"Use the gas tank, Ed," someone said. "You might need it."

"Critical," Dick said.

"I don't like that word."

But the carrier had turned and was steaming toward them. Dick, because he had a flap half shot away and was compensating as best he could, got the honors and the deck was smaller than ever. He was waved off on the first try. He thought of the guys up there on the last of the fumes in their tanks with a very big ocean all around and this time he'd go in regardless. He came in a little high because of the damaged flap and dropped her like a bag of stones. He felt the landing gear go and was scooting down the deck on his belly praying, Don't blow, don't blow! The cable didn't catch and the net was up ahead. At the last second, he put his arms up over his face and took a tremendous blow on his elbow and neck. It hurt like hell. As he jerked and pawed and prayed, Don't blow, for Christ's sake! he leapt down to land on his hands and knees and scurried away like a crab while the fire extinguishers gushed. She didn't burn.

"Dick," the flight leader took him aside after the debriefing. "I had to come in dead stick. It was hairy."

"Not many guys could have done it, Frank."

"I don't want to do it again. Now I know you had a bad flap—"

"She was bucking me around all over the sky."

"You didn't have a bad flap when you almost flew me into the ocean."

"Listen, I'm sorry—"

"Sorry don't cut it, Lieutenant. Now I'm going to tell you this one time. You shape up or I'll ship you out. You got that?"

"I got it."

It didn't make him feel a hell of a lot better to learn that the Japs had lost two battleships, three destroyers, one cruiser, two submarines and eleven cargo ships and that only a few of the troops intended for Guadalcanal got ashore. Damnit, he'd always been a good pilot, a guy others could trust, and there was something very wrong with him. He couldn't sleep.

Hell, he knew what was wrong.

He wrote in a cramped, nervous hand. "It's as simple as this, Laura. If your intention was to make me worry, to wonder what you're doing, you hit the nail right on the head. And so I'm going to put it to you this way. I want to know if you meant what you said. I want to know if you're doing what you said you'd do if I went back to sea duty. And I'll give you two choices. Either you let me know as soon as you can that you're being, as the saying goes, true blue, or send me a copy of the separation papers."

He sat there at his little desk looking at the letter for a long time and then with a curse, wadded it violently and threw it into the waste can.

Chapter 10

She was dressed in pink. The dress was chiffon, long, wide-skirted, flowing. Her hair was piled atop her head. She sat beside her father at the base commander's table. All around her were older people. The band was a special one—six saxes, six trumpets, six trombones. It was wild. It was beautiful and she'd danced only with her father and the base commander. Exciting.

She tapped her foot to the music. She didn't seem to know anyone anymore. There were younger officers in the club, of course, but all those she'd known before she married Dick were probably off on sea duty, or dead, or something equally boring. She wanted to dance, but she knew that it would take more guts than most junior officers had to brave the glares of all the brass at the base commander's table.

Now and then she'd catch the eye of a man dancing with another woman near the table and she'd flash her best smile, but an hour went by and still she'd danced only with her father and the other admiral.

She gathered up her evening purse and cigarettes and rose. Her father looked up at her.

"Powder room," she said.

It was almost like being a kid again. Since Dick had gone back to sea her father had been looking after her as if she were a teenager.

The ladies' room was a birdcage of chatter. She spoke to a woman she knew, checked her face in a mirror. Nothing wrong there. She took the long way back, passed by the bar, wondered if she could get away with sitting there and having a drink. She'd surely be asked to dance if she did that, but the bar was in clear view of her father. So she walked to an outside balcony and stood in shadows and lit a cigarette and looked out over the bay thinking that a few choice words of profanity might help things.

She turned when she heard movement behind her. A lieutenant commander in flawless whites stood there, outlined in the light from the door, fairly short and slim.

"Why is the most beautiful girl at the dance alone?"

"Who wants to know?" she asked, but there was tease in her voice.

"Mark Waring, at your service, ma'am."

"Mark Waring, I'm Laura Parker." She had almost said Laura Averell.

"You don't have a drink. May I get you one?"

"No, thank you. I was just enjoying the view."

"It is lovely," he said, coming to stand beside her. She had a hint of the aroma of his aftershave, examined his profile out of the corner of her eye. Not a bad looking man, about thirty-five, she'd say. "You were sitting at the head table," he noted.

"With my father, Admiral Averell."

"Ah." He flipped a cigarette out and down and watched the falling spark. "Would it anger your father if you danced with me?"

"I don't speak for my father," she said.

She put her hand on his arm. He led her back into the room and onto the dance floor. The band was playing "Don't Sit Under The Apple Tree." He was an adequate dancer. When the bouncy tune ended he held her hand and said, "Don't go."

Next was a smooth, slow number and she stepped into his arms with a little smile, looked up at him for a moment, then put her head on his shoulder.

A young officer tapped Waring on the shoulder to cut in. Laura looked at him and smiled. Waring said, "Shove off, Lieutenant," and swirled Laura away. The young man stood for a moment, undecided, and then came back to tap Waring's shoulder again.

"Look, son," Waring said, "I'm sorry, but no one is going to cut in on my honeymoon."

The lieutenant looked doubtful, but it was a way out for him. "Sorry, sir," he said.

"You've got your goddamned nerve," Laura hissed into his ear. First she'd been deprived of the pleasure of dancing, among other things, because the law and religion said that Dick owned her simply because she'd married him, and now this one, being the typical man, was taking possession immediately.

Mark looked at her and smiled. "Now you didn't really mind."

"Well," she said. He did have a nice smile. "It was a dirty trick on that poor boy."

"All's fair," he grinned.

"Do you have any more original sayings?"

"Yes. You're stunningly beautiful."

"That's fair, not good, but fair."

"How about, I'd like to take you away from all this?"

"Poor. Not a chance."

"I know, you're married."

"As a matter of fact, I am."

"So am I."

"Congratulations."

"So here we are, two lonely people, my wife in Omaha, your husband in—"

"To quote, 'Somewhere in the pacific.' "

"Where I'll be in a few days. What do we do in the meantime?"

The music ended. She pulled away from him. "I go sit down with my father. I don't know what you'll do."

"Live with your father, do you?"

She didn't answer for a moment, but, hell, it was only a game, a pleasant game. She'd played it well before she'd married Dick. "Yes."

"And the admiral keeps office hours. I'll call you."

"I think not."

"I'll need a number."

She smiled. "If you're as intelligent as you look, that shouldn't be too difficult."

Leave them guessing. She swayed her way back to the table and had the thrill of dancing with a grey-haired captain who told her that she was a pretty child and then the admiral was ready to leave. She didn't see Mark Waring as they made their way to the door.

When they arrived home, Laura said good night and started up the stairs.

"I don't think it's a good idea for you to be seen dancing with the younger officers," her father said.

She turned and smiled at him. "He was an old friend."

"Makes no difference," Averell countered. "You

know how people are. Give them something to buzz about and you've got a beehive of gossip."

"You're right, of course," she said. "Good night."

It was like being in prison. How ridiculous could you get? *I don't think it's a good idea for you to be seen dancing with the younger officers.* Nonsense.

She went shopping the next day. The Honolulu stores were low on everything, of course, damned war-time shortages, but she did manage to find a pretty little blouse and a matching scarf. She didn't see anyone she knew, but she got plenty of stares and a few whistles from men.

She returned to the house on the hill and looked forward to another long evening ahead. The radio. Records. A book. Dinner alone with the admiral.

"Hear from Dick today?" She'd heard that question every day since Dick left. She was sick of it. When a letter or a batch of letters did come she'd read the parts which weren't too private aloud to her father and he would chuckle. But not that night. She'd had a letter, but she wasn't in the mood to share it. The admiral was crafty enough to have figured out from Dick's cryptic references that Dick had been in on the action around the Solomon Islands and he was so proud. You'd think that Dick was his son instead of his son-in-law, Laura thought with contempt. Maybe she'd just tell Dick to write to the admiral direct and cut out the middleman.

She was out beside the pool when a houseboy called her, telling her that there was a telephone call for her. She threw her towel around her shoulders and went inside.

"Hi," she said.

"I can tell by the sound of your voice that you're wearing shorts and a halter."

"Close," she said. She recognized the voice immediately, the Nebraska accent, the sound of confidence.

"Ah. A bathing suit."

"A gold star for the commander," she laughed. Her mind was flashing in turmoil. She told herself to just hang up and not be available. And then she turned and looked out toward the deserted pool area and beyond to the sea.

She heard him say, "I'm about a mile away. I have a car and a picnic basket."

"You've done well. Let's see if you can find your way from there." She hung up then. Leave it to chance. The road to the house wasn't easily seen. One had to know where he was going. She went to her room, showered quickly, put on the new blouse, tied the gay scarf around her throat to accent it and stepped into a white skirt.

There was a knock on the door. "A gentleman to see you, miss."

He was standing in the entry. She walked toward him, face impassive, her mind still doing battle with itself, walked past him and out the door. He followed and opened the door to a Buick convertible for her. She tucked her skirt up so that the door wouldn't catch it and got in.

"Apparently I passed the test," he said as he started the engine and eased away. "Actually, I'm an old Hawaiian hand. I spent a few years here as a junior officer."

She turned to face him, holding her hair with one hand so that it wouldn't blow. "Look, Mark, I don't know why I'm doing this. Let me tell you in advance that this will be the last time, and that I'm going to spend about an hour with you, just long enough to convince you that I'm serious about what I'm saying, and then you're going to take me home and forget my telephone number."

"Your wish . . ." he said.

It was soon apparent that he wasn't lying when he said he knew the country. He was on a small road within minutes, winding up into the hills, and then he was turning off onto a track which was nothing much more than disturbed volcanic soil. It was less than three miles from her house. She knew the place well. She rode there often.

The car bounced over the rough road, strained, threatened to stall in loose soil areas, but made it through. He parked it on the back side of a little knoll. He came around and took her arm and helped her out, got a blanket and a picnic basket out of the trunk. She walked ahead. The knoll topped out in a tiny, cleared area. No one came there except young people looking for a secluded place to smooch. She'd been there herself with more than one boy, and the place seemed to stir something in her, making her feel the lips she'd kissed there, feel the hot, nervous hands on her.

The hills fell away in a steep cliff and below was the rocky shore. And the sea. Off on the horizon there was a smudge of smoke from some ship.

"Do you like my private place?" Mark asked as he came up and put the basket down. He spread the blanket.

"It's beautiful," she allowed.

"Since you're allowing me only an hour, I suggest we pop the cork on this wine right away and have one of my very tasty sandwiches."

She sat down, smoothing her skirt under her. "I'm not hungry."

He handed her a glass of wine. She sipped.

"Why did you get married?" he asked.

"What a silly question."

"No, I mean really. You're not wildly in love with your husband."

That didn't anger her. She looked at him, her eyebrows pulled together in thought.

"Are you?"

"Yes, I think so."

"Ah, if you qualify it, it means I'm right," he said.

"Do you love your wife?" asked Laura.

"I respect her. I love her for being the mother of my little daughter. I'll go back to her, just as your husband will come back to you."

"Are you a psychiatrist, or are you just taking a poll of married women whose husbands are on sea duty?"

He laughed. "I'm just trying to figure you out. I know that's impossible, where a woman is concerned, but I think I have a few clues."

"Tell me."

"You want to be here and you don't want to be here."

But Laura wasn't about to show her hand. "I came because I wanted to try to figure *you* out. I wanted to know why a married man would make such a blatant approach to a married woman."

"Ah," he said. "Because *I* might not live through the war. I'll be going back on destroyer duty in two weeks."

"Bull. Don't hand me that corny line. It won't work."

"What will work, Laura? Will it work if I say, quite truthfully, that I felt sparks when I first touched you?"

She looked away, out across the ocean.

"I have this strange idea that what I do is my business," he went on. "I know that society frowns on such an attitude, but I think anything two adult people do is strictly between them and involves no one else."

"Convenient," she said.

"How do you feel about that?"

"The same." She surprised herself. She hadn't expected that answer. "But putting it into practice is another matter."

"We have two weeks. Will we waste it?"

"I told you it was a waste of time. You didn't believe me."

"Because you don't want it to be a waste," he pressed, putting his hand over hers. She didn't withdraw her hand.

"I want you to listen very carefully," she said. He nodded. "Nothing is going to happen between us. Nothing. First, even if I do feel that what I do involves no one else, others don't feel that way. Second, there is no way I will risk getting pregnant with my husband off at sea. So that's that, Charlie. Finis. End. Period. Now let's see what kind of sandwiches you brought."

He lifted her hand and kissed her palm. Nerve endings exploded. "First, no one other than we two will know. Second, there is no need to risk that dire fate you mentioned."

"Ha," she said.

"There are more things under heaven and earth,"

he whispered, "which can give pleasure." He was leaning toward her. "Let me show you."

She allowed his kiss. No harm there. She was a big girl now. She could handle herself. But one kiss wasn't enough, of course.

"No way, Jose," she said, when his hand went exploring.

"Easy," he whispered. "Just let me show you."

She pulled away and sat up. "I told you, damnit."

"I agree to your terms," he said.

"Let me restate them," she said. Lord, she wanted to feel his weight on her. "Hands, kisses, period."

"Agreed."

She let herself sink into in Mark's arms for a few moments, felt his hands at her breasts, kept her guard up, pushed him away when his hand went to her soft thigh.

"If you try to force me, if you so much as touch me with—" She didn't say the word. "I'll scream, I'll scratch, and if you continue to force me I'll run to the nearest shore patrol and holler rape in capital letters."

"Just relax. Let me show you. There are ways."

He showed her. Lord, how he showed her, in ways she'd never had demonstrated before, and the reciprocal ways were not unpleasant. The two hours she spent on that grassy knoll on a navy blanket with Mark Waring were among the most wonderful hours she'd ever spent. It was as it had been before she was married, with some imaginative additions, and no worry, no baby-making contact, just kisses and caresses and hands and, ah, lips.

"Tomorrow?" Mark suggested.

"Anytime after sunrise," she whispered.

Chapter 11

Emi Pecora's life had settled into a routine. She had her room and it was comfortable. She had the radio and her record player and books. When Luke dropped out of her life she felt the pain. She tried to dull it through work. She had her regular shift in the hole at combat intelligence headquarters and she volunteered to continue the type of translating from Japanese publications which had been her first duty.

For a few weeks Tom Braddock tried to arrange escorts for her so that she could get out of the complex occasionally, but after several refusals he shrugged and told her that when she was ready to let him know.

There were many times when she found herself almost forming the words to ask Braddock what had happened to Luke Martel, but it was more and more obvious to her that Luke had been courting her merely as part of his job—to find out about her loyalty to the United States. She had her pride.

The work being done in the combat intelligence center was one of the most tightly held secrets of the war. Only a few knew that the interception and breaking of the Japanese battle code had contributed hugely to the American victory at the naval battle of Midway.

Emi's immediate superior, Lieutenant Commander Smith, was a serious, mostly silent man, but as the weeks passed and Emi's value to the unit grew he began to see to it that small things were done for her. A package would be left on her desk, for example, and on opening it she would find a new pair of nylons, or a carton of cigarettes, or a full box of Hershey bars.

Emi kept to herself as much as possible, but in working with the serious, dedicated men in the hole, relationships were bound to develop. She had conferences often with Lieutenant Colonel Alva Lasswell, a Marine, and she found that his knowledge of the Japanese mentality and language almost matched hers.

Where Lasswell and Smith were all business, some of the other officers had their lighter moments, and they vied with each other in seeing to it that Emi had fresh, hot coffee, that she had her pick of the food served on duty, and she had more than one invitation to go to the officers' club or on an outing into Honolulu. To all such invitations she returned a pleasant smile and a polite, "I'm sorry."

It wasn't a bad life. Regular letters from her mother encouraged her. Macimo Pecora had adapted well to her life in Chicago and had developed friendships among other Japanese exiles. She seemed to enjoy her job and was always urging her daughter to do her work with diligence. She hoped for a swift end to the horrible war so that they once again could be in their home together. Such letters, more often than not, caused Emi to weep, for she had access to information that most did not. She knew that although the war was going well for the Americans, the road to Tokyo would be a long and bloody one. The war, in the opinion of the officers in the hole, wouldn't end in that year of 1943 or even in 1944.

"We'll have to build the largest army ever put together," Commander Smith said one day. "We'll have to double the size of the navy, build transports and landing craft. And I hesitate even to estimate our casualties in an assault on the Jap home islands."

Guadalcanal was secure. The Japanese had taken the last of their troops off the island in daring destroyer runs. The final figures were in. American dead numbered around sixteen hundred. The Japanese had lost over twenty-four thousand men. Henderson Field, on the canal, was one of the busiest airfields in the world, the most forward air base, from which devastating air strikes were launched against the strong Japanese positions on Rabaul. It was from Rabaul that the Japanese army in New Guinea was being supplied and reinforced, but the battle for New Guinea was going in favor of the Allies, and the threat to Australia was past.

The Japanese had lost the war, it seemed. There were times when Emi had some faint hope that the Japanese themselves would recognize that fact. After all, Yamamoto had warned them repeatedly for years against war with the United States, the sleeping tiger.

She'd read much about Yamamoto. In fact, one of her assignments had been to study all written material about the commander of the Japanese navy and to write a character analysis. She'd found him to be quite a sympathetic character and she was concerned lest her report seem to be too pro-Yamamoto and thus too pro-Japanese. But she did her job and upon reading the report Braddock had questioned her.

"If he was so against the war why did he plan the attack on Pearl Harbor?" Braddock asked.

She shook her head and smiled. "I thought I'd taught you more than that."

"Yes, yes," he grinned. "I know. Honor, duty, the code."

"If Admiral Nimitz thought the planning of the general staff and the commander in chief was faulty, what would he do?"

"Yell like hell," Braddock said. "Then if he was overruled, he'd obey orders."

"So?" she asked.

"All right." He submitted her report, with his annotations. She had no idea where such papers went, probably into some top-secret file with huge locks to be lost from sight forever, but it wasn't hers to question, just to obey orders. She wasn't in the military, but she might as well have been. She was, in effect, a hostage.

Yet she'd lost her bitterness. Now and then she had letters from Ralph Izumi. He was an infantryman. He wrote of army life without complaint, looked forward to some large operation in which his Nisei unit would take part. Ralph, she knew, would do his duty, and he might be killed. This no longer seemed strange to her, a Japanese willing to fight his own race, for deep inside she knew pride at the triumphs, sadness at the reported casualties, fear for upcoming island invasions. She knew the plans that were in the works for such actions. She was American. Her country had been forced into a war it didn't want. Victory was necessary. That she and others had been treated unfairly was not the primary concern. The goal was winning the war, to return freedom to Europe and to the territories conquered by the Japanese.

Spring came. Seasonal change didn't mean much in Hawaii, for there was little difference in the weather.

find that military men tend to take the short-term view too often."

"Ouch," Braddock said.

She went on, unperturbed. "The army is probably insisting that if they were forced out of New Guinea, the Philippines and Java would be cut off. The navy is most probably pointing out their recent losses, the cost of sending supply convoys to New Guinea."

"So you would guess that they'll continue to try to hang on in New Guinea?"

"I'd bet the rent money on it," she quipped.

"Okay, Emi. I appreciate it. I hear things are slow in the hole."

"Very."

"Good time for you to go shopping or something. Shall I whistle up a polite young officer to escort you?"

"I think I'll just go home and read."

There was nothing else to do. She dug out books, periodicals, newspapers, refreshed her memory about Yamamoto, made notes to reinforce the things she'd told Braddock. She became involved, once again, in the character of the top admiral of the Japanese navy, a strange, often gentle man.

She couldn't know at the time that her analysis had been correct, that the Imperial Japanese navy had lost the argument over the strategic importance of their holdings in New Guinea, that even as men worked in the hole to break the new Japanese code, Admiral Isoroku Yamamoto was, indeed, in the Solomons, at Rabaul. His orders were to destroy Allied air and sea power in the Solomon-New Guinea area. His Operation I would first strike at the Solomons and then New Guinea.

In early April he moved his key staff members to

Rabaul in order to take personal charge of the offensive. His planes hit Guadalcanal and then he launched three large strikes at Oro Bay, Port Moresby and Milne Bay in New Guinea. His pilots reported the sinking of ships and the loss of Allied aircraft. Pleased, he scheduled his return to his headquarters on Truk with a one-day inspection tour of defenses elsewhere in the islands.

"Please arrange the trip as follows," Yamamoto ordered his staff. "I'll stop at Ballale"—that was a small island off the southern tip of Bougainville, where a division of the troops that had suffered so much on Guadalcanal was recuperating—"so that I may thank General Maruyama and his men personally."

General Hitoshi Imamura, conqueror of Java, commander of both the Seventeenth Army in the Solomons and the Eighteenth Army in New Guinea, heard of Yamamoto's plans. "Admiral," he said, "with all due respect, I advise you to reconsider. I, myself, was almost killed in an encounter with an American fighter plane near Bougainville."

"I'll have fighter protection," Yamamoto said. He gave his schedule to his favorite staff officer, Captain Yasuji Watanabe. Watanabe made a handwritten copy and carried it personally to Eighth Fleet headquarters. There he requested that the information, designed to give commanders at Yamamoto's various stops warning to be ready for a visit by the top commander, be sent by courier.

"That's impossible," Watanabe was told by the communications officer. "It will have to be sent by radio."

Watanabe had been with Yamamoto since the beginning of the war. In times of leisure he was the admiral's favorite chess partner and generally a sounding block for the admiral's formation of ideas.

"And if the Americans intercept the message and decode it?" Watanabe asked.

The communications officer laughed. "That's impossible. To break our code is inconceivable, especially since this code went into effect just days ago, on April 1."

The large air strike on Guadalcanal on April 7 had created an air of urgency in the hole at combat intelligence in Pearl Harbor. Now there was even more urgency, for a message had been intercepted from Japanese fleet headquarters on Truk. In the past such messages had signaled the beginning of important events such as the Battle of Midway.

Emi went in that morning even though the new code hadn't been broken. She saw at once that there was an air of tension. She made herself useful by taking fresh coffee to the men, who were working furiously. She saw Colonel Alva Lasswell, looking as if he hadn't slept in days, and talked briefly with Commander Smith.

There was a feeling in the room that the message from Truk was important and she couldn't tear herself away as the day advanced. It was April 13, 1943. Night came and still the message was a mystery, still the machines and the men labored. The sense of urgency was contagious, and she wished she had the skills and knowledge to help unravel the cipher, but in that area she was helpless. She could, however, stay there, run errands, serve coffee, wait for a plain Japanese text and then apply her knowledge to a clear interpretation.

It was midnight when Commander Smith came to

her and said, "Emi, you might as well go get some sleep."

She went off reluctantly, but slept in spite of the feeling that she would miss something important. She awoke before dawn with a growing excitement. It was as if she knew that something had happened. She dressed hurriedly. Lasswell looked up when she came in and handed her a piece of paper.

"Code symbols for place names," he said. "RR—check it with past place name symbols."

At last there was something to do. RR was Rabaul. RXZ was more difficult, but in the end, before dawn, it was agreed that RXZ was the small, insignificant island of Ballale, near Bougainville.

"Get Braddock in here," Smith ordered, and it was Emi who placed the call to hear Braddock's sleepy voice.

He was there within minutes. There was an air of tense expectancy when Smith handed Braddock the English translation of the message.

"My God!" Braddock cried. "All right, gentlemen, you've done a good job. I'm going to get this to Admiral Nimitz immediately."

"Let me go with you," Emi begged.

Braddock said, "No, sorry." Then he paused. "Smith, what do you think?"

"She knows the Japanese psychology," Smith pointed out.

Braddock nodded.

On the way to Nimitz's office he said, "Don't volunteer anything, Emi. Speak only if you're addressed directly."

It was just after eight when they arrived. The admiral had been informed. He was waiting, his hair slightly mussed, his face stern with that crusty, seaman look of his. He showed no surprise at Emi's presence. Nothing the intelligence people did surprised him. He spoke, smiled briefly, indicated two chairs in front of his desk.

Braddock put the message on Nimitz's desk and sat down. The admiral read it and looked up.

"Our old friend Yamamoto," Braddock said. "He will leave Rabaul at 6 a.m. on April 18 in a medium bomber escorted by six Zeros. He will arrive at Ballale Island at 8 a.m."

"I can read," Nimitz said.

Braddock's voice was low. "Do we get him, Admiral?"

Nimitz was silent for a long time. "I have one concern. Can they find a more effective fleet commander?"

"No," Braddock said. "He's the best they have."

Nimitz mused some more. "Tom, since you've brought this lovely young lady with you, I assume it's because she has something to contribute."

Braddock looked at Emi. "Sir," she said, "Yamamoto is unique. He's idolized by all the younger officers in the navy. His death would stun the navy, indeed, the entire Japanese people."

"But not enough for them to stop fighting," Braddock added.

"Miss—what was it?"

"Pecora."

"Miss Pecora. I've read a report of yours. You seem to have a command of the Japanese way of thinking. In your opinion, would we gain or lose by, ah, getting Yamamoto?"

''We would have an immediate gain,'' she concluded, ''but a long-term loss. If I may explain?''

Nimitz nodded.

''There's no one who could replace him fully, so the operations of the navy would suffer. However, Yamamoto is also unique among the Japanese high command in that he doesn't hate America. He spent some time in the States. He was a lone voice of sanity in the prewar hysteria, advising against going to war with the United States. It's my opinion that he would be very high up in the councils of the Japanese government when Japan is defeated, and that he would be, since he understands the American way of life, much more receptive, much more easy to negotiate with than any successor or anyone else in the upper levels of Japanese government. To put it very simply, sir, we would be, in spite of the fact that he's using all of his abilities to fight us, killing a friend, or at least a potential friend.''

''Sometimes, to save American lives,'' Nimitz said, ''we have to do the expedient thing.''

''I know,'' Emi said. Braddock looked at her quickly, praying silently that she wouldn't voice her opinion that military men always took the short-term view.

Nimitz swiveled in his chair, looked away and out a window. ''That's down in Bull Halsey's bailiwick,'' he said.

Emi held her breath. Then she felt she had to speak. ''Sir?'' Nimitz looked back at her. ''At the risk of convincing Commander Braddock and perhaps even you that I am what I've been labeled, I must say that it is my personal opinion that the murder of this man would work against us in the long run.''

Nimitz chewed on his lower lip for a moment. ''I

note your opinion, Miss Pecora. I reject the word murder. Tom, give me a few minutes."

They waited in the outer office. Then Braddock was called in alone. He was handed a handwritten order. "Get this to Halsey," Nimitz said. Braddock read. The order authorized Admiral Halsey to initiate preliminary planning.

"They're going to do it," Emi said, when they were in the car on their way back to the complex.

"If it'll make you feel any better," Braddock said, "the admiral bucked the decision upstairs to the Secretary of the Navy."

"I'm not sure whether it does or not," she said. "I'm not sure of anything, except that it just doesn't seem right. I know that men die in a war. But to deliberately seek out and plan the death of one particular man—"

"A man who planned the attack on Pearl Harbor."

It wasn't her decision. She tried to put it out of her mind, but it was the talk of the hole. There was endless speculation about what Secretary of the Navy Frank Knox would say.

The work went on. The new code was broken. Days passed. Tom Braddock called her into his office on the seventeenth. "I thought you'd like to know," he said, "that it's been approved not only by the secretary but by the President himself."

She felt a great and heavy sadness.

She awoke early on the morning of the eighteenth. She knew that it was under way. In her mind she could picture it. He'd be dressed in his whites. He always looked so immaculate in his uniform, so calm. In that she was wrong. Yamamoto's aides had persuaded him to wear green battle dress rather than his dress whites.

Major John W. Mitchell lifted his P-38 off Henderson Field on Guadalcanal and waited for his group to form up. There were sixteen of them, all heavy, weighted with wing tanks to give them the range to cover six hundred miles of open water. All he had was a compass and an air-speed indicator to guide him to a tiny speck of land right in the heart of enemy territory where the Zeros flocked like vultures.

It was, Mitchell knew, a touchy venture. He didn't know and he didn't care how the brass knew that a Jap bomber and six Zeros would be over an obscure little island exactly at a given minute. He was just obeying orders. He would have a few minutes over the island and that was all if they were to have enough fuel to get back to the canal. He looked around, checking. Twelve of the P-38s were assigned to take out the fighter escort. Four, under the command of Captain Thomas G. Lanphier, Jr., were to get the bomber.

After six hundred miles of open water, he could see Bougainville and then Ballale Island. He led his flight in at two thousand feet. There wasn't a Jap plane in sight. The sky was empty. The name of the airfield down there was Kahili. It looked small and ill kept.

When the silent radio boomed into his ear he jumped. "Bogies, eleven o'clock high."

He scanned the sky. Five, six, seven, eight. Two bombers! Damn. There was supposed to be only one. Now four P-38s would have to take out two of the Mitsubishi bombers.

"Switch to internal fuel. Dump tanks," he ordered. He felt the plane leap as his auxiliary tanks fell away. The Japs were coming down, readying for a landing at

Kahili. Then he saw the silver, gleaming belly tanks being dropped by the Zeros. The two bombers began to dive and the Zeros were coming down.

Tom Lanphier, leader of the killer group, was under attack, Zeros coming head on and high. He opened fire.

Mitchell, getting into position, said calmly, "Forget the Zeros, Tom. Get the bombers. Get the damned bombers."

The two bombers had dived low and were fleeing, just above the tops of the jungle trees.

Mitchell couldn't watch the killer group and fight Zeros at the same time. He saw, however, that two of Lanphier's planes weren't going for the bombers. One hadn't been able to drop his belly tanks. His wing man was staying with him to protect him. With the belly tanks the P-38 was a sitting duck. It was, Mitchell knew, as he dived on the Jap fighters, up to just Tom Lanphier and his wing man, Lieutenant Rex T. Barber, to shoot down two Jap bombers.

Lanphier had to worry about three Zeros first. He kicked rudder and turned the Lightning over on its back, caught a glimpse of a bomber down below and plunged. The Mitsubishi's right engine came into his sight. The heavy guns raked and the bomber shuddered, like a dog shaking off water. The tail disintegrated and then the two Lightnings were flashing past and looking back. Both pilots saw debris blown up from the jungle by the crash.

Now Lanphier was on the other bomber over water. Its wing caught fire under his guns and the plane dived and splashed.

The men in the hole, as a reward for their good

work, were sent a copy of the message which went from Guadalcanal, where the mission, one plane missing, did victory rolls before landing.

> POP GOES THE WEASEL. P-38S LED BY MAJOR JOHN W. MITCHELL USA VISITED KAHILI AREA ABOUT 0930, SHOT DOWN TWO BOMBERS ESCORTED BY ZEROS FLYING CLOSE FORMATION. ONE SHOT BELIEVED TO BE TEST FLIGHT. THREE ZEROS ADDED TO THE SCORE SUM TOTAL SIX. ONE P-38 FAILED RETURN. APRIL 18 SEEMS TO BE OUR DAY.

Commander Smith lifted his coffee cup. "Well," he said, "here's to it, whatever it is."

There was no cheering, no jubilation. Emi looked at each of the men in turn, wondering if they felt as she felt. She remembered how Luke had asked her if she'd have any hesitation in taking an action which would result in the death of thousands of Japanese and, in effect, she'd been doing that for months without guilt. But this was different. Here one man, a known man, had been involved, and he was dead, and she'd made a slight contribution to his death. No, she couldn't retract the word she'd used in discussing the matter with Admiral Nimitz. The word was "murder." That was a contradiction, she knew, but logic didn't make her feel any better. There was, somehow, a difference. This time, instead of planning to fight a battle in which men died, the plan had been to kill one human being.

"They can't tell the press about this," Smith said. "If they did the Japs would wonder how we knew. They might get the idea that that code of theirs isn't so safe."

"Just unsung heroes," someone said, but there was a touch of bitterness in his voice.

It was left up to Japan to announce the death of Yamamoto. And on June 5, 1943, a million people lined Tokyo's streets for a state funeral. Observers said that the death of the hero, Yamamoto, was a more bitter blow than the news that the United States had retaken the island of Attu in the Aleutians, with over two thousand Japanese dead as the result.

Chapter 12

Admiral John Averell obviously was not enjoying his dinner, although the Japanese cook had outdone himself. Halfway through his fish he put down his fork. "Laura," he said, "do you think I'm stupid?"

She looked up, surprised. "No, not at all. Why?"

"Don't you think I know you've been spending every day with that destroyer officer?"

For a fleeting moment she was a teenager again, a little girl being reprimanded, and then there was a flare of independence, of anger. "As a matter of fact," she said, her voice sweet and calm, "I thought I was being very discreet, not because I'm ashamed of riding with Mark, but because of your Victorian morals."

"I don't like it, girl," he fumed, his voice rising. "I don't like it one goddamned bit. I want you to stop it. You're an Averell, and you've got a goddamned fine husband off risking his life for his country."

"I hear and obey, Father." She bowed her head.

He was stunned. It was too damned easy. "What do you mean?"

"Mark is back at sea. Left yesterday."

"Laura, Laura," he muttered.

"So, you see, your concern is belated."

"What kind of person are you?" he asked. "Or let me put it another way. Why did you marry Dick if you intended to go on playing around?"

"I had no such intentions at the time," she protested. "In fact, I went to great lengths to see to it that there'd be no reason for me to, ah, play around. But—"

"All right, that's all over. That's past. Dick did what he thought was best. He did his duty."

"To hell with his duty."

"I will not have you speaking like that at my table," he demanded.

"I've been thinking about that, too," she said, so sweetly. "In fact, I was in town today and I've found a nice little apartment. Not easy this day and time, mind you. I'd intended to talk with you about that. May I take a few things from my room, and some of the old furniture up in the attic?"

"There's no need for that. This is your home."

"I'm a married woman. This was my home before I was married."

"Laura, damnit, make sense. What are you going to do down in Honolulu? You've got everything you need here. You've got people to cook for you and serve you and clean up after you."

"I suppose it's time for me to learn to take care of myself," she said. "After all, I can't have a house like this on a lieutenant's pay, can I?"

"I can't forbid you to leave." He looked down.

"No, you can't."

"I can ask you not to. I don't know why—" But he suspected that he did. After all, she'd been sneaking out with an officer for a couple of weeks. The thought hurt him, hurt him for himself as well as for Dick.

"If you lose him, Laura, you'll end up being very, very sorry."

"I'm sure I would," she agreed brightly. "I don't intend to. I've done nothing to cause me to lose him. I have been, in spite of what you might think, true blue, as they say. Except for my husband, I am virgin, and I intend to stay that way. Does that make you feel better?"

He cleared his throat. "Laura, there're all kinds of nuts in that town. I don't like to think of you being down there alone."

"I'll come up at least once a week for dinner," she offered.

He couldn't even threaten her with a cutoff of money. Her mother had left her a trust fund, hers and hers alone. She didn't need money. And she was a grown woman. "You're dead set on this?"

She softened. "Father, I think it's best. I'm going stir crazy. I'm lonely out here by myself all day. I'm thinking of finding some sort of job, just to have something to fill my days."

"Not a bad idea, but you don't have to go looking for a job. You could work with the officers' wives' club. They have some very worthy projects."

She pictured herself with a gaggle of the wives, all chattering away ninety miles a minute about who had kissed whom behind the potted palms at the last party, while knitting booties for sailors or some other worthy activity.

"I had something a bit more rewarding in mind," she declined. "Something which would give me a sense of accomplishment." She was just making it up now, knowing that he was hurt and concerned, trying to make him feel better. "Hospital work, perhaps."

He was silent. Her heart went out to him. She rose

and went to kiss him on the top of the head. He was growing more and more bald there, combing his hair up from the side to cover the sparsity at the center. "Don't worry, old darling," she whispered. "I'm not hitting out at you, really. You're the steady helmsman of my life, my rock. I promise I won't disgrace you, but I just can't go on this way. I've got to have a change. I think it'll be good for me to get out on my own."

He wanted to believe that her days with the destroyer officer were innocent. It was difficult, but he wanted to believe. "All right, pumpkin," he relented. "But I want you to promise me you'll be careful. And if you want to come back, this is your home. And it can be Dick's home, too. I haven't told you this, but I've been pushing for a sea command."

"Oh, no." Her face fell.

"Don't worry. Admirals are always behind several inches of steel on ship. I'm not even sure I can get it. There are those who think I'm pretty good at what I do. But if I should get out to sea, then this house would be sitting here empty. In a few months, after Dick has proven himself, picked up another stripe, he might be willing to come back here."

A few months. Now that Mark Waring wasn't around with his fun and games, each day was an eternity. "You're a love," she said.

She renewed an old contact with a transportation officer, and two army trucks were loaded with the things she'd selected. GIs, who took time out to admire her in slacks and blouse as she directed them, placed her furniture in the little cottage which sat on the outskirts of Honolulu a short distance from the ocean. Around it palm trees waved in the breeze. Her neighbors were almost all officers' families. She had her car and double gas rations, since the admiral always rode in navy staff cars and didn't use his personal allotment.

At first the novelty of it was enough. She made trips into town to buy curtain material and spent long hours doing things she'd done little of in the past—sewing curtains, hanging them, making the place look cozy. She spent a lot of time on the beach. It was nice to lie on a towel, sunshades in place, to bake in the sun, to be alone with her thoughts.

The family in the nearest house, a hundred yards away, seemed to be a happy one. She saw them on the beach—a boy of about eleven, a smaller girl, a mother just a bit too thick in the waist, and on a Sunday a tall man whose manner said military. The family made no attempt to make her acquaintance. It was left up to the man to do that.

She was on the beach alone early one morning, a Saturday. He came walking down on the harder sand just at the edge of the water and veered off to where she sat on her towel, hands locked around her knees.

"Hi, neighbor," he greeted. "Alan Enders, Commander U.S.N., at your service."

"Hi, Alan," she said.

He made some small talk and then sat down in the sand beside her. She'd seen him with his family. He wasn't bad looking, but at the moment she was content merely to be alone for the first time in her life.

He pointed to her wedding band. "Navy man?"

"Carrier pilot."

"Ah. Hear from him often?"

"Yes."

"I think it's rougher on wives than on the men," he ventured. "You must get lonely." He was smiling.

"Oh, it's not bad," she contradicted.

"I used to see you around the club a lot," he said.

She just smiled.

"Almost worked up the nerve to ask you to dance with me once." His eyes never left her.

"I like to dance." She wasn't being warm with him, just polite. She wanted him to go away and let her get back to her thinking.

"Now that we're neighbors, if you don't mind, next time I see you there I'll ask you."

Laura smiled cordially. "All right."

"As a matter of fact, I'm going to be alone for a while, myself," he let drop. He was watching her face carefully for a reaction. She looked away, her face impassive. "Wife and kids are off to the States. Hell of a thing to arrange in wartime, but her mother is dying and, well, you know."

"I'm sorry," Laura said.

"Listen, I cook up a fine batch of barbecued ribs," he said. "I'm planning some for tonight and I hate to eat alone. Maybe you'd like to come over."

"I don't think that would be a good idea," she refused the invitation. "After all, your wife has just left."

"I think we lonely people should stick together." He gave her a suggestive little smile. "You certainly would brighten up my evening."

"Thank you." She looked him in the eye. "Neighbor," she said coldly, "you're the one who keeps talking about being lonely. I suggest if you can't stand it that you go into downtown Honolulu. You'll see women standing on street corners. They don't mind shacking up with a man who's just sent his family off to the States. It's their business."

His face flushed. He rose. "Excuse me all to hell!" he stormed and tramped off.

So, Laura, she asked herself, what's with you? He was a man, and not a bad looking man, and wasn't it in the back of your mind that you'd be free to do exactly as you pleased when you moved out?

Yes. But it just didn't please her. Somehow it was just too raw. The entire family had been on the beach just the past weekend, the commander included, and he hadn't bothered to bring his wife and children down the beach to introduce them to a new neighbor.

Maybe it was Alan Enders' approach. Too sneaky. *Come over and have barbecued ribs*. Mark would have been open and honest about it. Mark would have invited her over for some adult fun and games and would've made no bones about it.

She'd had a lot of time to think. She didn't like making her father unhappy. She was proud of being an Averell. She was proud to be married to a fine young officer who, obviously, had a future in the navy.

She went back to the little apartment and fixed a salad and a sandwich. She sat on the small porch and watched the ocean as she ate. It was time to get off dead center. Time to do something. Seclusion was fine, for a short while. She felt more sure of herself now than she'd felt since Dick went back to sea. She knew who she was and what she was. Too bad it was a Saturday. She couldn't find much to do on a weekend to occupy herself. Then she remembered the old family friend, the navy doctor who'd attended to her when she pretended suicide, who hadn't put the incident on any record. He was an old-time Pearl Harbor man and had a permanent home.

* * *

"I'm very glad to hear you talk like this, Laura," the doctor said, after she'd told him that she wanted to make a contribution. "Hell, yes, we can use you. I guess you don't want to join the navy and go off to nurses' school."

"The war would be over before I went to work," she complained.

"Yeah, maybe. Well, I know a couple of places where volunteer ladies do valuable work. I can get you fixed up at the fleet hospital, for example. Or there's a couple of recuperation centers for wounded where a pretty face like yours would be a ray of sunshine."

"I think I might like working with the recuperating wounded," she said. Actually, she'd been doubtful about working in a hospital. All those sick people. So depressing! But it would be different in the recuperative centers. Guys there would be over the worst of their suffering. They'd be cheerful and working hard to recover so that they could get back with their units.

"Come by the office Monday," the doctor urged.

Which left the weekend.

Saturday night. She found herself humming the song "Saturday Night Is The Loneliest Night Of The Week." As it grew dark she didn't turn on the lights. She sat looking out the front window, watching the sun play a last chord on the ocean and then there was that velvet twilight. She got up quickly and turned on every light in the cottage.

She told herself that it was time to prepare an evening meal, but there wasn't much, as yet, in the larder. She turned on the radio. News. Music. The sounds echoed off the empty walls.

She had a new armor of determination. She'd turned

off the amorous commander without pity. She could handle herself. She dressed in a light and frilly gown, drove toward the base and arrived at the officers' club early. She had a fine steak in the mess and a glass of wine. It was still early. Only the bar was crowded with single officers. No one made any attempt to talk with her. She heard the band begin to tune up. The drummer was practicing a lick; the clarinet was going up and down the scale. Well, she was there. She went into the main room and found a small table. A few couples were at the tables, waiters wearing white serving jackets going to and fro with trays. The band was set up and began to play and two couples went out onto the dance floor. She didn't recognize anyone.

She had her dessert and coffee while the band played, from the sound of it taking advantage of the sparse crowd to work on new arrangements. Gradually the room and the tables filled. She was off in one corner and there were tables between her and the dance floor so that it wasn't easy to see her. She decided that was the way she wanted it. She could enjoy the music at least.

One of her father's contemporaries, a captain, spotted her, came over, bowed and sat down to chat. He was a bachelor. She'd known him for years.

"All alone?" he asked.

"Dick's still out playing war," she said. "I wouldn't be surprised if my father showed up."

"I'm sitting with friends," he said. "Why don't you join us?"

"Actually, I feel rather like a fifth wheel, unescorted," she excused herself. "I think I'd rather just sit here and listen to the music for a while and then go on home."

"Will you allow an old man one dance?"

"Certainly."

It was a slow number and the captain was a stately, precise dancer. He held her at a polite distance, chatting all the while about the war and how young men like her husband would win it handily for the United States.

When the dance ended he escorted her back to her table. "Sure you won't join us?"

"Thank you, no."

The waiter had replenished her coffee. Now the dance floor filled with younger people as the tempo picked up. It was one of her favorites and she began to tap her foot. She was so intent that she didn't see the man who approached her table from the side until he spoke.

It was not possible to refuse. The music was in her. She let him lead her out to the floor, threw herself into the jitterbug steps with a little laugh. He wore the wings of a naval aviator. But there was no time for talking, just dancing, and they stayed on the floor through three upbeat tunes before the band went romantic and she indicated that it was time to go back to the table.

He held her chair and then sat down without being asked. "If I'm intruding," he said, "just yell."

"Thank you for dancing with me," she said. "I was about to perish. My feet wouldn't stay still."

"My pleasure," he said.

She hadn't looked at him closely before. He was a smiling, bright-faced boy, in his early twenties, blond hair, perfect, white teeth, a scar on his cheek.

"I have nothing to do for the rest of the evening," he smiled. "I'll be happy to give your feet a workout."

"I can't stay long."

''Unless you run me off, I'll stay as long as you do.''

''What do you fly?'' Laura switched subjects.

''Fighters,'' he said.

''Tell me about it.''

''Boring, boring,'' he droned with a little smile that indicated he really didn't think so. ''I can think of better topics of conversation.''

''No, I want to hear about it. I . . .'' She paused. ''I have a friend who's a fighter pilot. Out in the Solomons, last I knew.''

''I might know him. I was on the *Wasp*.''

She made up a name. She picked the name of a boy she'd known in high school. The naval air arm, although swollen in ranks by the war, had always been a tight little club.

''No, I haven't run into him,'' he said.

''The *Wasp*,'' she repeated. ''Were you on her when she sank?''

''Wasn't I!'' He rolled his eyes. ''Just back. If it had happened thirty minutes sooner I could have landed on another carrier.''

''Were you hurt?''

''Not badly. Enough to give me some time in Pearl.''

''How is it out there?''

He shrugged. ''I could come up with a lot of answers to that. I could look grim and say rough. But I never lie to beautiful strangers. I love it. I've got the most expensive toys a man can have—war planes. I love the feel of it. I love being on one of those big ladies and seeing the organization and the skill and the sheer deadliness of her. I love strapping into a cockpit and feeling the launcher give me a boost, and I love most of all being up there playing grab-ass—" He actually blushed. "Sorry. We get that way. But I love the fight, outflying some Nip."

"You're not scared?"

"Oh, hell yes. Scared, but excited. It's like nothing I've ever experienced. You have to live it to know."

"Do you think most other fliers feel that way?"

He looked thoughtful. "I can't say. I'm sure some do. I think the good ones love it. I think those who don't love it get splashed."

What she was thinking was silly. This one was just a boy. Dick was a much more serious man.

I think the good ones love it.

Son of a bitch. Duty, hah! He'd gone back to play with his expensive and deadly toys. He loved it!

"Let's not talk about the war," he urged. "I'd rather talk about you." The last was delivered with an uneasy attempt at bravado that she found charming.

She smiled. All right, that son of a bitch Dick was doing what he loved and on Monday she was going to start hoisting bedpans to do her part for the war effort. So if he was doing what he loved, well. . . .

"I'd rather dance than talk," she suggested.

That was all she intended doing. She loved dancing. And he was good. And she didn't give a damn if she was seen by those who knew her, including her father. She, herself, rebuffed the young ones who tried to cut in. She'd smile and say, "Gee, I'm sorry." Because this one, this blond-haired one whose name she hadn't even asked was shy, young and safe—and a good dancer.

When she thought to look at her watch it was after one. Soon the club would close.

"I want to thank you for a wonderful evening,"

she told him as he held her hand walking back toward the table.

"Look, I noticed your wedding ring," he admitted. "So I guess it would be out of order for me to ask to see you again."

She didn't speak. Hell, why not?

"My husband was killed." She looked down a moment.

"Damn, I'm sorry," he said. He held her chair. Then he sat and leaned over the table. "When?"

"He was on the *Arizona*." She always had been quick on her feet.

"Tough." But she could see the wheels turning. Why had she lied? Because he would be going back on duty and men do like to talk about their liberty girls. But if she lied she'd just be another blonde back in Pearl.

"What are you doing tomorrow?" she asked.

"I hope that question means that I'm going to be with you."

She wrote the address on a matchbook cover and gave it to him along with her telephone number. "Come early. Say before noon and after ten."

"Hey, great," he said, reaching for her hand.

She let him hold it for a moment and then pulled it away. "I want this understood," she said, looking at him seriously. "I'm not a horny war widow—to put it bluntly. So there'll be no misunderstanding, you won't score. Still want to come?"

"Heck, yes," he grinned.

He arrived in a taxi at eleven in the morning. She'd been up only an hour, had eaten a light breakfast, piled her hair atop her head and had put on a bathing suit and a beach jacket. He was in whites and he carried a small bag.

"I hope there's a bathing suit in there," she said. "I forgot to mention it."

"That's the ticket," he said. "I remembered you saying you lived on the beach. Being from Nevada I can't get enough of the ocean."

"You can change in the bathroom," she said. "And when you come down bring those two lounge chairs on the porch."

"Roger," he said.

She carried a basket of soft drinks and little sandwiches, a blanket to spread them on, her towel and sun lotion and shades. He was there before she had the blanket spread. He pitched in to help, grinning and chattering about how nice it was on the beach. In addition to the scar on his cheek there was a jagged, new scar on the inside of his right thigh. He saw her looking at it.

"Pretty, isn't it?"

"What happened?"

"Piece of something, when a magazine blew, just as I was going over the side."

He was pale. The sun was scorching. "You're going to need some suntan oil," she said after they'd seated themselves in the lounge chairs.

"Ah, I'm tough."

She laughed. "No one is that tough." She got up and poured oil out on her hand and started rubbing it on his shoulders. "This is what I call service," he grinned. "Thanks."

She applied it to his chest. She was thinking only of protecting his pale skin. Then she put oil on his legs and came up the thigh with the scar and a little flash of sensuality went through her as her hand smoothed over the thigh and the scar. Then she sat down.

"Man, this feels good," he said.

"When do you go back on duty?"

"Couple of days."

"Back to a carrier?"

"Sure. Where else?"

She put on her shades and closed her eyes. The touch on his thigh had set things off in her, memories, Dick and those wonderful nights, Mark Waring.

He talked about his home town, his family.

"No special girl back home?" she asked.

"Not really. I write to a couple of girls I went to school with. They tell me about their dates. Just friendship stuff."

"Ah, the all-American boy."

"I guess so. I had a nice girl in college. Talked about getting married. Then I got into the navy air corps. Decided that marriage wasn't a good idea. She married a farmer."

"And you languished with a broken heart?"

He laughed. "Well, for at least two weeks. She wasn't as pretty as you."

"Thank you. That's nice." She spoke as if he were much younger, keeping him in his place. And yet she found herself looking at him out of the corner of her eye, from under her sunglasses. He was sprawled on the lounge chair carelessly. He was well built, sturdy, with a thick chest and strong arms.

After a while the talk faded. He seemed to be sleeping. She put one finger on his leg and pushed to see how much sun he'd had. "I think you've had about enough, mister," she told him. He hadn't been asleep. "Let's hit the water and then get out of the sun."

They swam out for a distance and rode the waves back in. Dripping, they gathered up the things she'd brought. They hadn't eaten the sandwiches. "This is your lunch," she told him, "whether you like it or not."

"I'll eat anything," he grinned.

"Why don't you go take a shower first," she suggested.

He came out in a few minutes in his white trousers, barefoot, with only his white tee shirt on. "May I be informal?"

"Sure," she said. "Put on some records if you like while I rinse off the salt water."

Her nipples were taut. She found herself soaping her breasts twice, thinking of him. He'd put on some moody Glenn Miller. She reached for her underwear, held the bra in her hands for a moment and tossed it back in a surge of pure excitement. She dressed in panties, shorts and a pullover blouse. Her nipples, as she looked in the mirror, were erect, making little marks in the blouse.

He was waiting as a bouncy tune began and she pranced toward him, feeling her breasts rise and fall with each step.

"Too small to get too fancy in here," he said, when the tune ended. They stood in the center of the small space in her living room, her hand still in his.

"Look, I remember the terms. Can I say one thing?"

"One thing," she smiled.

"I have never wanted to kiss someone so badly in all my life." His voice had gone breathy, low.

She hesitated. "That's within the terms," she whispered. And then, on her bed, she outlined the rest of the terms. "Like this," she whispered, positioning him just right. His weight on her, her blouse up around her neck, his mouth on hers and on the firm mounds and moving, moving.

He was almost frantic with his need when it was over.

"Take off your clothes," she told him.

"Let me take off yours." His voice was tense, choked.

"Not in the terms."

Later, they sat at the table, dressed, eating the sandwiches. "Terms all right, sailor?"

He grinned. "If they're the best I can get I won't knock them."

"That's it. Take it or leave it."

"I'll take it."

"Have to be anywhere tonight?"

"No."

Twice more. When she was sure she could trust him she stripped to her panties. And then, pleasantly exhausted, she slept in his arms. Morning activities made her forget, until around ten, that she was supposed to see the doctor at the hospital.

When she told him she had to go into town he kissed her. "I have just today and tonight, can't you postpone it?" he entreated.

"No, I'm sorry." She kissed him lightly. She, too, hated to have it end. "Why don't you wait for me here?"

"Great. I'll stay inside so the neighbors won't get suspicious."

"I don't care about the neighbors. Go get some sun. But be sure to soak down with lotion."

"Yes, ma'am."

* * *

It turned out that being late was fine. The doctor had just finished an emergency operation and was entering his office when she arrived. He asked her to come in. "I've talked with the folks at the recupe hospital. They're pleased to have you."

"Thank you." She was thinking that she could have gotten that information by telephone and be with—good God! She didn't even know his name.

"Just as well you came in, though. You have to have a health clearance. And I took a look at your records. You haven't had a complete examination in several years, Laura. So while you're here we might as well give you the 100,000 mile going over."

Blood tests. Thumpings and a cold stethoscope. Then heels in the stirrups. The doctor had pointed out to her that she'd never had a gynecological examination. Now a doctor was probing around and peering up inside of her, not her old friend, but a young man lately a civilian, a specialist in women's disorders.

"When did you last have sexual intercourse, Mrs. Parker?" the doctor asked.

"Hmm." It took her only a few seconds. "My husband has been at sea for four months and just over two weeks."

"Hmm," he echoed. "And you've never had this type of examination before?"

"No." She was getting frightened. "Is there something wrong?"

"I want to be sure. Do you mind if I ask Dr. Abrams to have a look?"

"If you think it's necessary. Look, you're scaring the hell out of me."

"Nothing to be alarmed about. Believe me." He

went out of the room, leaving her in the saddle. She wanted to be able to look down there, to see what was so damned scary. She didn't believe this. She knew that something terrible was wrong and she was so frightened that she didn't even bother to take her feet out of the stirrups. The doctor came back in with Abrams, the old family friend, and they poked and peered.

"It's nothing to be alarmed about, Laura," Abrams said. "I'm sorry to tell you, however, that you'll never be able to have children."

Jesus Christ! Was that all? She sighed in relief.

"Don't take it so hard, honey," Abrams said. "It's a tough break." He tried to explain but she wasn't really listening. All she knew was that there was some kind of a malformation which would, forever, prevent her from getting pregnant. And a maelstrom of thoughts surged through her head. That nice young man, blond, so solidly built. God, how he'd trembled and wanted her.

"So you'll just have to bear up under it, honey," Abrams was saying. "There are other worthwhile things in life."

"Thank you. I presume that I'm clear to go to work in the hospital?"

"Yes, of course."

He was waiting. All the way home she'd been thinking of it. No reason now to do the "everything but" bit. Now she was free, free. Lord, how many wasted opportunities!

He was just coming out of the shower, a towel around him. "Don't bother to dress," she whispered, as she went into his arms and kissed him. "Let me get a quick shower."

She decided to surprise him. She came into the bedroom in her panties with the knowledge that there would be no second-best measures this time. Her heart went wild in his arms and her body began to strain, to beg, to know a desperate need. They kissed fiercely, deeply, and explored each other, tension mounting, saving the best, the glorious moment. She reached down to pull off the last garment, to open herself to him, and she thought of Dick.

Except for my husband, I am virgin, she had told her father, and with the exception of that small, slight intrusion by that damned Marine, she'd been telling the truth.

She did not remove the garment.

"Darling," she said, "there's one other thing. I don't know if you'll like it."

"I'm game," he said.

She showed him. She'd learned it from Mark Waring. It was, he said, a first for him. It was not a last. It was a long and sleepless night. In her conscience, she was still virgin when he left the next morning and she drove to the hospital to begin a new part of her life.

Just before he left he held her close, kissed her. "I looked all over this place yesterday while you were gone to find something with your name on it."

She'd moved nothing, she suddenly realized, to give away her identity. No letters, no books with her name on them. Her name was on her social security card and her driver's license, but they were in her purse.

"Oh?" she commented, nonplused.

"I'd like to know. You probably have your reasons, but I'd like to know."

"I don't know yours, either."

He opened his mouth. She put her hand over it. "No, let's keep it this way. I don't want to know and you won't know mine."

"But I'd like to write."

"No. I won't be here next time you have liberty. No. Let's just keep our memories, okay?"

At the hospital she was sent to see a tough-looking navy nurse. "Glad to have you, Mrs. Parker. I understand that you're a volunteer, working without pay, but you'll be treated as an employee. Only way to keep discipline. We won't be hard on you. We'll start you on the book and magazine cart and you can work up from there."

"Do I need a uniform?"

"No. The men like to see pretty ladies in civilian dresses. Dresses, mind you. No slacks or shorts."

"All right."

"You'll be pushing the book and magazine cart, but the most important thing you can give these men is a smile and a friendly word. Some of them have been through hell."

The first ward she entered was filled with amputees. Men missing one arm, two arms, one leg, two legs and every other possible combination of missing limbs.

My God, she said to herself, what have I gotten myself into?

But she put a smile on her face. "Hi, need anything to read today?"

Chapter 13

Abby Preston found it hard to believe that she'd been living in the Luzon hills, surrounded by men, for well over a year. The time had gone by so quickly, despite the fact that individual days tended to drag. After the Japanese air attack on their first encampment, they'd been forced to move frequently. Sometimes they encountered other groups of guerrillas, but after spending some time with them, they always decided to go it alone. Some of the guerrillas turned out to be little more than bandits who preyed on civilians. They avoided the Japs because the Japs shot back.

New recruits told of rumors of other Americans in coastal areas. There was some talk of sending a party to try to link up, for the coastal and jungle groups seemed to have some American direction. One man who came up to the hills brought with him a battered copy of a propaganda magazine called *I Shall Return—MacArthur*. It was passed around until it became quite unreadable.

"They wouldn't be printing magazines aimed at guerrillas in the Philippines unless there were some known, organized groups," Red deduced. He wanted to go by himself to try to find Americans who might have a radio.

"Too dangerous," Tony argued. "Look, we're hitting the Japs every chance we get. We've helped to instill a spirit of resistance in the hill people. Hell, yes, we could get bigger. We could round up some of the tribesmen, but we wouldn't have guns for them."

"I'm not sure whether we've created the fighting spirit in the hill people or if the Japs have," Red reasoned. The Japanese periodically sent teams into the hills and when such groups encountered a native village they destroyed it. To save precious bullets, they would knife and bayonet the inhabitants—women and children along with the men.

"I think we should continue as we are," Abby voted. "The magazine says that we're on the offensive. We've taken Guadalcanal—"

"Wherever the hell that is," Red grumbled.

"—and we're whipping the Japs in New Guinea. It won't be long, surely, before we retake the Philippines."

"The lady is right," Tony concurred.

His approval caused her to smile. Inside, she was still fighting a great battle. Tony respected her, she knew, for after she'd rejected a couple of his amorous advances, he'd stopped trying to get her alone However, that didn't mean that he didn't look at her, look after her, see that she had the best of what there was to offer in camp.

As for Red, he was just good old Red. Always there when she needed him, holding her tenderly, in a big-brother way once, when a man died and she could do nothing and the tears came.

She could still remember, late in 1943, her last talk

with Tony. They'd been on the move and she was walking with him ahead of the main group.

"Abby," he'd said without warning, "you're driving me crazy."

"What do you mean?" she asked. They'd been talking easily about the countryside, the possibilities of this place or that for a new camp.

"To be so near and not be able to touch you," he said, his voice soft.

"Oh, Tony. Don't."

"I know, I know. I know all the reasons. It wouldn't be good for morale. I know that if I ever kissed you it wouldn't stop there."

She flushed, because she felt, deep inside, that he was right.

"And then we'd have each other and the men would have only themselves."

She thought it would end there. She didn't speak, and, in fact, started to fall back. He slowed too and took her arm. "I'm not finished," he said. "The minute this is over, the minute the Japs are whipped and we're safe, I'm going to kiss you until your toes curl. And then I'll marry you."

She didn't speak.

"You're supposed to say something," he reminded her.

"Okay."

"Okay what? Okay you'll say something or okay you'll marry me?"

She put her hand on his for one brief moment. "Okay, I'll marry you. But not the first minute. You'll have to promise me that we'll wait—"

"Hell no."

"—until things are back to normal, until we've

both gone home and you've seen other girls, other American girls."

He laughed. "You think I've fallen in love with you because you're the only girl in the game?"

"There is that possibility."

"That could go for you, too," Tony looked at her intently.

"I think not."

He'd left it at that and there were times later when she was alone in her tent that she ached to see him, actually made a move to go to him. What did it matter? They were thousands of miles from home, fugitives in a hilly jungle and they faced death each day. Any day they might be discovered by a huge Japanese force, or have the planes come down on them without enough warning. Why was she being so foolish?

Each time the men went down to raid for supplies, to kill Japanese, she suffered agonies. Each time they came back. Sometimes there'd be walking wounded, often a man missing, and no one ever mentioned those who didn't come back.

Early in 1944 the men returned from such a mission in exceptionally high spirits. She met them and found both Red and Tony grinning broadly.

"Hey," Tony yelled, as he saw her coming down the trail, "we've got a surprise."

It was a radio. A real short-wave radio, one which could be used in the field with a man turning a wheel on a portable generator. The raid had been made without loss and without wounded and there was food, a bolt of cloth from which she could make a dress and the radio.

All attention was on the radio. It took them a long time to set it up. At last Red sat down on the little stool and began to crank the hand wheel and Tony turned on the set and began to make adjustments. The sound of Japanese voices came, fading, static-ridden, the strange sounds startling the cockatoos in the nearby forest into making their warning calls.

Then came a voice in English and everyone, the Filipinos included, crowded around to listen. Armed Forces Radio, fading in and out, told them that the battle for Kwajalein, in the Marshalls, was over, with total American victory.

"Lord, they're getting closer and closer," Abby said.

Newscasts weren't written for people who'd heard no war news at all since early 1942. It took them several days and nights of listening, men taking turns on the generator, to piece it together. The American armies were in Italy and Italy had surrendered. The Germans were putting up stiff resistance. Astoundingly, the Russians had pushed Germany back into Poland, indicating to those who'd heard nothing about the early German victories that the Germans must, at one time, have been deep into Russia.

"They talk more about the war in Europe than about the Pacific," Red grumbled. "Where the hell is MacArthur?"

"Hush," Tony said. They were talking about a Marine invasion of Bougainville and the terrible losses suffered there.

Now and then they'd tune in to Tokyo Rose and hear the latest American hit tunes. They also heard the Japanese propaganda and they didn't know what to believe. If one believed the Japanese English-language broadcasts the Americans would all die in their attempt to island hop across the Pacific.

"Well, my guess is that we're here for another two

years,'' Tony said. He tried to put together what had happened since 1941. It sounded as if the Japs had almost conquered the Pacific, getting all the way to the islands off Alaska and that it was going to be an island-by-island campaign to beat them. They pored over a battered map of the Pacific, trying to guess the strategy. Red thought the main plan was to clean out the central Pacific, for there had been invasions in the Gilberts, the Marshalls and then at Kwajalein and Eniwetok.

''Naw,'' Tony said. ''I'll bet old Mac's running this show. They hit the Solomons first and now they're cleaning up New Guinea. That means he's coming from New Guinea into Mindanao.''

''I hope you're right,'' Red said. ''Be faster that way.''

''I've been doing some thinking,'' Tony mused. ''It's been over two years since the Nips kicked old Mac out of here. My bet is he'll be coming back soon. I think we oughta give him all the help we can.''

Abby had been listening to a Glenn Miller record being played by Tokyo Rose while one of the Filipinos turned the generator. She didn't like the sound of what Tony was saying.

''We need to get in touch with the other guerrilla groups, tell them what's going on. And then work together to tie down as many Jap troops in the hills and surrounding area as we can.''

Abby felt weak. She didn't want him going down deliberately to seek battle with the Japanese. In the past they'd gone down only when supplies were low.

''You're the boss,'' Red gave his consent.

Tony took a few men and went off to contact the nearest guerrilla group. Red stayed behind to help the experienced Filipino noncoms train a new group of men that had recently joined them. While the men played war, running up and down the hills ambushing each other, Abby cut up the bolt of cloth and sewed herself a rather attractive dress. She bathed herself in the stream and washed her hair with Japanese-made soap which left a lot to be desired, but it was the best she had. She told herself she was being foolishly feminine, but she felt good when she put on the dress, did her hair and used the juice of a bright red fruit to stain her lips.

Red came into camp just before sundown, hot and tired. He was pleased with the day's work. The new men were jungle-wise and willing to fight. He saw a stranger sitting on one of the hewn benches. She had her hair up and was wearing a pretty red dress.

"Holy mackerel," he whistled when he came near and recognized the stranger as Abby.

She stood up and twirled around. "Like it?"

"Lady, you're a sight for sore eyes," Red beamed.

"I guess that means you like it." She came toward him and gave him a light kiss on the cheek. She felt so good.

He cleared his throat and grinned at her. "Man, you bet I like it. I knew you were pretty, Abby, but, gosh."

"Don't overdo it," she laughed.

"You can wear that when we meet the first American troops and they'll think we've had a ball here, like a country club."

"Do you think Tony will like it?"

His smile faded. "Yeah, sure," he said. He turned and walked away. It was, she was thinking, a strange reaction for good old Red.

Tony came back, tired, grim-faced. "Cruds," he snarled. "They're a bunch of cruds. All they want to do is stay up here where it's safe, drink their homemade hooch and go down and steal chickens from the farmers now and then."

Not knowing when he was to return, she hadn't been wearing her new dress. She felt, since he arrived late in the day, that to change then would be too obvious. She was just the lady, dressed in faded GI fatigues, sitting around the campfire with her friends.

"But there was a Filipino who'd just come up from the coast," Tony told them. "He said there's a regular guerrilla organization down there and they're hitting the Japs hard. In some places the Japs can't come out of the coastal towns unless they're in force. What do you all think of going down to make contact?"

"I'm for it," Red proposed. "Time to do something."

"Lady?" Tony looked at her with a little smile.

"It scares me, of course, but whatever you men think best."

"You'll have to go with us," Tony told her. "We might not be coming back. If there's American leadership down there we'll plug into it and it wouldn't do to leave you up here alone."

"I'll be with her," Carlos protested.

"Sure, tiger," Tony said. "But you'll be coming too."

"I'm ready to fight the Jap," Carlos said. He'd obtained a rifle and was extremely proud of it. He kept it very clean. He'd been able to fire only a few practice rounds with it because of the shortage of ammunition.

The various moves they'd made had taken them higher and higher into the mountains. Tony's plan would lead them down the mountains to the east coast. There the coastal towns and villages were closer together than on the west coast of the island. There, it was said, the coastal jungles gave cover for the American-led guerrillas.

Many items that they'd accumulated since the fall of Corregidor had to be left behind. The men didn't like that idea, but after an explanation by Tony they agreed. The saddest parting was when they left their mules with some villagers. The mules would be more of a hindrance than an asset in the deep jungles of the coast lands.

Coming down from an elevation of over eight thousand feet was a shock to the system. On the eastern side the mountains were steep and they quickly descended into the steamy heat of the tropics. Vegetation became more dense, the going tougher, the mosquitoes worse. Fortunately they had an ample supply of quinine and Atabrine. Tony had a map and he used a GI compass to guide them toward the coastal town of Santa Cruz.

As they began to encounter more and more natives they found, to their pleasure, that they were greeted as heroes. They were given food when it was available and they picked up a few recruits. To the natives, anything American was good. The fact that this group had two Americans leading it made it a good group. Hatred of the Japanese occupation was practically universal, although they were warned against certain unscrupulous characters who were labeled fifth columnists, or collaborators with the Japanese.

Once they had to dodge a Japanese patrol. It was a nervous moment as an armored car passed on the road, infantrymen walking behind, but the Japanese seemed content not to scout the surrounding jungles.

Two of the new men from the coastal area were their guides. They knew of a group operating in the Santa Cruz area.

There was evidence of guerrilla resistance activities. Their guides led them around booby traps made by sharpening a type of bamboo into double-sided barbs. A wound from the bamboo picked up a poison from the sap and resisted healing.

In that jungle heat, their clothing quickly became soaked with perspiration. Great drops of sweat ran down their backs. But they were nearing their destination and it was time to find a safe camping place. The two Americans selected a site and tents were set up. One of the Filipino scouts, sent on ahead, came back with the word that there were plenty of Japs around but that they stayed mainly in the towns. When they ventured out they were ambushed by the guerrillas. He had made contact with the Santa Cruz group and a meeting was arranged with the commander, a Filipino colonel whose war name was Atabong.

"He has a radio," the scout reported. "He's in touch with MacArthur. A sub is coming, bringing many goods, many bullets."

"Sounds good," Tony said. "Red, you'd better come with me."

Red nodded.

"I go," Carlos volunteered.

"You stay and take care of the lady," Red told him.

Carlos was torn. He considered himself to be a man now. And yet he had his duty to look after the lady.

"Is it going to be dangerous?" Abby asked.

''Shouldn't be,'' Tony said. ''We're to meet this Atabong in the jungle. Shouldn't take us more than a day there and a day back.''

''Why don't you let Carlos go, then?'' she urged. She knew that the boy wanted so much to be considered a part of the group and not just a baby sitter for her.

''Why not?'' Tony grinned and Carlos threw out his chest.

She saw them off. At the last minute, as they were ready to leave camp, she had second thoughts. Any trip was dangerous. And the three people who meant the most to her were going away.

''Tony,'' she called, ''be very careful.''

''No sweat,'' he replied casually. But he did something then that he'd never done before. He put his arms around her and gave her a quick hug, a swift peck on the cheek.

Red, nearby, looked away and then, with a look of determination on his face, he approached her. ''See you in a couple of days, lady,'' he said and for the first time since she'd known him looked uneasy, unsure. He hitched his rifle higher on his shoulder, stepped toward her, and she was enfolded in his big arms. For a moment she thought he was going to squeeze the breath out of her. He kissed her on the cheek. ''I've told Juan and a couple of the others not to let you out of their sight.''

''I'll be fine,'' she assured him.

It was Carlos' turn. The two years of growth since he'd joined them had made him taller than Abby. He didn't put both arms around her. He put his hand on her waist and leaned and brushed his lips on her cheek. ''I told Juan if he didn't take good care of you—''

She smiled at him. "You go on. You're a part of the team now."

They took only five men with them in addition to Carlos. She watched them disappear in the morning mist, a steam which rose from the jungle with the emergence of the sun. She felt a pang of fear, then went back to her makeshift commissary. One of the men had fallen coming down the mountains, suffering a bad sprain of his ankle. She unwrapped it and let him test it. It was getting better.

The Filipinos set about making the camp livable. Trees were felled to form benches. A flat seat was cut with blows of their fierce, curved knives. Juan and two of the others made a bamboo sling for Abby's bed and raised her tent to cover it.

There was monkey meat for dinner and then another hot and breathless day. She found some relief in the stream. It seemed that the men could always find a stream.

She began to worry in the late afternoon of the second day. The men were taking advantage of the wait to rest. They lounged about, some slept, others played cards or just sat and talked quietly.

The party came back just before dark, bearing good news and booty. Red had almost more ammunition for his grease gun than he could carry. In his pocket he had a chocolate bar for Abby. They gathered over the coffeepot, steaming on the open fire, and she heard them talk excitedly about a guerrilla network that covered the entire island. They were in touch by radio with other groups on Mindanao and other islands. Submarines made regular visits to bring weapons and supplies. Best of all, to the north, around the inland town of Bangued, there was a very active group under the command of a naval officer. Tony had talked with him on the radio and he had his orders. He was to lead his group north and make contact with the navy.

"Atabong said they even have houses," Red told Abby. "How'd you like to sleep in a real bed again?"

"I can't even imagine such heaven," she sighed.

So they were moving again, the jungles thick and hot, the days exhausting. It was an uneventful march which covered about thirty hard miles.

In a jungle clearing they saw the first American they'd seen since the conquest. He was an air force sergeant. He had a brigade of hardened Filipinos with him. He stared at Abby, bug-eyed. "Lord, I'd forgotten what an American girl looks like," he said.

Now, in addition to the old short-wave receiving set, they had a two-way radio and could contact Commander John Barnes, leader of the Bangued group.

Sergeant Phil Woods told them the proper procedure for using the set. "When you make a contact, you move, and move fast. The Japs have radio direction finders and they usually send out an air strike if they can pinpoint the location of the radio."

Woods gave them their orders. They were not to consolidate with the main group, but, instead, were directed toward a little complex of huts in the jungle foothills, about three miles south of Bangued.

"What we do is make the roads unsafe for the Japs," Woods explained. "Now and then they'll come out of the towns. When they do we hit 'em hard and then run like hell before they can call in planes and reinforcements."

Woods had good maps. He outlined the area which was to be their territory. "You never want to hit the Japs too close to your headquarters," Woods warned. "That makes it rough, because it means you have to march a ways and hang around until you get a shot at them and then run back."

Tony and Red had no problem understanding the reasons for that.

"There's been some Jap patrol activity here," Woods informed them, indicating a road junction near a town called Candon. "The commander suggests that you do something about it."

"We'll see what we can come up with," Red nodded.

"By the way," Woods added. "There's a sub due soon. Anything in particular you people need?"

Tony and Red began to rattle off a list of needs. Woods made notes and then turned to Abby. "And the lady?"

"I'd give my eye teeth for some decent soap," she requested, "and some lipstick."

"This'll raise a few eyebrows," Woods predicted. He looked thoughtful for a moment. "I didn't know there was a navy nurse left on the island, except in the prison camps," he said. "I wonder if it wouldn't be best, Miss Preston, if you leave here when the sub comes."

Both Red and Tony looked at Abby quickly. "I think that's a great idea," Red encouraged. Tony was silent.

"No," she refused with conviction in her voice. "In the first place, I'm not navy. And anyway, I've stayed this long already and I'm needed."

Woods shrugged. "Your choice, I guess."

"Abby," Red coaxed, "I think you should consider it."

"I have considered it," she said. "I thought of it the minute I heard subs came here."

Red came to her tent later. He stood there for a moment, then cleared his throat. The men had raised her bed off the ground and the tent was suspended above it so that he had to stoop to look in at her.

"Abby, listen," he urged. "The more I think about it, the more I think you ought to go with Woods and get on that sub."

"Are you trying to get rid of me?"

His face was lit by the flickering flames of a fire. "You know better than that," he said in a low voice. "I'd miss the hell out of you. But . . ."

She reached out and took one of his hands between hers. "Red, you've taken good care of me. You saved my life several times over. I'm not very warlike, but I guess I feel that I'm a part of something worthwhile. I can't do much, but I can make it a little easier when a man is hurt or sick. If I left I'd never be able to forgive myself."

"Yeah, I knew you felt that way." He squeezed her hand. "It's going to get rougher, Abby. None of us can tell what might happen. And I wanted to say . . ." He paused and pulled his hand away from her.

"What did you want to say?" she asked.

He spoke so softly she could barely hear. "I wasn't going to say anything, not until after this thing was over. But . . ." Again he paused. "Well, we're going after Japs tomorrow, a lot more Japs than we've ever run into in the hills. I wouldn't want anything to happen to me without you knowing how I feel, so I guess, even though I think I'm putting an additional load on you . . ."

"Are you trying to say that you're fond of me?" she asked, wanting to head it off, not wanting him to humiliate himself.

He grinned. "A lot more than that, Abby. I wasn't going to say anything."

She took his hand again. "Red, you're the brother I never had. I love you very much. After the war I want to visit you, and when you have a wife and children I want to know them."

"Yeah, okay," he agreed in a choked voice. "I dig." Then his voice was firm. "Just promise me one thing."

"If I can."

"Don't make any decisions until we're out of this damned jungle, until the army comes back and it's all over."

"Yes," she said. "I can promise you that."

"Then talk to me. Give me a chance, okay?"

"Yes, Red, we'll talk."

Oh, Lord. She was a regular heartbreaker. Two fine men in love with her. And it hurt her to think that Red would be disappointed. Then she felt a bit of resentment. Why couldn't he have left it as it was, with her thinking of him as one of the finest men she'd ever known? As a man to whom she could talk, a shoulder to cry on, and not have to worry about him getting romantic. Oh, Red, damnit, I wish you really were my big brother!

The group went out the next day. It was five days before they came back and there were five vacancies in their ranks. They'd hit a Jap column on the road and they'd done well, but they'd lost five men and there were three walking wounded to be treated.

The sub came and she had her lipstick and some soap and some genuine canned soup. She met the Americans of the central group and the men went out to fight. The months slid by and still there was no American invasion.

Chapter 14

"God, what a beautiful sight."

Dick Parker had a new wing man. Now Lieutenant Parker was a flight leader and he'd drawn an early patrol, just a routine thing. The kid on his wing seemed to be all right. He'd been on the old *Wasp* when she went down and he had three Japs to his credit, so he was a cut above most of the new pilots. Most of the new ones were fresh from training and had never fired a shot in anger.

The task force had formed in the Marshall Islands. This was the first time Dick had been up since the massive force set westward, destination unknown, but obviously another Jap-held island. Dick's carrier was now attached to one of the most potent naval strike forces ever assembled, Task Force 58.

"Right pretty," Dick said, acknowledging his wing man's awed comment.

The eight hundred ships were spread out below them—carriers, battleships, cruisers, destroyers, supply ships, a hospital ship, troop carriers. The destroyers prowled the outskirts like worried guard dogs.

The patrol assignment was to scout ahead. He flew

a compass course, timed it carefully, saw nothing but empty sky and empty ocean. Damn, the Pacific was big. It was big enough to swallow up all those eight hundred ships and all those thousands of men and not even burp. A lot of his buddies had died in it.

It was quite unlikely that they'd see any Japs, ships or planes. And yet he was alert. He'd come to grips with his problem. Laura's letter writing had improved. He didn't like the idea of her living alone, but he was rather proud of her for working in the convalescent hospital. Maybe she was growing up a little after all.

He reached the end of his assigned flight, turned the group and headed home. He could relax a little then and let his thoughts do some rambling. Sometimes he thought Laura could read his mind by long distance. There had been that time right after he came back to sea duty when he was worried because of the things she'd said when he left, and then out of a clear sky he'd had a letter which addressed itself to precisely those worries in Laura's own straightforward way. That letter must have caused quite a stir in some little room where the censors read everything. He had it memorized.

> I said some terrible things, darling, because I was worried about you, and hurt. I take them all back. To make myself perfectly clear: While I lie here on the bed dressed in your favorite little black nighty, I'm thinking of you and how I wish you were here to lift the nighty off over my head. You're the only one. Only you have sampled what you jokingly called the best part of me, and I think you know what I mean, darling, because it's the part that twitches uncontrollably when I

think of you and those nights in my father's house. Speaking of my father, he's on your side. He's always after me to be, as he calls it, true blue. And be assured that I am. That best part of me is yours, darling. I promise you that.

Your virgin wife

Jesus. It was still a long way to Tokyo. And getting liberty, at least all the way back to Pearl, was impossible. Things were picking up in the war. Mac was on his way back. And it was everyone's guess that this huge task force was aimed at the Mariana Islands, because any fool could look at a map and see that air bases were needed there to put the Jap mainland within reach of the new monsters, the B-29 bombers.

But a guy could think about it and dream.

He made a perfect landing. A.D. Adkins, his wing man, right behind him, bounced the F-4F a little, but got it down in one piece. They went through debriefing, which was routine since nothing had happened to report, and then they sat in the wardroom with coffee.

"Makes me proud," A.D. beamed. He was a happy kid, sharp looking and friendly.

"Know what you mean."

Gradually the others in the wardroom cleared out and Dick was thinking of going to his quarters to write a letter to Laura.

"How long you been out, Dick?" A.D. asked.

"Too long."

"Know what you mean. Damned shame a guy has to lose a ship to get some liberty."

"Well, I wouldn't want to get it that way," Dick laughed.

"I didn't like the idea of seeing the *Wasp* take the deep six, either, but it got me a few weeks at Pearl."

"Not bad duty."

"Whew," A.D. whistled. "You don't know the half of it. Dick, I met this chick. I mean, she was something else."

Dick grinned, refilled his coffee cup.

"She had this little cottage at the beach. Nice. And we sat in the sun. She rubbed suntan oil on me. Man! Said her husband was on the old *Arizona*. Don't know why she was still in Hawaii."

"So all you did was sit in the sun," Dick teased.

"I didn't say that," A.D. laughed. "I said we sat in the sun *first*."

"You wouldn't know what to do with it anyhow," Dick chuckled.

"Wouldn't I." A.D. got up, walked to the coffee-pot, came back.

"She laid down the rules, buddy. No ficky-fick. Just funzies. I said to myself, oh hell. But you know me, old A.D. Adkins, an officer and a gentleman."

"One of those anything-but gals, huh?"

"Yep. You hit it. Ever tangle with one of those?"

Laura. She'd laid down the rules. Before they were married she liked to pet, liked all of it but . . .

"Wow, could she kiss! These nice, smooth, sorta wide lips, you know? And almost pulled me on top of her. Dry humping like crazy. I was going wild and she said, in this sweet little voice—"

Dick's manhood was throbbing. So like Laura. Well, with the threat of getting knocked up, maybe lots of girls got their kicks that way.

"—'Take off your clothes.' "

"Huh?"

"She said, 'Take off your clothes.' I said, 'Let me take off yours,' but she wasn't having any of that. So I did, and she did."

"Did what?"

"Well, I didn't have to tell her suck, baby, suck, blow is just an expression, because she was good. Mmmm."

Laura never did that. Didn't need to. The best part of her was his.

"That was on a Sunday. I spent the night. Man, oh, man. I tell you I didn't get a heck of a lot of sleep."

"But you stood up under the strain," Dick said dryly.

"She had to go into town the next day and she asked me—that was my last day—to stay and wait for her. Had to see about a job at a hospital or something."

He set his coffee cup down. No. That was damned silly. Lots of women worked at hospitals.

"So I waited. I guess she saw that I was a man of my word. Man, I wanted to slice that, but she'd laid down the rules. When she trusted me, she stripped to her skivvies, I mean, just a little ole pair of panties and—"

"And then you did some muff diving."

"Naw."

But A.D. wasn't a good liar. He looked away and Dick snickered. "You did."

"Didn't have to. She loved the finger."

"Liar. What was her name?"

"A gentleman doesn't kiss and tell."

Dick was musing. Maybe he'd been a little hard on Laura. He'd always thought she was a little too interested in sex. But they all seemed to be that way.

"I'll tell you the truth," A.D. went on. "I never knew her name. She wouldn't tell me. And she didn't want to know mine."

"Ha."

"She just wanted loving, buddy. Man, she was hot to trot. All blonde and pretty, with a figure like you wouldn't believe."

"Blonde? You're lying, A.D. Every joker's story is about a blonde."

"No lie. Beautiful gal. Put her hair up like this." He made a motion. "These nice, big eyes, perfect teeth. Gorgeous titties—soft but firm, and she loved having her nipples nibbled. Liked having her back tickled too."

Dick was growing a little uncomfortable. But then what the hell, maybe all girls liked having those things done. "This girl laugh a lot?"

"Yeah, why?"

"Seeing your face, dummy."

"No, she was happy. Laughed this low, chuckly little laugh while she was coming, you know?"

Dick got up, went to the coffeepot. He was telling himself it was all coincidence. There must be a lot of girls who lived in beach cottages and laughed when they climaxed.

The best part of me is yours. Your virgin wife.

They'd had a talk, once, about sexual morality. Laura had some strange views. He hadn't pushed it. She'd told him he was the only one ever to have her, and he hadn't asked, for fear of what she'd say, if she'd ever made out heavily with other men.

"A.D., tell me more." He was sick inside. He was picturing her, bending, her blonde hair falling down around her face. Her mouth opening . . .

"That's about it. I've never had a sexier woman, but she wouldn't put out. Hands and lips, she'd say. Hands and lips. And boy she used 'em well."

"You didn't get her name?"

"No. She said she wouldn't be there when I came back. Hell, I even looked, while she was gone, to see if I could find something with her name on it. She had a lot of clothes, and one of those big R.C.A. record players, with the drawers, you know? I even looked in that."

Coincidence after coincidence. But she wouldn't. She just wouldn't do that to him. He told himself to forget it, to drop it. It wasn't Laura. She'd promised to be true. But there was acid in his stomach. He felt as if he needed to throw up.

"A.D., this is damned strange. I think I know that girl."

"You're lying."

"No. House on the beach, right near the water. Wears real sharp and expensive clothes. Has this big record player with the big band stuff."

"Right," A.D. nodded, still smiling.

"Tells you right up front she won't lay, but when you start kissing her she melts and lets you do any damned thing you want to as long as you don't prong her because she says she's not about to risk getting pregnant."

"All the way."

"Has this little blue birthmark on the inside of her left thigh, just below the crease."

"Small world, ain't it?" He was grinning. "Hell, skipper, I guess we got more in common than I thought."

A.D. Adkins never knew how close he came to getting hit in the mouth. He sat there grinning and inside Dick the forces were battling. He turned and walked out.

"Hey, where you going?" A.D. called.

"Get some sack time," Dick hollered back. It wasn't A.D.'s fault.

Laura, Laura.

How many more? The best part of her was his. He owned a vagina, and the rest of her was A.D.'s and God only knew how many others.

He was sick. He bent over the head and vomited and fell into his bunk.

They were briefed a couple of days later. The target was the Marianas. The Fifth Fleet, that massive array of ships, had several targets. First Saipan, headquarters of the Japanese Central Pacific Fleet, then Guam and Tinian. Saipan was fourteen miles long by six miles wide, rugged and hilly. The Marines went ashore on the fifteenth of June and had heavy going. The pre-invasion bombardment had been spectacular. And it was all lost on Dick Parker because he could think of nothing but Laura and A.D. in bed, she clad only in her panties, doing obscene things to the smiling man.

While the Marines were still slugging it out on Saipan, Task Force 58 was on the move. The combined Japanese fleet had come out of hiding. There were Japanese civilians on Saipan. The Americans were beginning to hit territory which had been Japanese before the war and the Japs were going all out.

Dick told himself to forget Laura. Out there was the whole Jap fleet and when he lifted his fighter off the deck he knew that it was going to be a day.

They called it the Marianas turkey shoot. It began

early. Just after dawn Dick Parker led his flight in support of a group of dive bombers and there they were, the Japs, ships everywhere and the sky full of Zeros and then Laura was out of his mind because he was fighting to stay alive in a dizzying dogfight, seeing one, two, three Japs go into flames before his guns. A.D. got one and yelled out.

They went back to the carrier and off on another strike. It was all too easy. The Jap pilots were unskilled, not using the maneuverable Zero as he'd seen it used in the past. Sitting ducks. They came in in droves at the fleet to be blasted by the antiaircraft guns.

When darkness called a halt to the slaughter they gathered in the briefing room and a smiling, jubilant officer told them, "After today, gentlemen, the Japanese air will not be a major force. Reports are incomplete, but by our best estimates we knocked down over four hundred of them today."

There was a cheer. More than one ace had made his mark that day. Dick Parker, with his three confirmed kills and a probable, was a double ace. But it was all like sand in his mouth because A.D. was sitting next to him, grinning, and there beside him, in Dick's mind, was Laura in her panties.

The orders were in. The advantage would be pressed home. The twentieth of June began with maximum strike force, everything the American carriers could put into the air. The range was long. All night the fast carriers had been steaming toward the Philippines and still the planes had to fly long distances to find the Japanese fleet.

Dive bombers slammed torpedoes into the Japanese ships while the fighters engaged the Zeros in the air above. One Zero pilot was good, bringing his Zero up and over to get on Dick's tail while he tried madly to dislodge the bastard. Then there was A.D. and the Jap flamed. They dove to scratch two at once on an easy pass. Then the gas was getting critical and the Japs still were coming. It was a game of deadly grab-ass and then for the second time in his flying career he felt the hammer blows of machine gun rounds on his craft. He threw it over on its back to fall like a screaming leaf and get out of it but there was something wrong.

He managed to pull the plane out of the dive. It wallowed.

"Buddy, you're hit!" came A.D.'s voice. He'd come up on the port wing.

"What's it look like?"

"If your tail fin stays on you'll be all right."

"Jesus. Thanks."

A.D. read out a bearing.

"Roger," Dick said. "Look, A.D., stay with me. Tell me if I start falling apart."

"Roger. You couldn't get rid of me. We got a date in Pearl. Maybe that blonde chick will take both of us at once."

Dick knew A.D. was just trying to be light, to get Dick's mind off his problems, off a plane which handled as if it might decide to fall out of the air any minute. But it had the opposite effect. "You smiling son of a bitch," Dick whispered, but not into the radio.

"Going home, da-da-da-da-da-da, flying home," A.D. was singing.

"Fuel," Dick said.

"I'm scared to look."

"Do it anyhow."

"Thirty minutes, max."

"Ditto."

"Hey, skipper, I'm not a goddamned good swimmer."

"Don't feel like a lone ranger."

"Tally ho."

He could see them up ahead. Blessed ships, and there she was, big, coming along with a bone in her teeth, home sweet home.

"Got a hurt chick," A.D. was telling ship's control.

He could see them falling out down there, crash crews, red fire-fighting equipment. There was a blurring of his vision and he put his hand up and it came away red. Nothing serious. He wiped the blood out of his eye.

"You're all right, buddy," A.D. said. "Put her down gentle."

"Holy Christ!" Dick shouted as he turned into the wind. The plane bucked. "A.D., what the hell happened?"

"You lost a piece. That's all. Nothing vital. 'Bout a quarter of the tail fin surface. Take it gentle, buddy."

He almost lost her when he let the wheels down. The breaking effect jolted him and the plane tried to nose over. He fought it, brought up his hand to wipe blood out of his left eye, saw the deck up ahead, pitching and heaving. He saw the signal officer waving and he went down. A little high, he eased her nose down, lost some more speed.

"A.D., how're my wheels?"

"Looking good!" A.D. sang out. "Down and locked."

"Lost instrumentation," Dick warned. "You sure?"

"Right as rain."

Lower the nose and hang on. Damned thing wanted

to drift over toward the side, go barreling off and land in the water. Oh, Jesus.

He felt the portside wheel collapse when he hit the deck. The broken plane screamed toward the cable and the net and the port wing hit in a shower of sparks.

"Don't blow, you bastard! Don't blow!"

Flames roared. Burned to a crisp right there on home plate, right on your own carrier! Not much gas in the tanks, thank God, only fumes by now. Come on cable, grab, you mother! The plane began to come apart with a snarling, crashing, banging, cracking scream. The cable caught and he felt as if his head would snap off. Then blackness arose amid the smell of gas and heat on his face and a red glare.

Good-bye, Laura! Good-bye, you bitch!

He hurt like hell. Burned all over. He was able to open one eye and see the sky filling up with the planes coming back. One came in while the crews were using heavy equipment to push what was left of his F-4F over the side. He saw the incoming plane dropping, dropping. He raised himself on one elbow.

"Easy, sir," a corpsman said.

The plane hit the water in a great splash, bounced off a wave, went airborne and came down nose first. It sank up to its tail and bobbed like a cork.

"Is he out?"

He didn't recognize his own voice.

"Is he out, damnit?"

"I don't see him, sir." And then he was being carried off. Blackness descended again.

Chapter 15

"Thanks for stopping in." Tom Braddock stood as she entered his office. He wore new rank insignia. Emi sat down in front of his desk. He'd ordered coffee. The navy seemed to run on coffee. She took the cup he offered. He sat on the corner of his desk.

"I just wanted your opinion, Emi," Braddock said. "We've had a rush call for a good interpreter. I'm thinking of young Ellis. Just how good is he?"

Ellis was new to the hole. He'd learned his Japanese at U.C.L.A.

"He's not bad," Emi hedged.

"But not good?"

"I don't want to say anything bad about him."

"I want your honest opinion. Here's the situation. There's a native Japanese population on an island the Marines have just taken. Hell, you know everything else, why not this. It's Saipan, in the Marianas. And in addition to the Jap civilians, they've taken some pretty high ranking Jap officers. Lost a couple of interpreters in the fighting and the intelligence boys want help fast."

"I think that Ellis probably would be fine with the

officers,'' she judged. ''But if he runs into any rather uneducated Japanese, he'd be lost.''

''Yes, I thought so.'' Braddock frowned. ''And he's all we've got that I can spare. I guess he'll have to do.''

''How important is the assignment?''

He shrugged. ''Maybe routine, but you never know. Some of these Jap officers won't talk at all. Some, considering themselves to be worse than dead, open up all the way. Their shame, in their own minds, at being alive and a prisoner, can't be deepened. So they spill everything they know.''

''The civilians?''

''I don't know about them. Maybe nothing. But they've been around and have watched the Japs prepare Saipan for battle. We could probably get some good information about Jap methods from them. Some of them probably worked on the defenses. We'd know a bit more about what we're likely to encounter on other islands, I'd guess.''

She sipped her coffee. ''There's someone else who isn't necessary to the running of the hole.''

''Oh?'' he looked at her innocently.

''You know damned well who I mean,'' she snapped. ''Or don't you trust me to go off where there are real Japanese?''

''I can't ask you to go, Emi.''

''Okay. So I'm volunteering. It'll be a change.''

''It's a long, hairy flight. They've pretty well cleaned up on the Jap air, but you never know when you get up close to a fighting front like that.''

''As I said, it'll be a change.''

''You're sure?''

''I guess.'' She smiled at him. ''When?''

"You have about an hour to get ready. There's one thing, though. You can't go as a civilian."

She looked puzzled.

"I have here a form which gives you the temporary rank of ensign in the U.S. navy," he said. "And I guessed at your size, so I hope the uniform fits."

"You bastard," she said. "You knew I'd go."

"Well, I hoped so." He grinned. "No hard feelings?"

"No more than usual," she sighed.

There was a frantic rush of activity. She found the uniform—blue skirt, natty little hat, white blouse—to fit perfectly. "You're a good judge of the size of women," she told Braddock, who was with her as she was being hustled from place to place.

"Years of practice," he chuckled.

Finally they were ready. She had the necessities, all government issue except for makeup, in a little bag. He escorted her out of the complex. The sun was bright. When she got back, she decided, she was going to give up her life as a recluse and get out into the open air more. He helped her into a staff car.

He had her orders, and when he handed them to her in an envelope she felt for the first time as if this were real. He told her to whom to report on Saipan.

"You're sure there are no Japs there?" she asked.

"They declared the island secure on the tenth," he said. "You'll be well protected. I'd say there are a few Marines there who'd go out of their way to protect a pretty girl like you. Really, it'll be fine. The only risk is in getting there, and you'll be flying with one of the best."

They were approaching the giant navy base. It was

bustling with ships in for repair, men scurrying everywhere. He helped her out of the car. A launch was waiting.

"He'll take you out to the seaplane anchorage," Braddock said. "Get the job done and get back to us soon, Emi."

"If you tell me you're going to miss me—"

He smiled. "I will. We all will. Emi, you're part of the team. *You're* the one who refuses to join."

"I do my job."

"And very well." He took her hand and shook it as if she were a man. "Good luck."

The salt spray as the launch plowed through the harbor felt good on her face. She hadn't been swimming in years. And up ahead a nest of amphibians and seaplanes rode the gentle waves. The sailor at the tiller eased the launch alongside a PBY and threw a quick lash up to hold it. He helped her step up onto the float. A hand and arm came out and she took the hand, was hoisted up.

She stood up, brushed down her skirt and looked at the man who'd helped her in.

"Emi!" Luke Martel cried. "Emi, my God, I was just going to come and see you when they yanked me in for this flight!"

She felt her stomach do a little flip. She had thought she'd put Luke Martel out of her mind and yet just seeing him made her feel dizzy.

"You're my VIP passenger?"

"It would seem that way," she answered coldly. He'd come into her life like a bomb blast and disappeared as quickly as the puff of smoke after the explosion.

"Hey, great. You make yourself comfortable over here and strap in. I'll get this turkey airborne and come back and talk. You don't know how good it is to see you, Emi."

The PBY was one of the VIP planes, well fitted inside with comfortable seats. She strapped in and heard the engines howl. She wasn't going to let Luke complicate her mission. She'd just tell him to go back to his pilot's seat and leave her alone. There were magazines to read.

They were flying through little fluffy clouds when the port to the cockpit opened and Luke came out, smiling, his hat in his hand, his hair tousled. He sat in the seat facing her.

"You can unstrap now if you want to."

"I'm fine." She didn't look up from the magazine that lay open on her lap. He reached over and pulled it away, tossed it onto an empty seat.

"You have a right to be a little down on me," he said.

"Do I?"

"At first I *was* just doing a job, Emi. They told me to find out as much about the way you think as I could. But it got to be much more than that quickly."

Well, it had to be faced. She was strong now. "I noticed."

He grinned. "At least I have you as a captive audience. Since it would be difficult for you to walk away, you'll have to listen."

"Is there a lady's room?" she asked, with a little smile. He was so damned confident, so pleasing to look at.

He laughed. "Okay. I was going to explain. I was going to tell you that I was assigned to pick your brain. Then someone had the bright idea that I was needed elsewhere." He rolled his eyes. "Comes from being the best amphib pilot in the navy, you know. I went out and I thought about writing you and decided that by then you'd stumbled onto the fact that I was acting in a double role when I was taking you out. So I decided that it would be best to let things ride. I'd be home soon, I thought. The assignment was supposed to be temporary. Trouble was I was acting as personal pilot for a big-shot admiral and he liked me. So the days and the weeks and the months went by and then it really was too late to write. I got back to Pearl late yesterday, no sleep in twenty-four hours, sacked out and was on the way to see you when Braddock nabbed me.'' He spread his hands. ''The defense rests.''

She was looking at him thoughtfully, examining the line of his brows, the strong statement made by his nose and his mouth.

''Are you going to say anything?''

''How long will it take us to get to the Marianas?'' she asked. She wanted to say something, but even though his story sounded plausible at first hearing, she would have preferred that he'd written. At least then she'd have had something.

''You'll know when we get there,'' he said. ''Look, Emi, I'm damned sorry. I wouldn't hurt you for the world. I want you to believe that. How about we just start all over. I'll prove to you what a nice kid I am.''

She smiled in spite of her uneasy feeling.

''There, that's better. How about some coffee?''

She sighed. ''Lord, if it weren't for coffee this war would have been lost a long time ago.''

He poured from a large thermos.

''I guess you're going to be very busy where we're going,'' he said. ''And I have orders to come on back to Pearl.''

She looked up, startled. Her mind was working in strange ways. It upset her to know that he would leave her alone on the island with strangers. Why? Until a short time ago he hadn't been a part of her life at all, and now suddenly she was upset to know that he wouldn't be around.

"But I'll be around," he said. "Now that I've got that admiral off my back I'm back on the old routine, jockeying the spy boys around, and I'll be back to the Marianas if you stick around there for a while."

"I don't know how long I'll be there."

"I'll find you, where ever you are," he pledged.

"You're assuming that I want you to find me."

"I'm hoping that, yes."

She couldn't get her brain to work properly. When she spoke she knew what she wanted to convey, but she wasn't sure she was saying it right. "I don't really know how I feel. I'm caught up in the war in a way I don't think anyone who hasn't experienced it can understand. I'm not sure I'm ready for any other involvements."

"No involvements." He took her hand. "I'll state my intentions. I intend to court you in a gentlemanly way and convince you that I'm not really a snake in the grass. I'll put it all up front. I've known a lot of women. I've spent a lot of time lately, a lot of long and lonely hours, flying here and there in the Pacific. The flying is a mixture of boredom, fatigue and moments of complete terror. But I've had a lot of time to think. I'm not a career man. When the war is over I'm going home, and if I can find a flying job which will support the traditional vine-covered cottage and put shoes on the feet of a couple of little kids, okay. If not, I'll find something else. The thing is I know what I want. I want to have a wife who thinks that I'm king of the world. I've always wanted a wife and I've looked a lot. I haven't, not until I met you, found the right woman for the job. So, up front, I'm in love with you, Emi. I want you to hang on until this is over and go home with me."

She felt a wetness on her cheeks.

"Comment?" he asked.

"I've never heard it put more beautifully," she said, her voice choking.

"Heard it a lot, have you?" He was grinning.

"No. This is the first time."

"You're stalling."

"No. I'm just overwhelmed, I guess. Confused. There are some complicating factors. My mother. And we have a grape ranch. I've always thought I'd go back there, with my mother."

"We can work all that out."

"You're a nice guy. I think it would be easy to love you."

"Hey, that's a start. We can go from there."

"But I can't give you an answer. I'll have to think about it. I thank you for saying such nice things to me, and for selecting me."

He squeezed her hand. "The war isn't going to be over tomorrow or next day. We have time. I'm going to haunt you."

"I like being with you."

He kissed her. He leaned over and nothing but their lips touched at first. Then he was pulling her across the little space between seats and placing her on his lap and the kiss deepened. The feel of his arms gave her a security she hadn't known since the men came knocking on the door of her home to take her and her mother away. Her blood sang and her nerve endings tingled all over her body.

Once she came up for air and said, "What about your copilot? He'll think you've deserted him."

"The joker is gung ho. Loves to fly. He's happiest with me out of the cockpit."

"Are you going to kiss me all the way to the islands?"

"Any objections?"

"No," she sighed.

"Say you'll marry me."

"That's unfair. I can't think. You've got me all giddy."

"That's an answer, honey. That's an answer. That's a yes."

"If you continued to fly I'd worry all the time."

"I'll quit flying."

"No. I wouldn't ask you to give up something you like."

"I like you better than anything."

"Would you want boys or girls? Girls run in my family."

"Girls would be great if they looked like you."

"You've made my chin raw." Whisker burns. A sweet little irritation. He kissed it.

"Honey, I'm sorry. I shaved early. Damned things grow like weeds."

"Guess I'll have to toughen up my skin."

"Damn, Emi, I can't get enough of you. I feel as if I'd like to just absorb you into my body, to have all, every cell, every sweetness of you."

"You're going to, if you don't quit squeezing so hard." But when he eased off the pressure of his arms she said, "No, don't stop."

He had to stop eventually. The plane droned on, high, flying through occasional clouds, and down below was the vast stretch of water.

"Don't go anywhere. I'll check on the navigation and be back."

He was back in half an hour. "Everything's okay. We're headed for Kwajalein and refueling. Weather's fine." He sat down.

"I've been thinking." She looked up at him shyly. "The answer is yes."

He grinned broadly, lifted her from the seat, swept her into his arms, kissed her swiftly, little pecks. He eased her back into her seat. "If I start that again I'll forget some of the things I want to say. You mentioned your grape ranch and your mother. I think I can find something to do in the valley. I've been thinking in terms of a flying school, or maybe a small air freight line. That way you can be close to your mother."

"She'd like that."

"How's she going to feel about me?"

"I think she'd like me to marry a good Japanese boy, like Ralph Izumi, but she'll accept you."

It was so lovely making plans. They sat side by side, holding hands. It was as if they had their own private airliner. The copilot never intruded. The hours melted away and then Luke went forward to make the landing in Kwajalein's lagoon. Suddenly they were surrounded by the trappings of war. Emi was reminded that all those nice plans, all those visions of the future, would have to wait.

They ate in an officers' club. "First building that goes up on a captured island," Luke laughed. They walked. The ravages of the invasion were still visible in the form of shattered palms and a ghostly array of junk, ruined vehicles, shell holes. Luke told her they should get some sleep and they parted reluctantly. She'd been assigned a room in a new transient officers' quarters.

Back in the air, Luke visited her as soon as the plane had attained altitude. "Is there really someone up there, or do you just leave the plane to fly itself?" she asked.

"Actually, I've trained a monkey I picked up."

"You're crazy enough so that I half believe you."

They sat drowsily listening to the drone of the engines, holding hands and dreaming.

"What are you going to be doing on Saipan?" he asked.

"I'm to help in the interrogation of captured Japanese officers and civilians."

"Any qualms?"

She looked at him. "Is that question in the line of duty?"

"No. I swear. In the line of being interested in my future wife."

"All right. A few. I guess we have to talk about this sooner or later. I'll start from the beginning. I'm a true-blue American girl who happens to think that the Japanese were pushed into this war."

"Whew," he said.

"I'll admit that they had no right to invade China, a backward nation, tanks against horses and all. But they have one of the most concentrated populations in the world, and they're a dynamic people. It isn't the first time a dynamic, expanding population has sought room."

"What about the atrocities in China?"

"There have been atrocities in every war. We're not lily-white. Off New Guinea American planes sank a troop transport and the water was full of men in life jackets. They called in an air strike and strafed the men in the water."

"Because of that damned code of theirs," Luke heatedly replied. "The American commanders knew that the Japs wouldn't surrender. That they'd make their way ashore and go on fighting. It had to be done."

"And yet we scream atrocity when the Japanese kill a pilot who's parachuted from his plane. Their thinking is that this is a highly trained man who will come back to fight again if they don't kill him."

"Touché."

"Okay. China aside. That wasn't our business anyhow. But what gives us the right to be moralist for the world?" Emi grew animated. "Japan has no oil. The British cut them off from the southeast Asian and the offshore oil. They're a highly developed industrial nation and they faced industrial extinction. They had to go find oil. They were put into a position where they had to fight or become a vassal of the British, begging for oil."

"There is some justification there, I'll admit."

"They are different. They put a different value on life. It's their religion. Death in battle is honorable. But they're not savages. They made a vast miscalculation. Men like Yamamoto knew that if America was aroused Japan couldn't win the war. The planners counted on the Americans accepting a certain Japanese influence in the Pacific. And now it's David against Goliath, only David doesn't have a slingshot. All you have to do is look at the casualty figures on any island. We mourn casualties in three figures, say at Betio. The Japanese lost thousands. Seventeen Japanese were left alive. *Seventeen*."

"Don't talk like that in front of a Marine who waded the lagoon."

"Now you're getting angry. Just listen. I think something could be done to stop this senseless slaughter. I think we could talk. I think the Japanese would be willing to pull back to prewar positions, except in China, if we gave them concessions for oil."

"Honey, you're dreaming. The Japs themselves have made it impossible for us to settle for anything less than unconditional surrender. There have been too many beheadings of captured Americans, too many sneaky tricks, and we're getting some fragmentary reports out of the Philippines that would stand your hair on end."

"I think the thing that disturbs me most is the cold-blooded planning that went into the killing of Admiral Yamamoto. When you take the might of a great nation and aim it at one man, that ceases to be just war, and it becomes murder."

Luke pondered that for a moment. "I guess I can accept all that. I don't agree with it, but I can see why you'd feel that way." He turned to her and smiled. "Anyhow, you and I don't make the plans in this war. We just do what we're told."

He kissed her. She let the war go out of her mind and sank into the comfort of his arms and chest. After long, heated kisses, she felt the strength and warmth of his hand coming down her side to her breast. His hand felt as if it belonged there and everything else faded away.

"I think we've set a record," he joked a few hours later. There'd been some tentative exploration, some heated pressings, some kisses that seemed to suck all of her up, up, into his heated mouth.

He checked his watch and left her. He came back in minutes.

"Right on schedule. Here's where it gets a little nervous. We've got some good clouds. We'll stay in them until we're near Saipan. I think the navy has pretty well cleared out the Japs, but if we should make any sudden maneuvers, don't worry. Strap in just in case."

The flight continued smoothly. Outside the ports she could see the fluffy clouds and then they were in them, mist whipping past the wings.

The clouds gave way to a clear, blue sky and she saw below the endless ocean. She was looking for an island below when the plane banked suddenly, steeply, and made a hundred and eighty degree turn, racing back toward the bank of clouds. Her heart leapt. She peered out the windows and saw the Zero as it came down from high and behind them. The plane seemed to leap and things were crashing and smashing and she screamed. A wisp of smoke came from under the port leading to the cockpit and she unstrapped and ran forward. As she ran she saw the light dim and glanced at the windows to see that they were back in the thick clouds. She opened the door.

There was blood everywhere. "Luke!" she screamed.

"I'm okay, honey."

It was the copilot. He was the man she'd never seen until now. He was slumped in his seat, half his head shot away. His blood was splattered all over the cockpit and there was blood on Luke.

"You're hit!" she cried, putting her hands on his shoulder.

"No, no. I'm all right. Now listen, Emi. I need your help."

She tried to keep her eyes off the dead man.

"I need for you to get him away, out of the seat. Away from the controls."

"I can't. I just can't."

"You can. Look. We've taken some damage. I can't turn this thing loose. You have to do it. Unstrap him and roll him off between the seats and then pull him into the back."

She fought her fear, her revulsion. Luke used one hand to help her free the body from the tangle of wreckage and then she used all her strength to pull him clear, back into the passenger area. She wept. His blood was all over her. She leaned against the doorjamb.

"You'll find a couple of blankets in a locker back there."

She spread one blanket over the dead man. Luke told her to put the other over the copilot's seat. She was shaking when she sat down. The instrument panel was a mess. Shattered glass and blood were everywhere.

"We've got a few challenges, Emi," Luke told her calmly. "We're all right, but I want you to know where we stand. I don't know where those Nip sons of bitches came from. Down Guam way, I'd guess. They're not our main concern now. They can't hang around too long out there waiting for us. What I'm doing right now is flying circles inside the clouds until they have to bug out. The main problem is that they got all our navigation equipment. The compass is gone. The radio is gone. Ditto the air-speed indicator. Otherwise we seem to be in one piece and we've got enough fuel."

"So you can't tell where you're going?" she asked, still shaking, but gaining confidence from him. She felt that the danger was past. He would get them to Saipan.

"We were just over three hundred miles out when

they hit us. I'll aim for the islands by dead reckoning. Fly into the sun."

After another quarter hour he eased the plane out of the clouds. The sky seemed to be empty. The sun was getting lower ahead of them. Luke talked reassuringly, chatted about how they'd build a fine little house in the valley. The plane droned on slowly, so slowly, the sun getting lower, the ocean still empty.

"What if we miss the islands?" she asked.

"Well, we'll just put down on the water just before our fuel runs out and hope that the navy finds us. They know we're coming. We checked in with Saipan just before the attack."

She saw the low smudge first. Was it just a darker blue of the water? No. She pointed.

"Ah," he said. "The old Eagle Scout comes through."

He was getting a little worried. Apparently the damage hadn't been confined to the instrument panel, for the fuel was shrinking at a rate indicating a leak somewhere. He hoped it was all going outside and not into the engine compartments. He strained his eyes. It was getting to be twilight down there. Up here there was still light. He told her to hand him a chart and examined it closely.

Saipan had a couple of mountains which made good landmarks, two peninsulas on the east side. That island down there was shaped like a peanut and it was too big. He'd been just enough off course during the past three hundred miles to fly a long way south of his line. Because that was Guam down there. And the Japs were still on Guam. He was faced with a hard choice. He had enough fuel for another hour of flying. He could turn north, fly until the gas ran out and put her down at sea. If he got her down without busting the float she'd stay on the surface. They had the life rafts and he knew that a landing was scheduled for Guam, although he didn't know the exact date. The invasion force would find them.

Maybe.

And maybe the weather would change and they'd be in the raft in the broiling sun and he knew what that meant. He'd been a part of a rescue operation. Men in a raft for twenty-one days. Some of them dead. The others burned, ruined.

If he'd been alone he'd have turned north. But he had Emi with him. He made his decision. He flew on toward the peanut-shaped island. He was soon convinced that his decision had been a wise one. The starboard engine coughed and quit. He feathered it and checked his fuel gauges. They were crazy. Now he had no idea how much fuel was left for the other engine, and he had enough problems keeping the plane on an even keel.

He was south of Pago Bay. A fringe of coral reef outlined the shore.

"Emi, chances are we'll be captured by the Japs. Here's what I want you to do. I want you to tell them you're a prisoner, just as you felt for a long time. Tell them you were forced to wear the uniform, that your mother is being held hostage. They'll believe you. The Marines will be landing on Guam within a few days at the most. Whatever happens to me, you play it cool and stay alive and you'll give some Marine unit the surprise of their lives."

"I'll stay with you."

He turned to glare at her. "You'll do just as I tell you. If they take me they'll want to question me for a

while. I'll tell them just enough to keep alive until th
Marines come."

The last engine quit as he was picking out a wide
smooth lagoon behind the reef. He brought the plane i
dead stick, smoothed it down on the water just as if h
had power.

"Damn," he grinned, "I didn't know I was tha
good."

He looked around. The shore was mangrove swamp
They were lucky. No Japs. No tracers. No pockmark
in the water from machine-gun bullets. He began t
hope. Guam was a big island, the largest of the Mari
anas. Maybe the Japs were all on the east side, the bes
place for amphibious landings.

He got out a raft and inflated it, filled it with
number of items from the plane, including the surviva
kits. He rowed the raft into a little creek where mosqui
toes attacked in swarms and it was a choice of bein
eaten alive or going inland with the possibility of facin
the Japs. He went up the creek.

They left the raft when the creek gave them acces
to solid land. They began to climb a gradual slop
through dense jungle. His plan was to find a decen
place and hide out until the Marines came. They ha
plenty of food and water.

They found a little hillside glen just as the darknes
made it impossible to see. They had water and foo
from the survival pack. They huddled together, Em
calm, confident that he would see her through.

They awoke to distant thunder, but the mornin
sky was clear. It was July 21, 1944. The Marines ha
come back to Guam. He had to try to see it. He led he
up the slope, but the eastern beaches were too far away
The naval bombardment ceased and now the day wa

quiet, except as now and then a dim chatter of small-arms fire would come, and now and then the low, hoarse cough of a mortar.

"They'll be here in a couple of days," he told her.

They found a cave in a rocky outcrop and set up housekeeping. She slept with her head on his arm, his arms around her, and woke to the sound of voices.

He jerked and she put her hand over his mouth. The language was Japanese. Men were shouting orders. He crept to the mouth of the cave and she followed. There was a good view of the slope below them. A squad of Japanese was prodding two battered Marines along in front of them at bayonet point. Each of the Marines had a rope around his neck. In the center of a clearing the Japs jerked the men off their feet, and an officer drew his sword. It happened in seconds. The sword flashed. Blood gushed. The other Marine tried to crawl away and was almost decapitated when the sword came down in the nape of his neck.

She gasped and hid her head against Luke's shoulder. But the voices were still yelling and now a group of the native population of Guam, brown-skinned, ragged, two women weeping, were pushed into the clearing and the slaughter began again. A woman's shrill scream ended in a gurgling sound.

Luke pulled his forty-five. If the Jap death squad came toward the cave he would take a few of them with him. But they left. The clearing was quiet. A body twitched, legs kicking out the last faint impulses of life.

He pulled Emi back into the cave and held her close. She was weeping quietly.

"Savages," she whispered fiercely. "They *are* savages."

"Hey, hey," he soothed, kissing her tears away.

A flood of grief, anger and terror swept through her. She clung to him, needing to know that there was something in the world other than death and murder and fear. He understood, knew the need to be close, to reaffirm life. Clutching and whispering, they tossed clothing all over the cave to come together with a burning, frantic, life-seeking need.

They saw two battle-clad Marines emerge from the jungle and halt at the sight of the bloated bodies in the clearing.

One of the scouts went scampering back. "Sarge, they's two Americans up there. And wait'll you see one of them."

They had stayed in the cave for over a week, not going out, clinging together. No doubt now. They would be married at the first opportunity.

"You'll lose your commission," Luke joked.

They were taken on board a cruiser offshore where they were given fresh clothing, hot food and a medical examination.

"They told me I was a little weak," she said to Luke, when they were alone. "I wonder why?"

"Don't blame it on me, sex fiend," he laughed, reaching for her.

"Luke, not here. Someone could come in."

He rolled his eyes. "Already being a woman."

"There'll be time," she said. "Plenty of time. Just wait until I get you alone, mister."

Duty came first. She insisted that she was fit enough to go on to Saipan and do the long delayed work. Once she got there, there was something she had to know.

"How many Jap casualties on Guam?" she asked an officer.

"Still counting," the officer said. "Maybe as many as twenty thousand."

"Good," she said.

It was terrible. The whole goddamned war was senseless, but now she knew. Now she knew what they meant, those serious officers who talked about the Japanese tenacity. Defeat would have to be so total in those small island wars that the Japanese high command would be reluctant to go on. An invasion of the Japanese mainland would make all of the islands look like Sunday school picnics.

Chapter 16

Laura Averell Parker was having a lovely war. At first, the men she encountered in the convalescent hospital depressed her with their horrible injuries, but gradually she became accustomed to the multiple amputees, the boy who couldn't speak because his voice box had been shot away, the other ruined victims of a war that was still, to her, far away and barely real.

She did her best for them. Most of them were cheerful, just happy to be alive, the shock of their injuries still upon them. But some brooded and were immune even to the pretty smile of the blonde lady with the book cart. She liked the cheerful ones best. One of her pets was a boy just over twenty who'd lost both feet at the ankles. He playfully threatened to chase her around on his stumps. Now *that* was accepting fate and making the most of it.

She flirted with them, smiled at them, talked with them, helped those without arms write letters home. But once she left the hospital, she stopped thinking of them. They didn't intrude into her private life. But there was a doctor, a New Yorker, tall, with a most mischievous smile, and after a few dances at the officers' club and a real physical struggle, he agreed to the "Laura Rules," and they had some exciting moments together.

The boy with no feet was from Arkansas. He was a Marine. His name was Earl McFall.

"I wish I was rich," he said one day, while she was joking with him. He was in his wheelchair on a verandah overlooking a cliff.

"So do we all," she laughed.

"Because if I was rich I'd buy you and take you back to Arkansas with me."

"How much would you pay for me?" she teased.

"Whatever it took. A million. Two million. Twenty million. I'd set myself up in a fine place and we'd hire other people to do the work and all you'd have to do is just walk around looking pretty for me."

"Sounds like a soft job."

"Well, there might be a few extra duties now and then."

"Ah," she said. "Naughty, naughty."

That's the way it was with Earl. Long, slim, almost gangly, shortened cruelly by a Japanese booby trap, he was always happy, so when he turned glum on her she was concerned.

"Who licked the red off your candy?" she asked him, finding him alone in his wheelchair on the verandah again.

He tried a smile. "Hi, blondie," he said.

"Something wrong?"

"Naw." He looked away, swallowed. "Well, can I ask you something?"

"Sure." She smiled and winked. "I won't guarantee, knowing you, that I'll answer."

"No, I'm serious," Earl said. "You're married. Your husband is off fighting the war. What would you o if you got word that he'd lost, oh, say, an arm, or a ‹g?"

"I'd cry for him," she said.

"Yeah, sure. What else?"

"I'd try to get to him as soon as possible and tell im that I loved him, that I could love what was left of im even more because there was less to go around." ‹eep it light, Laura.

"I'll bet you would too."

"Sure." He wouldn't look at her. "What is it, ‹arl?"

"All my folks know is that I've been wounded."

"Shame on you. You should have told them. They ›ve you. They won't think any less of you."

"Yeah. Well, it isn't them so much."

"Ah. A girl."

He grinned. "I've been trying to work up the ›urage to tell her that I'd sort of be out of it as far as ancing is concerned."

"I think you should tell her. Is she waiting for ›ou?"

"Yep."

"I'm sure you wouldn't fall in love with anyone ‹ho isn't nice," she said. She moved close and ruffled is hair. "And I'm jealous. All that talk about taking ıe back to Arkansas."

"You really think I should write to her and tell er?" he asked.

"Want me to help you put it in words?"

"No, thank you. I'll do it, I guess."

After he'd done it he seemed to feel better. He was ıe old Earl again, wheeling along behind her to help er distribute books and magazines to the other patients ı the amputee ward.

In addition to the doctor, who had become some thing of a regular, there was a nice young air force ma who was in Pearl after losing a B-24. Her days wer fairly pleasant, but there were exceptions. Not bein able to go all the way because she was being true blu to Dick. Then there were the boys at the hospital wh couldn't seem to cope with fate. Then Earl McFall wer over the two-hundred-foot cliff in front of the veranda in his wheelchair.

She learned about it one day shortly after arrivin for work. A pall of gloom hung over the ward. She' left the air force pilot asleep in her bed, liking th manly way he sprawled there, wishing she could sta and wake him up and continue their activities of th night before.

"Have you heard about Earl?" a man asked.

She felt sick when he told her. And then angr Why would the fool do a thing like that? He'd had t work at getting that wheelchair over, because there wa a chain-link fence there about three feet high and then guardrail.

A nurse was gathering up Earl's personal belong ings. Laura stood watching. When the nurse picked u Earl's box of stationery she said, "That's where he kep the letters from his girl."

"Poor kid," the nurse said.

"I have the girl's address," Laura said. "Woul you like for me to send her letters back to her? I'd lik to write to her myself to tell her what a fine boy Ea was."

She left early with the box of letters under her arm The letter was, she found, difficult. She might d better, she felt, if she knew more about the girl. Ea wouldn't have minded her reading the girl's letters to him.

She quickly learned more about Earl's Arkansas belle than she wanted to know. The lást letter was on top of the pile. As she read she felt her face flush with sadness and anger. The girl in Arkansas "owed it to herself and to the children she wanted to bear" to have a "whole man."

"You screaming little bitch!" Laura yelled. The girl had, the letter said, returned Earl's ring to his mother and she was going to marry the local preacher, who'd been after her for a long time.

But that's all right, Earl, wherever you are, because your Arkansas belle was "really, really sorry you had to go and get hurt so bad." Rest in peace, Earl.

"I hope your goddamned preacher gives you the clap!" Laura said, throwing the letter as far as she could.

She was so upset that she had to get out of the cottage. She dressed and drove to the club and had a drink at the bar, ignoring the attentions of two young officers. When she felt a hand on her shoulder she turned angrily to tell some barracks commando to shove off. She just wasn't in the mood.

"I thought I'd find you here," her father said. "I have a table over in the mess. Come with me."

It wasn't a request and there was something about his face that warned her of heavy seas ahead. She was in no mood for that, either. If he started on her she'd tell him to shove off, because it was her life, damnit, and like the girl in the song, she was always true to her man in her own fashion. If Dick didn't like her way of being in the state of wedded bliss while he was off playing with his expensive toys and having fun, then to hell with him.

So she was primed to take no guff when she followed her father away from the bar and to his table. He held her chair for her and then sat down heavily. "I went by your cottage."

"I wasn't there," she said brightly.

"Laura, what's happened between you and Dick?" The question came without warning. It was obvious that her father was upset.

"Nothing," she said, genuinely puzzled.

"Nothing?" He sighed. "When a man has his wife's name removed from his records as the one to be notified in case of emergency something is wrong."

She felt the blood drain from her face. "Notified?" She half rose. "Oh, God. Dick?"

"He's not dead."

She sighed in relief, then leaned forward, panic growing. "How bad?"

"I don't know."

"But I've heard nothing. Nothing."

"As I said, he'd given instructions that you weren't to be notified. Then he had his records changed. Now I want to know why, Laura."

"I don't know. I swear I don't. I just had letters from him. Everything was fine. How did you find out?"

"Being an admiral has it's little perks," he said. "A friend. I'd sort of asked him to keep an eye on Dick, to let me know, on the q.t., how he was doing. I like that boy, Laura. I've got the wheels rolling now to find out how badly he was wounded. All I know is that he crashed landing on his carrier and was transferred to a hospital ship. The ship is due here at Pearl, with casualties from Guam and Saipan, in two days."

"I'll be there," she said.

"There is one thing which might help shed some light on this," Averell said. "While I was looking into Dick's strange actions I asked my friend, who happens to be the exec on board Dick's carrier, to see what he could discover. There was this letter, sealed but not mailed, on Dick's desk. It's for you."

She seized it, ripped it open. It did not start "My love" or "My dearest Laura."

"Laura," it began. "I just met a friend of yours. He knows you well. In fact, he spent a couple of nights with you in your cottage. You don't know his name, but that's all right. He's the one who told you, suck, baby, suck, blow is just an expression."

Silly. No one had ever told her that.

"What you have done to me is something—"

Done to him? What in hell had she done to him? She'd been very, very good, and all because of him.

"—is something I shall never forgive, or forget. But I won't be vindictive. Since you're building the reputation for giving the best head in Pearl, I'll send some troops your way. One of them will be carrying the divorce papers."

It was signed Lieutenant Richard Parker.

It began to sink in. It had to be the smiling boy with the wounded thigh. The nice one. She'd rubbed suntan oil on him. And he'd—oh, damn!—she should have known better than to play with a naval aviator. It was such a tight little club. But what the hell was he so upset about? Did he expect her to rot away while he was off playing games? She'd kept herself pure for him. Not one man had taken his place inside her.

Nor in her heart. It hurt. God, it hurt.

"Well?" her father asked.

"Nothing. It's just the usual."

"Well, we'll see when he arrives."

She was at the dock when the hospital ship came in. She watched the wounded being taken off, but there were so many of them. They came off in stretchers, some grinning and waving, some deathly still. And the burn cases, swathed like mummies, black holes for mouths, tubes running out of their wrapped arms into glass containers, all being handled very, very carefully.

It took the admiral and the navy to find him. He was at the new burn center in intensive care. She went there, found he was allowed no visitors. Specifically, at his own request, she was told, he was not to be visited by his wife. She pretended to leave. Like most service facilities, the hospital was well marked with signs telling where everything was. She entered from another direction, walked as if she knew where she was going, following the signs. She'd learned that hospital security is always lax and all you had to do was act as if you belonged and you could go anywhere.

It took her three tries to find his room. She could tell only by the chart at the end of the bed. Lieutenant Richard Parker. She stood by his side. His eyes weren't damaged, thank God. There were holes there in the bandages. His lids were closed.

"Dick. Dick. Wake up, please."

His eyelids fluttered, then shot open, turned toward her. A feeble croak came, then words, which she had difficulty understanding. She bent, put her ear in front of the hole over his mouth.

"Don't want to see you."

"Please, Dick."

"Never again. Bitch."

"Dick, Dick." The tears came. "I was true. I was. No other man has ever—"

He was speaking. "—you went all the way with them. Rather you went all the way."

"Oh, darling."

He tried to move and a groan came. "All right," she said. "I'll make it up to you. I won't stay now. I don't want you to hurt yourself. But I'll be back. If I have to come crawl to you, I'll be back."

"Wouldn't have you if you crawled all the way around the island. You're filth."

She had trouble seeing the road. Tears blinded her. She pulled over. And then came the anger. He had no right! How could he condemn her for having a little fun while he was off playing with his airplane? If he only knew how much she loved him. Oh, God. But he was sick. He'd change his mind.

The lawyer called her four days later. She'd made no further attempt to see Dick, wanting to give him time to begin a recovery, time to think. The lawyer wanted her to sign divorce papers. He was charging her with adultery.

"That's not true, you know," she told the lawyer calmly.

"You'll have your chance in court," the lawyer said, "if you care to fight it. I'd advise you, Mrs. Parker, to allow the divorce with no contest. You obviously don't need money from Lieutenant Parker. If you contest, there'll be a messy trial."

"But it's not true."

"He has a witness," the lawyer said. "His wing

man, as a matter of fact. He's at the hospital with Lieutenant Parker. Crashed into the water on the same mission where Lieutenant Parker was hurt. He'll testify that he spent two nights with you and enjoyed sexual intimacy."

"But—" She closed her mouth. Damnit, they were just too stupid to realize that what she'd done was just entertainment, kids' stuff, that she'd never done the real thing except with Dick. She signed the papers, consenting to allow the divorce without contest.

Oh, the silly bastard! He just didn't know what he was giving up. She dressed in the most revealing little sundress she had and got into her car. She'd show him. She'd show them all. They were blaming her for something she'd never done. If she was going to bear the name, she'd damned well play the game. She'd been depriving herself of something she loved very much and her reward was to be accused falsely.

All right, if he got so upset because she'd made out with a fellow officer, how would he like it if she laid it on the line with an enlisted man? Better than that, a civilian. An able-bodied civilian. The lowest of the low in the eyes of a fighting man.

She cruised the streets, saw a stalwart man walking toward an intersection. He wore a sports jacket and an open shirt, collar out over the coat collar. She pulled to the curb and honked her horn. He came over. He wasn't all bad. He'd been drinking, but he seemed to be reasonably sober.

"Get in," she said.

"Honey," he said, observing the expensive car, her obviously expensive dress, "I don't think I can afford you."

Okay, that's what she'd been labeled, so that was fine. "Get in, you fool," she said. "I'm not sure why, but this one is on the house."

He had a pint of bourbon in his pocket and she took a pull, coughed. He drank deeply. She soon had second thoughts about taking him to her cottage. He was drunker than she'd thought. He was vile-mouthed and he began pawing her as she drove and there was no pleasure in the touch of his clumsy hands. She drove into the hills and parked. Get it over, Laura. Get it over.

She didn't take her dress off. It was swift and passionless, and his orgasm was just a feeble little throbbing in her and then he got up and vomited. Some of the spray got on her legs, on her car seat. She caught the rank, acid smell and leaned her head out the open door and imitated him. Then a black gloom descended on her, making her hate herself, hate the velvet, warm night, hate the man who's name she hadn't asked. She put her feet on his back and kicked as hard as she could. He tumbled to the ground and lay there, in a stupor. She threw his pants and underwear on top of him and pulled out in a fury, leaving a shower of dirt from her spinning wheels.

"Dumb!" she said aloud. "Stupid!" Because Dick would never know. No one would ever know. It was Laura who'd been punished back there, spread out on the seat, one leg thrown up over the back. It was Laura who had been soiled, who would never feel clean again, who would never think of the man-woman relationship as she once had. That hadn't been a fun game between consenting adults back there. That, as Dick had said, was filth.

She drove to the beach. Now she realized what

she'd lost. Oh, God, if she'd only had a little more patience. If she'd only waited. Now she'd never know the thrill of Dick's love again, never feel his arms around her, never be able to laugh with pure happiness when he gave her that glorious pleasure.

Poor little rich girl. She undressed and walked from the road down a rocky path to the deserted beach. She didn't hesitate. Her mind was made up. There wasn't enough water in the ocean to cleanse her. She waded until she was submerged by a wave and then she swam. She was a good swimmer and it would take a long, long time.

She didn't get fifty yards from the beach.

Idiot! she gasped. Who's this going to hurt?

All right, so she'd lost Dick. So she couldn't even think of another man right now. She swam back to the beach, dried on a towel from the trunk of the car and dressed. Looking at it from a practical viewpoint, her death wouldn't have hurt Dick because he hated her so much. It would have hurt her father and he was an old dear.

She moved back home the next day. She told the admiral that she and Dick hadn't hit it off, that he was asking for a divorce.

"Look on the bright side," she said, when he got upset. "You're getting your baby girl back."

She threw herself into her work. And there seemed to be a new sense of understanding in her. She remembered the flirty, friendly young man from Arkansas, and she saw a little bit of him in each of the men who came into the amputation ward. She made that ward her pet project.

They called her blondie. Once a wise guy Marine

with just one arm reached out and grabbed her breast. Two amputees, one without a leg, one with no right arm, threw the Marine out of his bed and told him if he ever touched blondie again they'd amputate something he'd miss more than his arm.

Chapter 17

The news that Mac was back came by radio on the morning of October 18, 1944.

"Leyte!" Red said. "Oh, Jesus."

Tony groaned. Leyte was midway in the chain of the Philippines. And the landings had been made, apparently, by relatively small Ranger units on offshore islands.

But, God, it was good to know that Americans were back in the Philippines.

Orders came from the main group. All guerrilla units were to maximize activity, to keep as many Japanese troops as possible occupied to prevent reinforcement of the Leyte area.

"It won't be long now, honey," Tony told Abby. "Old Mac will come storming up the island with the damnedest army this part of the world has ever seen."

Why did the news frighten her? It was strange. It was news they'd been waiting for, praying for, and yet it made her uneasy. Soon the American army would be on Luzon and they'd be safe after so many years of living from day to day.

And then Tony would ask her to marry him.

Well, wasn't that what she wanted?

And then Red would ask her to marry him.

But you love Tony, silly.

Don't you?

Yes, yes, yes.

"You two don't do anything silly," she said, a
they prepared to go. "We're too close to home to hav
anything happen now."

"Never you fear," Tony said.

Red flipped her a salute. "We shall return with ou
shields or on them."

Carlos spoke up. "I bring you some Jap goodies
lady."

She watched them go and then settled in. Ther
were some American magazines, brought in on the las
trip by the submarine, and she was fascinated by th
pictures. She could hardly wait to get home to try som
of the new styles.

It would be soon. The U.S. First Army was i
Germany. The Russians were in Yugoslavia, closing i
on Germany's eastern frontier. And best of all, the wa
in the Pacific was picking up and all of them were sur
that Mac's landing of Rangers on the islands off Leyt
was just the beginning.

Why, she even looked forward to seeing her mothe
and her aunt. She smiled. They'd probably be so ex
cited that it would be almost fatal. They'd be taking t
their beds for a three-day rest while she—

What?

With Tony?

All this time she'd watched him, coveted him
committed the sin of carnal thought with him. Wha
was the matter with her?

Just cold feet. It would work out. She was ju

remembering the doctor, the liar. Tony wasn't like that. With Tony, love would be sweet and tender and wonderful.

And with Red? Big, gentle, big brotherly Red?

A burst of sound, surprisingly near, brought her out of her dreaming. Good Lord. They'd run into Japs not more than a couple of miles away, judging from the sound of the machine guns, the small arms fire, the crump of grenades.

And so many guns! There were fifty-two in the group and she didn't think so few could make so much noise. Oh, God, how many Japs?

A man with a leg wound got off his bed, reached for his rifle. "No, no, you can't!" she argued with him.

"Lady, they hit many Japs. I go."

She was left alone with two malaria victims as the man hobbled into the jungle. She paced, listening to the fierce fire fight, hearing it diminish and feeling a mixture of fear and relief, for she had to guess, had to pray that the Japs had been defeated. Then it began again a few minutes later, a bit closer, and she realized that her men were trying to disengage and get back into the jungle.

The fighting was close enough now for her to recognize the characteristic chatter of Red's faithful old grease gun. It spoke in short bursts. The volume of fire diminished and then there was only a scattering of shots. Someone came running through the jungle toward her. She waited, a hand to her mouth, and then Carlos burst into the camp area.

"Lady, you come," he yelled, waving his arm wildly. There was a raw slash of red across his neck. She grabbed her medical bag and ran to him.

"You're hurt!"

"Just a scratch, lady," he said. "You come. Quick."

"Who is it?"

"You just come."

He ran. She followed, trying to keep up, the sweat beginning to roll down her back under her fatigue jacket.

They began to encounter the men. Those who weren't injured helped others along.

"Bad, lady," one of them said as she ran past.

They'd obviously ignored the rule that wounded men who couldn't walk were to be left behind. The war was too close to being over.

The last battle had been fought at a stream. She saw dead men, her own men, Filipinos. Carlos ran down the stream, pushing aside the undergrowth.

"Here, lady!" Carlos called.

She saw Tony's back. He was kneeling. Thank God it wasn't Tony. But where was Red?

"He's hit bad, Abby," Tony said, looking over his shoulder.

Red lay on his back. His eyes were open and when he saw her he tried to smile. He was hit in both legs. Tony had applied a tourniquet. She pushed Tony aside.

"Don't sweat it, big boy," she said, forcing a grin. "It's just a scratch or two."

There was arterial bleeding.

"You two go on," Red whispered. He was weak from shock and loss of blood.

"Not a chance," Abby said. "We can fix you."

She thanked God for her operating room experience, for having watched doctors like Fraleigh patch up just such wounds.

A quick examination showed her that the wounds looked a lot worse than they were. Both were flesh wounds, but he'd die from loss of blood unless she stopped the bleeding.

She popped him with a shot of morphine as she began to clear away the tattered fabric of his trousers and cleaned the wounds.

Red was breathing easier as the morphine began to cut down his pain. "You know the rules, Tony. Take her and go. We didn't get all of them. They'll be back."

Tony's eyes flicked back toward the jungle, then to Abby's face. "How long will this take?"

"Thirty minutes, maybe an hour," she said, preparing.

She had clamps. She exposed the artery and clamped it and the bleeding stopped. Her hands were steady. She'd done it before.

"Abby, I've got the other men to think of. A lot of them were hit. The Japs were moving right toward the camp. They must have been tipped. We've got to move."

"You go. I'll stay with him."

"Abby, damnit," Red moaned. "Go on."

"I can't let you stay," Tony said, taking hold of her arm. She jerked it away.

"Tony, don't try to force me. If you feel you have to go, I understand."

He seized her and lifted her to her feet. "You've got to come with me, damnit."

She struggled, slipped out of his hands. "No, Tony!"

He moved toward her.

A click. The safety of Carlos' rifle being released. "Sarge, sir, you don't touch lady."

Tony's rifle was lying on the ground. He turned slowly. "Put that damn thing down, Carlos."

"You don't touch lady. We're not letting Red die. You go."

"Please, Tony," she said. "Please, just go. I'm wasting time. I have to stop the bleeding."

He looked indecisive. From somewhere not far away he heard the sound of engines. "Look, even if you stop the bleeding we have no plasma, no whole blood. We can't carry him. He's too heavy. You hear that?"

Trucks. On the road not over a mile away.

"Me and lady, we carry him. You go," Carlos said.

"Abby, I've got the men to think of." He was pleading. He shrugged as she knelt and began preparations for the delicate job of repairing the artery. Fortunately it wasn't completely severed. She had only to take a few tiny, careful stitches.

"I'll send someone back to help you," Tony said. "I'm going to pick up my rifle and go, kid." He looked at Carlos as he bent. Carlos kept the rifle trained on him. Then he was gone.

She held her breath as she released the clamps and the stitches held. There was no leakage and blood began to pulse back into the leg. Capillaries were still bleeding. She applied sulfa. He was unconscious, but he was breathing well. He was pale. She wished for just one bottle of plasma. For one unit of whole blood. And while she was finishing up, then bandaging, a roar of fire came from the direction of the road.

"Get down, lady!" Carlos yelled. He threw himself down and pulled her with him. They lay beside Red and listened and there was a fury of gunfire and then silence, followed by a crashing of men moving through jungle. She wept. All this time on the run and now she'd spend the rest of the war in a Jap prison camp—if they didn't kill the three of them on the spot.

"Japs come, lady," Carlos whispered. "I kill them."

"No," she said. "We'll surrender. Hide the gun, Carlos. Hide it quickly."

He dug in the mulch and buried the gun. The crashings came closer. And then a voice. Tears of joy came, for the voice was speaking the Philippine dialect.

"Over here, Joe!" Carlos yelled.

The Filipinos gathered around Carlos, Red and Abby and began exchanging stories of the big fight. Red had regained consciousness. Sergeant Phil Woods came up.

"You lost quite a few men," Woods said.

"Too many," Red said. He was in pain. The morphine was wearing off.

"How about Dunking?"

"He left," Abby said. "He thought the Japs knew the location of our camp. He went to move the men."

"He left you?" Woods was sorry, immediately, that he'd asked the question. He knew the rules.

"It was his duty," she said, but it was the soldier speaking and she was not a soldier. She was a woman caught up in a war and Red, during all that terrible time, had never left her. He'd half carried her. He'd dragged her. He'd risked his life for her. When it meant death to even look sideways at a Jap, during the march up from Corregidor, he'd killed a Jap soldier who'd hit her.

"Whew, heavy," a Filipino grunted as Red was lifted onto a stretcher.

After a march they were in a clean, neat little sickbay and she was lying on a bed beside Red. They had the same type blood. Afterward Phil Woods had a buffalo steak for her, to make up for the pint of her blood she'd given Red.

She sat beside him, listening to an Armed Forces Radio report of the battle of Leyte Gulf. "The Japanese navy," said the newscaster, "is no longer a significant force in the Pacific."

"They'll be here soon, big brother," she said.

He grinned. There was a doctor with the Bangued group, and he'd praised Abby for her field surgery.

"Lady, how'd you like to have a platter of hamburgers with fries and two big, vanilla milkshakes?" Red asked.

"I can't think of anything closer to heaven." She went to sit on the side of his bed. "That appetite is good news."

"I'm indestructible. Got too much to live for."

Oh, Tony, Tony, if you'd only stayed a few minutes longer. I know you had your duty. I know. But . . .

What was love? She'd known several kinds in her life. She'd had the thrilling, exciting puppy love of a high school crush, the all-consuming, passionate love she'd felt for the doctor, the love she'd known for Red—a sweet, sexless, mother or sister kind of love. And her love for Tony. She'd burned for him, and in those frozen, fearful moments when she thought the Japs were coming, she'd seen that the way she felt about Tony was to be equated with letting Dr. Frank Charles coax her into his bed, a body love, a selfish, seeking, hedonistic love.

If you really love someone, you're ready to lay down your life for that someone. Aren't you?

Chapter 18

"You're looking good, Lieutenant," a male therapist said.

Dick Parker had been moved into a convalescent ward. The skin grafts on the left side of his face had taken well. He was walking with a cane, his twisted left leg getting stronger all the time.

"Just get settled in here," the therapist said. "I'll see you every day. Blondie will be around after a while with some books and magazines. If you need anything she'll shop for you. And there'll be a movie tonight in the rec room."

"Thank you," Dick said. He hobbled to his bed, hoisted himself up with a grunt.

He saw her come in at the far end of the ward. She was wearing a frilly little dress. She was so goddamned beautiful that his eyes blurred for a moment and then the nasty pictures were back and he turned his head.

He could hear her laughing. Men sat up and smiled, chatted with her. She handed out books and magazines and ruffled one young man's hair, causing him to blush.

"Great gal," a Marine officer in the bed next to him said. "You'll find yourself looking forward to the mornings just to get a look at her, but don't get any ideas.''

Dick didn't answer.

''Blondie lost her husband,'' the Marine said. ''She won't talk about it, but she must have loved the guy. I've tried to tell her that she works too hard. Spends her own volunteer shift here and then comes back to do another one.''

''Bully for her,'' Dick said, and the bitterness in his voice caused the Marine captain to look at him with narrowed eyes, then turn away.

He made a move to leave his bed, then decided to hell with that. He could face her. He could tell her exactly how he felt about her.

She saw him when she was about four beds away. She felt her stomach fall away and for a moment she had to grip the foot of a bed to stand. Then she recovered, smiled and talked and distributed her magazines.

''Hello, Dick,'' she said, standing at the foot of his bed. ''Want something to read?''

The words were there, the scalding words. He wet his lips. ''Yeah, I guess so.''

''Take your pick,'' she said, fanning out a handful of current magazines. He pointed to a *Life*.

''You're looking good,'' she said.

''Doin' all right.''

''The admiral would like you to come and see him.''

''Yeah, well.''

''I'm not home during the days.''

He looked away.

''You know blondie?'' the Marine captain asked after she'd left the ward.

''Yes.''

"Lucky."

Hell. It looked as if the whole ward loved her. Maybe she'd loved all of them. He was filled with a pain that didn't come from the healing skin grafts.

"She was my wife."

"Was?" The captain gawked at him. "You dumb son of a bitch, letting her get away. There's not a guy in this ward wouldn't give another limb to be married to her."

"Well, she's available," Dick said. He turned away.

The Marine wouldn't let it lie. "I don't know what the problem was, son, but I'll tell you, that's one hell of a lot of woman, in all ways. I've seen her pull a guy up out of depression and make him laugh. And I've seen her wipe the tears away while she was writing a letter for some Joe without an arm. And I've seen her so tired she could hardly stand and smiling and talking all the time."

"Okay, drop it."

"Suit yourself."

A saint. She was a goddamned saint. Every man in the frigging ward thought she was Florence Nightingale. You couldn't talk with anyone without hearing about blondie, blondie, and how great she was. And the thing that hurt was she was so beautiful that he got this pain in his gut each time she came in.

"How are you, Dick? Something to read?"

"I'm going up to see the admiral tomorrow."

"That's good."

The word had got around. That navy joker was so damned stupid he was divorcing blondie, and the way she looked at him indicated she wasn't in favor of it. Each day men watched as she approached Dick's bed and there was a silence in the ward. He must be some kind of rotating son of a bitch, was the consensus of opinion. Couldn't be blondie's fault.

She handed him a magazine. "He's looking forward to having a visit with you."

"Yes, I am too." He swallowed. He was confused. All those things that A.D. had told him. It didn't seem possible. She was beautiful and clean and he could smell that perfume she used.

"Laura?"

It was the first time he'd called her by name. She smiled. "Yes?"

He motioned. She went to his side. No damned privacy in the ward. He looked into her eyes and whispered. "It was true, wasn't it?"

A tear formed, slipped down her cheek. "Yes," she whispered. Lord, how she wanted to hold him, to weep on his shoulder and beg his forgiveness, to tell him how much she needed him. The twisted leg, the smooth areas of his face which would never be fully mobile, she didn't even notice. He was Dick and she saw him as she'd always seen him.

His eyes lowered.

"Can we go somewhere and talk?" she asked.

He swallowed and wouldn't look at her.

She was whispering so that no one could hear. "I told you I'd crawl to you. On my belly. Would that help?"

He couldn't speak.

She felt a fierce determination growing in her. She turned, pushed the cart down past his bed out of the way, walked, head high, toward the far end of the ward. His bed was near the end. It was over a hundred feet from door to door. And at the door she turned. All of them were watching her, wondering, wanting to go down and punch that jerk who was upsetting their blondie.

She stood across the ward from him. ''I'm sorry, Dick. But I can't undo anything. What happened happened. What else can I do now, besides apologize and try to make it up to you in the future.'' She paused. ''And I could crawl. Would that help?''

''You don't have to do that,'' Dick answered.

''You son of a bitch!'' someone called out to him.

''Are you sure, Dick?'' Laura asked. ''Can you forgive me?''

Dick pulled himself out of bed and began to hobble toward her. ''I forgive you, Laura, I forgive you. Do you forgive me?''

Laura took a few halting steps. Tears filled her eyes. ''Dick!'' she cried, and then she ran across the ward to meet him.

His arms went around her and held her tight. ''I've missed you so much, Laura.'' He pulled back and looked into her face. The other men, the ward, the hospital, ceased to exist. There were just the two of them and when he kissed her he heard a strange sound which he didn't recognize at first.

Cheering. All of the men were cheering.

He looked around, grinning. ''I guess the only thing I can do with you is keep my eyes on you every minute.''

''I'll love that,'' she promised.

Chapter 19

It was one hell of a Fourth of July. In a ruined city a few Americans stood, backed by a large group of ragtag Filipinos. A big man in baggy pants walked down the line, shaking hands, offering his congratulations for their bravery. He paused for an extra minute in front of Abby Preston.

"We can tell our grandkids about this," Red said, when it was over. "What'd old Mac say to you?"

"He said I was the prettiest guerrilla in the Philippines."

"Always knew that man had good taste."

They were married by a navy chaplain in the ruined chapel of a great church. Red had lost weight, but his legs were as good as ever. The honeymoon began aboard a PBY. They were getting VIP treatment. And then Hawaii.

"My God." Red gave a long, low whistle. He'd heard the amount of back pay he was entitled to. "We're rich!"

"Buy you more hamburgers than you can eat," she said. She was always touching him, holding his hand, clinging to his arm. He was Red. Her Red. And in a Honolulu hotel she found, quickly, that love can be many things, including much pleasure and wicked, wicked passions which, with one's husband, become so sweet.

She'd seen Tony at the grand Manila review. He was fit, smiling, unconcerned. Both he and Red were awarded medals for their activities in the Philippines. But the medal was just icing for Red. He had all he needed or wanted in the arms of a little woman with the sweetest face and the wildest love he'd ever known.

Chapter 20

You did a great job out in the islands, Emi,'' Tom raddock congratulated her. They were in Braddock's ffice, coffee, as always, in hand. ''We're going to iss you around here.''

''I've heard that before,'' Emi said. ''But this time can say it too. I'll miss you and the gang in the hole.''

''Well, San Diego isn't a bad place to live. Luke's lucky guy, marrying you and getting a stateside as- gnment too.''

''Well, it's just because he's the best amphibian ilot in the navy,'' Emi smiled. ''And they want him to ass on his skills.''

''I think we'll all be going home soon,'' Braddock aid.

''Oh?''

Iwo Jima. Okinawa. The bloodiest of all, and ahead nother string of islands leading up to the Jap homeland here the real fighting would begin.

''Sounds strange, doesn't it. I can't tell you why I eel that it'll be over soon. Maybe it's just a hunch. laybe not.''

She knew that he was telling her something.

"There's one thing I'd like your opinion on," he said, "before you go off and practice being Mrs. Martel."

"Shoot," she said.

"It's a little game we've been playing. Suppose we could mass enough B-29s to obliterate a Jap city."

She shuddered. She knew about the fire raids. She knew that many Japanese cities had suffered heavily under the raids from the bombers flying from the Marianas.

"It's just a game, just a study, but if we could totally destroy a city, which city would you think would have, through its loss, the greatest effect on the Japanese?"

"Tokyo, of course," she said.

"But if it's completely obliterated, everyone dead, there'd be no one left to make an official surrender. No government left. No emperor. It might be chaotic and the war might go on by default, just because no one would have the proper authority to say, hey, we've had enough, we quit."

"Then there's world opinion," Emi said. She'd engaged in these thinking exercises many times while working in the hole. Many were meaningless. This one had to be, because even with massed B-29s it would be difficult to kill everyone in a large city. "I think I'd pick a heavy industry town, something vital to war production."

He tossed a paper at her. On it were listed several Japanese cities. She studied the list. "Something which is large enough to make a terrible impression, which is a legitimate military target—discounting the fact that there are civilians there—and not so large, like Osaka, to seem brutal." She underlined two cities, handed the list back.